MAIL ORDER BRIDE

Montana Luck

Echo Canyon Brides

Book 4

LINDA BRIDEY

This is a work of fiction. All characters, names, places and events are the product of the author's imagination or used fictitiously.

First Printing, 2015

Dedication

This book is dedicated to all of my faithful readers, without whom I would be nothing. I thank you for the support, reviews, love, and friendship you have shown me as we have gone through this journey together. I am truly blessed to have such a wonderful readership.

Contents

Chapter One

Lucky Quinn sat in the sweat lodge that he and his friend, Wild Wind, had built. Looking at sixteen-year-old Adam Harris, Lucky's gray eyes filled with concern and sympathy for the asthmatic boy. He'd started with an attack the day before and Erin Avery, Echo Canyon's doctor, had brought him out to the sheep farm to use the sweat lodge.

It usually helped ease Adam's attacks when other remedies didn't work. However, this attack was very bad. Wild Wind, a Cheyenne brave, knew the medicinal uses of many plants. He made Adam a mustard poultice and gave him very strong coffee to drink. He also made a boiling pot of eucalyptus water and had Adam breathe in the steam to help clear his lungs.

Adam had just finished the steam and coughed as his lungs began to rid themselves of mucus. It didn't help that he had a bad case of hay fever. He suffered most in the fall and spring, but the September weather of 1892 bothered him more than usual.

He hadn't been able to go to school the past couple of days and had missed a test that he would have to make up. Adam loved school—so much, in fact, that he wanted to be a teacher. When he wasn't plagued by his ailments, he liked to work outside, doing chores and other activities.

However, at night and in his spare moments, he loved to read and study all kinds of things. There wasn't any subject that he didn't do well in. He was a big help to Hank Winston, Echo's schoolteacher, because he often helped the younger kids with their lessons.

Lucky watched Adam cough and struggle to breathe and prayed that the young man's affliction would subside. Adam's brown hair was soaked with sweat, his dark eyes red and swollen from the hay fever. Finally, the coughing began to lessen and Adam was able to take deeper breaths. Then the poor boy began sneezing and Lucky's eyes moistened. He couldn't stand to see anyone suffer, and Adam was special to Lucky.

He'd met him a little over two years ago when he'd come to Echo Canyon, commonly referred to as Echo. Sheriff Evan Taft's wife, Josie, had been a mail-order bride from Pullman, Washington, whom he'd met on the train to Montana. He and Josie had become fast friends after he'd saved her life when their train had derailed.

Lucky had also been on his way to Echo to see the property he'd bought from an old man from the region. The land was perfect for sheep farming and he'd begun a sheep farm with the help of his friends, Billy Two Moons, Winslow Wu, Ross Ryder, and Travis Desmond. Over the past two years, the farm had prospered, making them all proud.

Adam's mother, Charlene, worked at Erin's medical practice as a cleaning woman. She had other cleaning jobs, too. The widow spent all of her money caring for her son, but during the warmer season, Adam did odd jobs to bring in money.

Lucky had hired him part-time to help on the farm, but they didn't let him do jobs that would set off his asthma. He was good at mending pens, milking goats, butchering, and running errands to town for them. Other than his asthma and hay fever, Adam was a healthy, robust boy.

"Oh, God love ya," Lucky said, sniffing. The Irishman was sometimes moved easily to tears, especially when people were sick.

"Don't make me laugh," Adam wheezed, blowing his nose. A stack of hankies sat next to him, most of which he would use.

Lucky frowned. "Why's that funny?"

Pushing his sweaty hair away from his forehead, Adam said, "Because if God loved me, He wouldn't have given me asthma."

Lucky could understand Adam's bitterness, but he didn't like Adam's lack of faith. He'd certainly suffered enough of his own misfortune, so he knew how hard it was to keep a positive outlook. However, it wasn't in his nature to give up, as the two tattoos on his back denoted.

On his left shoulder blade, a griffin stood poised to strike; on his right one, a bull prepared to charge. The griffin represented a protector and the bull stood for determination and a strong will. Lucky possessed both of those traits, along with a tender heart and a good sense of humor.

Erin entered the tipi, her brown eyes settling on Adam. "How is he doing?"

Lucky shook his head. "A little better. He just finished the steam part about ten minutes ago, so it should start takin' effect soon."

"Ok. No school for you tomorrow, buddy," Erin said.

Adam's free hand clenched into a fist and anger glinted in his eyes. "Test," he managed to get out before he started coughing again.

Erin said, "Adam, I know you're frustrated, but you have to calm down. When you get excited, it makes it worse. Think about something you like reading about or try picturing someplace you'd like to go."

Lucky got up, scooted Erin out of the way, and went outside into the chilly air. It felt great after sitting in the hot sweat lodge. He trotted over to the tipi where he and his son, Otto, lived. The four-year-old was Lucky's greatest joy. Right now, the tyke was in town at Josie and Evan's house. Evan's Aunt Edna, a sassy lady in her mid-sixties, had become a surrogate grandmother for Otto, and he loved visiting with her. Otto also called Josie and Evan his aunt and uncle. He had gained many aunts and uncles since coming to Echo.

Inside their tipi, Lucky found Adam's schoolbooks that he'd brought with him and grabbed a book Adam was reading on the Mayans. Then he returned to the sweat lodge and sat back down.

"All right, then, lad. I'm gonna read to ya," Lucky said. "That'll take yer mind off things."

Adam smiled a little, but kept his mouth shut as he concentrated on his breathing.

Lucky settled in and said, "Close yer eyes and rest the poor things."

Adam leaned back, relaxing as much as he could, and let his eyelids shut. Erin used Indian sign to say, "Thank you," to Lucky. She left the sweat lodge before the smell from the eucalyptus steam got the best of her. She took several deep breaths to clear the scent of it from her nostrils and sighed in relief.

Now in the early stages of pregnancy, her sense of smell had heightened and the medicinal steam was one of the scents she couldn't stand. By her calculations, she was due in March or April and she and her husband, Winslow Wu, the town veterinarian, were thrilled by the prospect of becoming parents.

She wondered if Lucky would mind if Adam spent the night, but she wasn't going back into the sweat lodge again right away to ask. Most likely, he wouldn't be opposed to it. Erin didn't think it was a good idea for Adam to ride back into town in the chilly air. It would be better for him to go home early the next afternoon when it was warmer, provided his symptoms had subsided enough.

Normally, Adam was a sweet kid, but his asthma attacks angered him, especially when he had to miss school. She decided to pay Mr. Winston a visit to ask if he would go to Adam's house the next evening just long enough to give Adam his test. That way, Adam would at least have that much peace of mind.

Then she groaned. Win had forbidden her from riding since she was pregnant, and he wasn't home to hitch up the buggy for her. Then, inspiration hit her and she went to the goat barn.

"Wild Wind? Are you in here?" she called.

"Yes. Back here," he responded.

She found him near the back of the barn, playing with a couple of kids that had been born late in the season. The frisky Nubians liked to play and Wild Wind had taken a special liking to them. He knelt while they ran around and butted him playfully. Erin laughed at the sight of the tough

Indian brave playing with the young goats.

He smiled at Erin. "They're full of themselves." He stood up and brushed straw from his buckskin pants. "How is Adam?"

"He's been better, but I think the steam is starting to help. He's angry because he can't go to school tomorrow again."

"Mmm. He's worried about that test," Wild Wind said.

"Will you do me a favor, please? Can you hitch up our buggy for me? I can't ride and Win's not around to do it and I really shouldn't."

"Sure. Where are you going?" he asked as they left the goat barn and walked towards the horse barn.

She explained her errand to him and he nodded. "Do you have other business in town or would you like me to go for you? I'll pick up Otto, too."

"That might be a good idea. Lucky's reading to Adam to keep him calm," she said.

Wild Wind nodded. "Ok. I'll stop at the post office, too. Do you need anything from the store before it closes?" he asked, looking up at the lowering sun to gauge the time.

"No, thanks. I really appreciate it," Erin said.

He smiled. "It's no problem. I'll be back soon."

Wild Wind's horse cantered along the road into town, its hoof beats making a steady beat to which he sang a Cheyenne song. He'd come from the Cheyenne reservation in Oklahoma to Echo with Lucky in April and had settled into life in a mostly white society fairly well. It hadn't been a completely peaceful transition, but eventually people had warmed to him, and he'd made some good friends.

He'd become best friends with Lucky when the Irishman had lived with his tribe a few years ago. Lucky had fallen in love with a Cheyenne maiden named Avasa. They'd married, but a couple years later the military found the tribe and forced them onto the reservation. They wouldn't let Lucky go with Avasa since he was white. She had hurriedly divorced him and told him to go live his life.

However, Lucky hadn't been able to forget Avasa, especially since she'd been five months pregnant with their child. Wild Wind had known about Lucky's vow to return for Avasa, so when he'd found out that they were being moved further west, he'd gotten word to Lucky. He'd told Lucky what day to arrive so he could bring her to him.

When they'd arrived at the meeting place, Lucky had discovered that Avasa had fallen in love and married another man, whom she wouldn't leave. However, she'd given Lucky their son to take and raise in Echo. She'd felt that Otto would have a better life with Lucky than he would trapped on a reservation. Although brokenhearted, Lucky had agreed. Wild Wind had decided to accompany Lucky and Billy back to Echo.

Entering town, the brave first went to the post office before it closed. Going inside, he greeted Ian, the postmaster.

"So how's our other Indian today?"

Wild Wind smiled. Billy was a mixture of Nez Perce, Lakota, and Cheyenne Indians. His medium brown hair with reddish highlights and his somewhat lighter skin was a result of his small percentage of white blood. Because the talented artist was often with Lucky, they'd been given the nickname of Irish and the Indian. Now there were two Indians, so Echo's residents had started calling Wild Wind "the other Indian." He didn't mind. Having a nickname made him feel accepted.

"I'm fine. Do you have mail for any of us out at the farm?"

"Let me look." Ian checked and handed a few letters to Wild Wind.

"Thanks," Wild Wind said as he left the post office, heading for the Taft house.

When he arrived, Josie was chasing Otto around in the yard while the boy laughed. They ran around the trees, his long, slightly curly blond hair bouncing as he ran. Josie put on a burst of speed and caught him. Playfully, she pulled him down to the ground and tussled with him. He let out shrieks of laughter as she tickled him.

They looked up at the sound of approaching hoof beats.

"Hi," Josie said to the brave. "Are you here for this guy?" she asked, pulling Otto to his feet, only to tickle him again.

He sank back to his knees and giggled, making both adults laugh.

"Yes. I had a couple of other things to do in town so I figured I would pick him up for Lucky."

Josie let Otto up and picked leaves out of his hair.

In Cheyenne, Wild Wind said, "Time to go home, nephew."

Otto said, "I have to say goodbye to Grandmother," and ran into the house.

Josie chuckled, brushing leaves off her coat. "He's so much fun, and he's so curious. He helped me make cookies today."

Wild Wind smiled. Yes, he likes helping Lucky cook, too."

Josie said, "You better go in and see Edna or you'll be in trouble."

Grinning, Wild Wind jumped up onto the porch and said, "I know. I don't want to face her wrath." Entering the parlor, he saw Otto hugging Edna.

"I have to go home, but I'll see you soon," he said to her.

Edna smiled, her blue eyes twinkling. "Ok. You have a good night."

Otto nodded. "Ok."

Josie and Evan's year-and-a-half-old daughter, Julia, caught sight of Wild Wind. She got up off the floor and walked towards him. He picked her up and said, "Hello, pretty girl. You're looking well."

She smiled and nodded. "Yes." That was her favorite word right at the moment.

Edna said, "There's the other Indian. I guess I'll forgive you this time for forgetting your entrance fee."

Wild Wind grinned. "Thanks."

Edna and her male friends played a private game where the men took off their shirts in exchange for admittance into the house. Evan always made the men put their shirts back on.

Edna rose, saying, "I'll get your cookies. Otto can hold them for you."

"I helped make them," Otto said proudly.

"I heard," Wild Wind said. "That was nice of you. I can get them if you tell me where they are, Edna."

Edna suffered from rheumatoid arthritis that had settled in her knees and ankles. "No, no. I need to move around now. I've been sitting long enough." She shuffled out to the kitchen, her knees cracking a little as she did.

Otto followed her out to the kitchen as Josie came in the front door.

"It's getting cold out now," she said. "How's Adam doing?"

Wild Wind frowned. "Not good. He has to miss school again tomorrow, so Hank is going to go to Adam's house tomorrow night to give him his test."

Edna came back carrying a tin of cookies. "Here we go. You tell Adam we hope he gets better soon. These cookies will help."

"I'm sure they will. I'll see you soon, little one," Wild Wind said. He kissed Julia and sat her down.

She toddled over to the sofa, trying to get on it. Otto went over and gave her a push, making the grownups smile.

"He's always so helpful with her," Josie said. "It's so cute."

Wild Wind nodded. "Are you ready to go, Otto?"

"Yes," Otto said, giving Josie a hug around her legs. "Goodbye, Auntie."

She bent down and hugged him back. "Goodbye, honey. Thanks for all your help today. We'll see you later. Be a good boy."

"Ok. I will."

After thanking them again for the cookies, Wild Wind and Otto left.

Chapter Two

Lucky put down the letter he'd just read and sighed before looking over at his sleeping son. Adam also slept, but his breathing was still a little labored. Lucky had propped him up on few blankets so his lungs didn't have to work so hard.

Lucky wanted Otto to have a mother. He firmly believed that children should have two parents if at all possible. Therefore, he'd had Edna write a mail-order-bride ad for him a couple of months ago. He'd gotten a few letters, but he hadn't written back to any of the senders yet because his heart wasn't in it. He still hurt over Avasa, even though he knew he had to get on with his life.

For the most part, he had, working on the farm, raising his son, and spending time with his friends. But not romantically. Even if he'd been so inclined, there weren't many single women around Echo, which was why men from the dying town had started advertising for brides. In its heyday, Echo had been a bustling mining town, the gold, silver, and copper mines creating wealth for many of the town's citizens.

However, when the mines had dried up, many families had moved away to find work. Therefore, most of the people who remained were single men who worked on the ranches, as well as a few other surviving businesses. Jerry Belker, who was running for mayor in November, had come up with the mail-order-bride idea.

So far, the plan had worked. Evan had been the first to try it and after his success, Win had given it a whirl. Billy had come next, although he hadn't married the woman who'd come to Echo, Callie Carlisle. It hadn't taken long for her to find someone, though. Ross Ryder, the town butcher, and she had been attracted to each other right away. They'd been courting since then.

When Lucky had returned from Oklahoma, he'd been incredibly dejected. However, like in the past, he'd concentrated on getting through one day at a time and, sometimes, one hour at a time. He was trying to let go of the lingering grief and do the right thing for Otto in finding a mother for him.

Lucky again looked at the letter he'd just read, trying to work up even a little enthusiasm about it. He couldn't. After putting more wood on the fire, he lay down, fighting down the anger that bubbled up inside him. Letting it consume him would do no good. He prayed that the Great Spirit would open his heart enough to find a woman to share his life with, if only for Otto's sake.

"Let him go," Evan said. "Just let him go."

Deputy Shadow Earnest growled, tightening his grip on the neck of the thief he'd caught. "But he's guilty."

"I know, but you can't kill him," Evan said. "We need him for information."

Shadow winked at Evan from where he stood behind the crook. "He's not going to give up his cohorts, so we might as well get rid of him. I know a good place—"

"Please, Sheriff! Don't let him kill me! I'll tell you anything you want to know!"

"Shadow, just handcuff him and we'll take him to the office," Evan said, barely suppressing a grin.

Shadow sighed dramatically. "Can't I at least break something? A leg? An arm?"

"No."

"A finger?"

Evan almost lost the battle of hiding his amusement. "No! Just cuff him and let's go! That's an order, Deputy!"

Shadow let out a louder growl, pulled the man's hands behind his back, and put handcuffs on him. His rough treatment made the thief grunt in pain.

"Happy?" Shadow asked, practically snarling.

"Yeah. Let's get going," Evan said.

Shadow shoved the guy forward and they left Temple's General Store. Sometimes Shadow still wanted to flinch away from the sunlight, but the tinted glasses he wore made that unnecessary. It was his instinct after years spent trapped in darkness and then only being active at night.

Every so often, he pushed their prisoner a little hard just to satisfy the violent part of his personality. He'd been a deputy for almost three months now and he still didn't understand the world of law enforcement. He'd rather just snap necks and rid the world of the criminals, but Evan wouldn't allow him to do that. However, Evan let him cause pain and create mayhem to a certain extent. Since he had a badge, Shadow figured he had permission to do so as long as it ended up serving justice. Of course, he was still a little fuzzy on exactly what justice meant.

He thought about his fiancée, Bree Josephson, as they walked along. Bree was six months pregnant now. He thought about the first time he'd felt the slight fluttering movements of their baby underneath his palm a couple of weeks ago and smiled. His pleasant thoughts were the only thing that made his treatment of the thief kinder than normal.

Evan saw Shadow's smile and knew it didn't have anything to do with their current activity. "Deputy Mayhem, that looks like the smile of a happy man."

Shadow's smile broadened. "Very astute of you, Evan. Feeling our baby move is one of the greatest joys I've ever known."

"You're having a baby?" the crook asked. "Heaven help us."

Shadow immediately seized the man by the back of the neck and squeezed so hard the man went to his knees. "Do not ever, ever say anything negative about my child or I will make your death very slow and agonizing no matter who is around. Are we clear?"

"Yes! Yes! Sorry! Please stop!"

Evan put a hand on Shadow's arm. "Let him up, Shadow." His green eyes met Shadow's and a moment of understanding passed between them.

Shadow relented and hauled the man up again. "Move and keep your mouth shut unless you want me to slap your teeth right out of your head."

Evan did laugh then. "He means it, too, as you can see."

"Can't you keep him on a leash?" the man asked and then cringed.

Evan chuckled. "This *is* on a leash. You'd really hate it if I let him off it."

Shadow let out a low laugh. "Every so often, I break the leash, though."

"Yeah. I know," Evan said, sounding displeased.

At the sheriff's office, they put the guy in a cell. This was the worst part of the job for Shadow. After being kept in a cage for the first sixteen years of his life and suffering brutal, cruel abuse by his father, Shadow hated anything resembling a cage. The cells disturbed him so he always made short work of jailing people. He would even avert his eyes from the cell room if possible.

Sitting down at his desk, Shadow said, "I suppose you want me to write up a report?" Evan was a stickler for this.

"What do you think, Deputy Mayhem?"

Shadow liked his nickname, thinking it suited him perfectly. "I think I'm going to get it done quickly. This is the other part of the job I hate."

Evan said, "We all have to do things we don't like." *Like what I'm going to do someday soon.*

"True. I'm glad Marvin is back on his feet now. It's been a long recovery," Shadow said about his twin.

If it weren't for the difference in their hair color and Shadow's slightly bulkier build, it would have been impossible to tell them apart. Shadow wore his dark brown hair long while Marvin's golden blond hair was shorter and stylishly combed. Both men were beautifully handsome and intimidating.

During the summer, a fight had broken out at Spike's, one of the two saloons in Echo. Evan had been busy fighting one of the culprits who'd started it when another man had sneaked up behind him, intent on smashing a bottle of whiskey over Evan's head. Marvin had intervened, knocking the man down, thus saving Evan's life.

One of Marvin's disgruntled ranch hands, Corey Allen, had taken advantage of the situation, attacking his employer. As a teenager, Marvin had had a botched inguinal hernia repair and that area in his groin was weak. Corey had kicked Marvin viciously in the abdomen, rupturing the hernia. Emergency surgery by Erin, Win, and a doctor from Dickensville, a neighboring town, had saved his life. However, a lot of damage had been done and it had taken several months for it to heal properly.

Evan and Marvin had been enemies after Marvin had slept with Evan's fiancée several years ago, but since Marvin had saved his life, Evan had slightly softened his attitude towards Marvin. "I'm glad he's coming along. I'll bet you're excited about Saturday," Evan said.

Shadow smiled. "Yes. I'm very ready to wed my lady. Marvin's healthy enough to be my best man and enjoy the festivities. There won't be a large crowd, but big enough, and I didn't want him to be in pain during the event."

"I can understand that. The wedding might be small, but that doesn't mean it won't be beautiful," Evan said.

"Thank you. While we're on the subject of weddings, I have a confession to make," Shadow said. He'd been meaning to talk to Evan about this for a while and he figured that he might as well do it now. "I was the one who kidnapped you on your wedding day."

Evan sat completely still, his green eyes filling with fury. His jaw clenched and his face became slightly flushed. "That was you?"

"Yes, it was. I thought in light of our new friendship, I should come clean," Shadow replied.

Slamming a fist down on his desk, Evan said, "You almost cost me the woman I love! If I weren't the sheriff, I'd put a bullet in your head. You're just lucky we made that immunity agreement or I'd put your ass in a cell."

Shadow felt slightly remorseful. "I'm sorry. At the time, you were my enemy, and we were trying to thwart your efforts to grow the town. In retrospect, it probably wouldn't have worked. You and Josie love each other too much to have stayed apart permanently. But, if I hadn't intervened, you wouldn't have been here to help during the earthquake. So I suppose I actually did the town a favor."

Evan put his face in his hands, trying to rein in his anger. However, even though he wanted to beat Shadow, he still saw the humorous aspect of Shadow's skewed perspective on his actions. He took a huge breath and expelled it slowly, using the technique to calm himself down.

Getting a grip on his emotions, Evan lowered his hands and stared at Shadow, meeting Shadow's blue eyes hidden behind his tinted glasses. "I understand that you went through hell for a lot of years and that Marvin shaped you in a lot of ways, but you had to know right from wrong."

Shadow cocked his head a little. "What I knew was right at the time was to do whatever was necessary to keep my existence a secret," he said in low tones so that the robber didn't overhear them. "When Marvin found me that day, I had a speech impediment, I was emaciated, and I barely knew how to read and write. If someone else had found me in that condition, I would have been thrown in an institution.

"Once I understood how different I was from other people, I begged him to keep me a secret, and he did without hesitation. I've told you this before; Marvin became what he is to protect me, so in a way, I'm as much to blame as he is."

Evan grunted and shook his head. "It always amazes me the way you stick up for him."

Shadow's temper flared. "You've no idea how much he did for me. None. He was the first person outside of my father that I'd ever seen. From the first moment we met, he showed me kindness and unconditional love. That's not something that's easily found. I don't expect you to understand, but don't try to turn me against him because that will never happen."

A few months ago, that had been Evan's plan, but he'd since realized that the brothers' bond was too strong for them to ever turn on each other. Their brotherly love had been forged by torture, darkness, and cruelty; they would never be torn apart. So the intelligent, insightful sheriff had given up on that idea and now simply sought to make Shadow a good deputy and friend.

"I'm not trying to do that. No one could ever turn you guys against each other. I guess I'm just trying to understand, but I doubt I ever will because I've never been through anything like that," Evan said.

"You're right. You'll never understand and I don't expect you to. I only ask that you respect my relationship with Marvin. Unlike many people, we can look past all of the negative aspects of our personalities. We see the people within; we know each other's thoughts and can feel each other's emotions much of the time. I would die for him and he for me," Shadow said.

"Why did he intervene that night at Spike's? Why would he come to my rescue like that?" Evan asked.

Shadow smiled. "I think you should talk to him about that. It's really not my place to answer that."

Evan nodded. "Ok. Fair enough. Well, Mayhem, you write up your report. I'll go out on patrol."

"Am I forgiven for my transgressions?" Shadow asked.

"Not yet, but I'll work on it." Evan put his hat back on and walked out the door.

Chapter Three

Lucky had just read another response to his ad and, although it was nice, it just didn't move him. When he groaned, Win looked over at him from his chair on the porch of Erin and Win's cabin.

The Chinaman asked, "Don't like that one, either?"

"It isn't that I don't like them. My heart isn't in this. I'm doin' it for Otto's sake," Lucky responded dejectedly.

"If you're not ready for love, be more practical about it, the way I was. It started out as a bargain, but it turned into love. Maybe that might work for you," Win said. "You're not looking for romance right at the moment. Approach it from a different angle and you might get excited about it," Win said.

"Explain that a little more."

Win propped his feet up on the porch railing. "Ok. I've come to see that you're a very results-driven person. When you set a goal for yourself, you achieve it, no matter what it takes. You're one of the hardest working, most determined people I've ever met. Look at this as another goal instead of an emotional issue."

"I see," Lucky said and thought about it. "Ya wanted to bring a doctor to Echo and find a wife at the same time, so ya advertised for a female doctor. It worked out, too, and yer finally havin' a wee bairn."

Win grinned. "Yeah. I can't wait to be a father. I also can't wait until Erin's anytime sickness goes away. I've never understood the term 'morning sickness' since pregnant women can be sick at any time of the day. I know it's more prevalent in the morning, but Erin's proof that it can happen no matter what the hour is. She's even felt sick at bedtime."

Lucky nodded. "I know. Poor thing." He fell silent a few moments, his thoughts returning to his predicament. A smile spread over his handsome face. "I have it! By God, yer a genius! I'll go back through my letters and see if there's a woman who has a skill that'll help the town. There's gotta be somethin'. I'll call on my good luck. It is my name, after all."

Win chuckled. "I don't know about genius, but I have my moments. I wouldn't have thought to do that, though. Good idea. Now you have a goal. Find a woman who can do something that Echo needs."

"With help, she might even be able to open up a business the way you and Erin did."

Win started getting excited about the idea, too. "Yeah. Hey, let's go look through the ones you already have. I have a little time before I have to go into town."

"Good idea," Lucky said, looking up when he heard Otto let out a shout of laughter.

The boy was riding Sugar, Win's eccentric burro, and she'd sat down on her haunches, dumping him gently onto the ground. This was usually her indication that she was done giving rides. Otto got up and leaned against her, scratching her back and neck while she grunted in delight.

As they descended the porch steps, they smiled at the duo. Adam was feeling better and had gone home the day before, so there was no one else around to watch Otto.

"Otto, come with us, lad."

"Why?" Otto asked, walking towards them. "I want to play."

"I know, but we're goin' inside a little. We'll come out again. Besides, it's lunch time," Lucky replied.

"Ok," Otto said, as he caught up to them. "Da, can I have a pony?"

This was probably the hundredth time Otto had asked. Lucky smiled. He remembered how it had felt when he'd gotten his first pony, but he wasn't sure Otto was quite ready for one of his own. Of course, he did well enough with Sugar.

"Da!" Otto said.

"What? Oh, sorry. I can't promise, but I'll think about it," he said.

Otto frowned, but at least his father hadn't said no. "Ok." He'd learned that whining and nagging didn't move Lucky any more than it had Avasa. He let it go for now, but he would ask again sometime.

Win fought a smile at the thoughtful look on Otto's face. Many of his expressions reminded him of Lucky and this was one of them. They entered the tipi and Lucky began heating water for tea and slicing some leftover ham from that morning for sandwiches. Some kids might complain about having the same thing for lunch that they had for breakfast, but Otto had grown up doing that, so he thought nothing of it.

Once he'd served the food, Lucky began going back through his letters, which he kept in a rectangular wicker basket. After taking a bite of sandwich, he started reading one.

"Nope. Nothin' useful there. Cookin' and cleanin'. That's about it."

Win said, "It's useful, just not to Echo as a town."

"Right. Um, next one. More of the same." He kept going until he got to the seventh letter. "Glory be!" he almost shouted.

Win jerked and a little of his tea slopped out of his cup onto his jeans. "What? You scared the sh—crap out of me."

Otto nodded. "Me, too."

"Sorry. A cobbler! This one's a cobbler," Lucky said.

"You eat cobbler," Otto said.

Lucky laughed. "Aye, but a cobbler is also what you call someone who repairs shoes, lad. That's a skill we're lackin' around here."

"You're right. We have to take all of our shoes to Dickensville for repairs. We also have to go there to buy shoes. Temple's only carries a few styles and sizes," Win said.

Lucky's quick mind began going over figures—what size store she'd need and how long it might take to get everything operational. "She can start out by makin' repairs until such time as she's got enough inventory to start sellin' shoes. I wonder what sort of equipment she'll need."

Win smiled. "If you write and ask her, I'm sure she'll tell you."

Lucky laughed. "Don't you ever just think out loud?"

"Rarely."

"Figures. You never talk more than you have to," Lucky said.

"And you talk all the time," Win shot back.

The tipi flap moved and Sugar stuck her head inside. She'd gotten lonely outside and was curious to see what they were doing. The burro also wanted to see if she might be given a treat.

Otto laughed at her. "Sugar's funny."

"Too bad Billy's not here," Lucky said. "He'd want to sketch her doin' that."

"Billy's a bad influence on her."

Sugar was Win's constant companion. He'd saved a farmer's foaling mare and Sugar had been his payment. She'd quickly attached herself to Win and would chew through ropes and break fences to follow him; Win just let her go with him now. She was popular and if she was waiting outside a store for Win, people petted her, which she enjoyed.

Evan was unusual because he crocheted, something very few men did. He had crocheted Sugar three different sweaters: a red one with a white lace collar and gold buttons down the back, a green one with a black satin collar, and a very colorful one made out of scrap yarn that he'd had laying around.

Evan had learned the craft from Edna when he'd been ten and he'd been doing it ever since. He often sat at Spike's working on a project. It relaxed him and he enjoyed giving his creations to other people. Josie and Evan were a perfect match because she enjoyed doing the same sorts of things. Evan was also a great cook, and he and his wife liked cooking together.

Billy was the only other person Sugar would stay with, so when Win had work to do, he often had Billy watch her so she wouldn't get in the way. Sugar was a mooch and liked many types of food; she also adored coffee, but it wasn't good for her and made her very hyper. Billy had a tough time saying no to her about things.

Lucky chuckled. "I can't wait to see what he's like with their kiddies. If he can't discipline a burro, how's he gonna discipline a child?"

Win laughed. "Yep. It'll be interesting, all right. Thanks for lunch. I have to go open up the office for the afternoon. I have one appointment coming in and there might be more people who stop. I hope."

"Don't worry. You've been gettin' more business right along," Lucky said.

Win pushed Sugar's head back through the tipi flap and smiled. "Thanks. I'll be back tonight." He ruffled Otto's hair. "Be good and keep your da in line, ok?"

"Ok, uncle."

After Win left, Otto asked, "Can I go outside?"

"Sure. I'll be right there," Lucky said, gathering up a tablet and pencil. He also grabbed a large woven blanket and took it outside to spread on the ground. The sun shone, warming his shoulders as he sat down to write while Otto ran around with the animals. They'd bought some black sheep, and the two colors made a nice contrast with the grass that was still tinged with green. The woods that half enclosed the meadow created a nice backdrop. He watched Otto play while he thought about what he wanted to say and then got to work.

Dear Miss Carter,

I was very glad to receive your letter. You sound like a very nice lass with a good heart, which is important to me. I'm a single father looking for a woman who's willing to become a mother to my lad. He's been through a rough time this year and he needs a steady woman in his life who can take him into her heart and love him.

That won't be hard to do. I realize I'm his father, so I'm

> *sort of biased, but even if I weren't, I'd say the same thing. He has dark blond hair, dark brown eyes, and my smile, or so my friends say. His mother is a Cheyenne woman whom I was married to for two years before we were separated by the military and she was forced onto a reservation ...*

Leah read Lucky's account of what had happened with Avasa and the subsequent journey he'd gone on in order to be reunited with his wife and child. Tears welled up in her eyes as she read how brokenhearted Lucky had been after he'd lost his wife to another man. She also thought how unselfish it had been for her to give Otto to Lucky to raise so that he could have a better life. She didn't think she'd have the kind of strength it had taken Avasa to part with her child.

> *So as you can see, it hasn't been easy for us, but my main concern is his welfare. Every child should have a loving mother and father and that's what I want for him.*
>
> *Now, here's where I turn a little businesslike. Your letter stated that you're a cobbler by trade, and Echo can really use a cobbler. I'm not sure what your circumstances there are regarding your profession, but if you come to Echo to marry me, I'd be willing to help you set up your own store.*

As she excitedly read the rest of Lucky's letter, Leah began pacing in the parlor of the apartment she shared with her sister. She could see that he was an intelligent, thoughtful man from the way he outlined how they could establish and grow the business. The tender way he spoke about his son practically melted her heart and the funny things he said about his friends made her grin.

He explained why the men in Echo were looking for brides and that three good matches had been made so far. Leah liked his forthrightness about both the situation and why he was looking for a bride. He seemed to possess many good qualities, but would he want someone like her?

She felt a vibration on the floor behind her and turned around to face her sister, Sofia, who said, "Time for supper."

"He wrote back," Leah signed. "And he sounds really nice."

Sofia signed, "Tell me about it during dinner," and smiled. She was excited to hear what this man had to say.

As they ate, Leah told her about Lucky and Sofia liked the happy light in her sister's dark eyes. She knew that it was Leah's dream to marry and have a family, but there weren't many men who wanted a deaf wife. Lucky sounded nice, but it was too soon to tell.

When Leah had first told her she wanted to become a mail-order bride, Sofia had tried to talk her out of it, but Leah wouldn't budge. Her argument for going ahead with her plan had been sound, so Sofia had stopped trying to dissuade her.

"He says that Echo needs a cobbler and that he'll help me set up a shop," Leah signed. "You should just move there with me."

Sofia smiled. "I can't. I'm certain that Gary is going to ask me to marry him very soon."

Leah made a face. "Why do you love him? He's boring and he won't even learn sign language."

That did frustrate Sofia about Gary. He was kind and steady and had a good job at one of the accounting firms in Glendale, California. It was true that he wasn't very witty, but she didn't find him all that dull. She'd tried to teach him sign language, but he'd refused after trying a couple of times.

"I'll just never catch on to it, Sofia. I'm sorry," he'd said.

As a result, he didn't talk to Leah very much. Leah read lips very well and could speak, but she didn't like to because she knew she didn't sound like other people. Therefore, she wrote down her answers to anything he asked her, and he grew impatient waiting for her to finish.

"Gary is a good man and he'll be a good husband," Sofia said.

"And you'll be bored to tears," Leah replied.

Sofia rolled her eyes. "Let's not argue about it anymore. We've been through all of that. Let's concentrate on your Irishman instead."

That was perfectly fine with Leah. They finished dinner talking about the possibilities of a cobbler shop.

Chapter Four

Dear Mr. Quinn,

I hope this letter finds you and Otto well. Your story greatly moved me and I can see what a good father you are. Your farm sounds idyllic, although it also seems as though you have excitement there. I'm happy that your friend Billy found a wife, even if it wasn't the woman he was supposed to have married. It seems as though things worked out well for all four people.

When I told you that I worked as a cobbler with my father in our store, I didn't know that it would impress you so much. I grew up watching him work and began learning at an early age.

You asked what equipment I would need to get started, so I've sent you an itemized list. I hope you don't mind, but my father sent along the name and address of a friend of his who sells us most of our supplies. He's very reputable and knowledgeable. It's in the other envelope he gave me to send with my letter.

Otto sounds very sweet and I'd be honored to be a mother to him. I've always wanted to get married and have a family. Of course, it's only fair that I explain why I haven't. I'm stone deaf and have been since I was around six years old. I'm fluent in American Sign Language and I'm an excellent lip reader. I can also write very rapidly so that I can respond to people who don't know sign language.

I haven't found a man willing to take on a deaf woman, so at the age of twenty-six, I feel like a spinster. By society's standards, I guess I am. I had a series of severe ear infections when I was little that ruined my hearing. My parents took me to a lot of doctors, but they couldn't help me.

I'm very independent and self-sufficient. I can cook, take care of a house, and I'm very good with children. I'll understand if my deafness puts you off, but I wanted to be upfront about it.

Lucky read on, enjoying the rest of Leah's letter. She was plucky, witty, and sweet. As he read, he could envision how pretty she was. Leah had said that her paternal grandmother had been from Spain and that she'd inherited her grandmother's dark eyes and black hair, but had her English mother's pale skin.

When he was done with her letter, he opened the one from her father.

Mr. Quinn,

I understand that my daughter is interested in possibly becoming your bride. If after you read her next letter, you are still interested in her, I feel it only fair to warn you that if you hurt her in any way, I will personally come to Echo Canyon and do you bodily harm. Although it sounds like you're a good man, I'm protective of both of our girls. I'm especially watchful over our Leah and I won't tolerate anyone abusing her or being cruel to her.

I've enclosed the contact information of my friend who makes and sells shoe-making equipment. Again, I warn you; do not get her hopes up if you aren't serious about this.

Mr. Carter

"Well, that does it then," Lucky said.

"What does what?" Billy asked, his dark eyes shifting from the painting he worked on to Lucky.

"What?" Lucky hadn't realized he'd spoken aloud. "Oh, well, let me tell ya about Leah's letter."

By the time he was done, Billy had almost finished with the first part of the painting.

"I'm gonna marry her," Lucky said.

Billy suddenly turned to Lucky in his shock and his paintbrush went right across the rest of the canvas. "Damn it! Look what you made me do!"

Lucky said, "What do ya mean? I didn't make ya do anything."

"Yes, you did! You said you were gonna marry the deaf girl! I've told you before about saying surprising stuff while I'm painting," Billy complained. "Warn me before you do."

Lucky laughed. "So I'm s'posed to say, 'Billy, lad, put yer brush down because I have somethin' shockin' to tell ya?'"

Billy ground his teeth together in anger. "For the love of God, yes! I don't think I can save this. I have to start all over." He sighed resignedly. "Are you kidding about this?"

"I'm not. I don't care that she's deaf. She's bright and funny. She's got a skill we need and it sounds like she'd be good to Otto."

"How are you gonna communicate with her?"

"Weren't ya listenin' to me? She reads lips."

"You didn't mention that part."

"Oh. Sorry. She uses sign language, too. If I learned Indian sign, I can learn hers, too. I'll teach her Indian sign."

Billy sat down next to Lucky on the old sofa in his studio. "Are you saying this because you feel sorry for her?"

"I'm not. I admire her for working so hard at bein' independent and not lettin' her hearing loss stand in her way of doin' anything. I'm glad I had the good fortune of findin' someone like that. It was also lucky for me that other fellas were stupid and couldn't see past it," Lucky said.

"Good. I'm glad to hear you say that. You better be sure, though. Her pa doesn't sound like someone to mess around with," Billy said as his wife came into the studio from the store.

The same night as the fight in Spike's, a group of miscreants had set fire to Billy's old store, burning it to the ground. That had been horrible enough, but the culprits had tried to kill them by attempting to lock them inside the building. Fortunately, Billy had been able to break the window in the kitchen door so that he and Nina could escape. Evan and Shadow had brought the culprits to justice.

The original building had been a large, two-story structure, but Billy had only had enough money from his insurance to build a single-story building. The studio was in the back of the building. Once they had enough money, the Two Moons planned to build an apartment over the store. For now, they lived with Billy's parents in his large, childhood room. Remus and Arlene Decker lived next door to the Tafts, and the two families had become good friends.

The beautiful young blonde woman with huge green eyes walked over to them and sat on Billy's lap. She took Billy's hand and put it on her slightly rounded stomach. "He moved a little," she said. She was certain that they were having a boy, but Billy insisted they were having a girl.

Billy grinned and ran his hand over the area where she'd placed his hand and felt a little movement. He laughed and hugged Nina with his free arm. "Our baby just moved! When did it start? Does it hurt? How many times did it do it?"

"Slow down, Billy," she said laughing. "I wasn't sure at first if it was my imagination or not, but then he did it again. It just happened. That's why I came back here. It doesn't hurt; it's wonderful."

Billy felt it again and tears pricked his eyes. "That's such an amazing feeling. I mean, I know what it felt like when Julia kicked Josie, but it's a little different when it's your own baby."

Lucky saw the happy, loving look Billy and Nina exchanged and felt like an interloper. He was glad that Billy had found someone to love him who understood what it was like to be someone of one race who'd been raised in a completely different culture. Deciding that he should leave the young couple to enjoy the special moment in private, he got up off the sofa.

"I'm very happy for ya both. Ya deserve it. It's a wonderful thing feelin' a wee one move like that. I'll see ya tomorrow," Lucky said, smiling.

Billy grinned. "Thanks. Off to write your girl?"

Lucky kissed Nina and smiled. "Aye. And her father. I think I'll have Evan write him a letter. Sort of like a reference letter or somethin'. It'll sound good comin' from the sheriff."

"That's a good idea," Nina said.

Lucky smiled and exited out the back door.

Pastor Sam Watson had just sat down behind his desk in the church office when he heard someone knock on the doorjamb and saw Evan standing in the doorway. Sam's brown eyes shone with a happy light.

"Hello, Sheriff. Have a seat," said the six-foot-seven tall man who was built like a lumberjack.

Evan closed the door and sat down. He stared into Sam's brown eyes for a minute.

Sam frowned. "What is it?"

"How could you do it to me, Sam? How could you do it to your wife?"

The pastor sat frozen in his chair, completely stunned by Evan's remark. He knew exactly what Evan was referring to.

"I thought we were friends."

Sam had to clear his throat a couple of times before he could say, "We were. We are. I'm so sorry—"

"Friends don't sleep with their friends' fiancées!" Evan said. "And good husbands don't cheat on their wives! And you're a pastor! You're not fit to stand in that pulpit and yet you're up there every Sunday preaching about the Ten Commandments!"

Sam's face flushed crimson. "I know, Evan. I know. It was a mistake. A huge mistake and I'm so sorry."

"You got Louise pregnant, for Pete's sake! Pregnant! Did you know that?"

"Yes. I knew. I told her that I would take care of the baby when she had it, but—"

"She had an abortion. I know the whole sordid story, thanks to Marvin. He gave her the money. Not only did you betray me and Bea, you let someone else take the blame for Louise's pregnancy!"

Sam said, "I know what I've done is horrible and I know there's nothing I can say or do to make it up to anyone. That was the only time I've ever strayed, Evan. I swear. Please don't tell Bea. I love my wife. I don't want to lose her and the kids."

"I'm not gonna tell her, but you and I are through as friends. Do you hear me? I can't trust you. When I think of all the times you've looked me in the eyes and called me your friend, all the while knowing how you'd betrayed me, it makes me sick. I want you out of town after the holidays. You're not the man I thought you were, and this town deserves better," Evan said.

Sam asked, "Where am I supposed to go? It's not that easy to just pick up and go. What do I tell Bea and the kids? What reason do I give them for leaving? Please, Evan, can't you try to understand?"

Evan's eyes locked on Sam's. "Would you have ever told me if Marvin hadn't?"

Sam's jaw flexed and he looked away.

"That's what I thought." Evan stood up. "You have until February. If you're not out of town by then, I'll tell your wife. I don't normally resort to blackmail, but I can't stand the idea of a hypocrite preaching about morality. I don't care what excuse you give your family. I'm sure you'll think of something since you're so good at lying."

Evan slammed the door after him and Sam jumped from the sound. The preacher stared at the door, rage at Marvin filling his chest.

Chapter Five

Dear Mr. Carter,

Thank you for sending the contact information of your friend. I appreciate the help. I understand why you're protective of your daughters. All good fathers are. I can assure you that I have only the utmost respect for Leah. Her deafness doesn't bother me. I admire her courage and determination to be independent. Those are both good qualities to have in a wife.

I'm not the sort of man to take advantage of a woman in any way. Ma and Da raised all of us right and I would never harm your girl or any woman in any way. I'm absolutely serious about your daughter and about helping her set up a business here. Echo Canyon is in dire need of a cobbler and I know that we could build a profitable business.

I've got a good head for business. The sheep farm I started with some friends has started turning a good profit even though we've only been at it for a couple of years now. We've diversified and started selling goats' milk and cheese, which has increased our profits. I've looked at three possible locations for a shop and sent along pictures to Leah so she could see which one she'd like the most. I'm sure she'll show you.

I've decided to build a one-story, three-bedroom house for a couple of different reasons. Keeping in mind Leah's deafness, I've designed a special sort of doorbell that will work well with a one-story house. I'm not sure what else you'd call it, really. It's a series of cords rigged up to pulleys with brightly colored cloths on each of them. When someone comes, they tug on the rope outside and the rags move. She'll be able to see them and know that someone is at the door. I don't want people just walking in and scaring her ...

Broderick Carter finished Lucky's letter and sat back in his wingback chair, tapping a finger thoughtfully against his knee before opening another letter he'd received from a Sheriff Evan Taft. It outlined all of Lucky's good qualities and told Broderick what a great man Lucky was.

Broderick didn't take this sheriff's recommendation lightly. He thought Lucky sounded like quite a fellow. An Irish sheep farmer with business savvy, a kind heart, and ingenuity. Leah could certainly do worse. He and his wife, Constance, just wished that he didn't live so far away. The father in him just wasn't ready to give his blessing quite yet, which he knew was going to frustrate Leah, but he just couldn't. However, there might be something he could do to test the man.

"Papa! How could you?" Leah signed furiously to him the next week at the shop. "You sent him a letter without my knowledge demanding he come here to meet us? Are you insane? You've ruined any chance I have of getting married!"

"I understand why you're angry with me, but if he's really serious about you, he'll come here to get to know us a little."

"You're not thinking clearly," she signed. "He has a business to run just like you do. How is he supposed to just leave it to come here? I can't believe you've done this to me!" She turned away and went to the coat rack, putting her cloak back on.

Broderick got in front of her. "Where are you going?"

"Anywhere but here," she said, her dark eyes flashing fire at him. "I'm too angry with you for going behind my back as though I'm some child who can't make up her own mind. I'm deaf, not stupid."

With that she flung the door open and hurried out onto the sidewalk. Broderick's instinct was to go after her, but he knew it was best to let her calm down before trying to talk to her again.

Marvin looked at his reflection in the mirror in his room and straightened the tie on his tuxedo a little, smiling as he remembered the way Shadow had balked about wearing something so fancy.

"You want Bree to have the best, don't you?"

"Yes, of course," Shadow had said.

"Then a tux it is. You want your wedding pictures to be perfect. Believe me, these things matter, especially to women. You want her to look at them and remember how you went above and beyond for her. Trust me, Shadow," Marvin had replied.

Shadow had groused about it a little more but had agreed on the tuxes. Marvin knew that Shadow was much more comfortable in casual clothing, but this was a very important occasion and he didn't want his twin to have any regrets about the day—or their honeymoon. He knew Shadow was nervous about that, too, even though they were only going to Helena.

Since his existence had been discovered in the spring, Shadow had come a long way with his social skills, but he would probably never be fully comfortable around a lot of people. However, he would do anything for Bree, and he'd wanted them to have a nice honeymoon, even though she hadn't asked for one.

"Come in," Marvin said when someone knocked on his door.

It opened and Shadow entered. "I feel ridiculous."

Marvin turned to look at him. "Well, you certainly don't look ridiculous. What a handsome fellow you are, brother mine."

Shadow grinned. "You're only saying that because we look alike."

Marvin chuckled. "You know me well. But you do. You're going to give your bride a case of the vapors with all of that virility of yours."

"Shut up. Now you're just having fun at my expense," Shadow growled.

"No, I'm not. Don't think I haven't seen women look at you with that particular hunger in their eyes," Marvin said. "With your looks and charm, you could have any woman you wanted."

Shadow smiled. "The only woman I want is down the hall in Ronni's room. So when are *you* going to marry *her*?"

Marvin snorted. "I have to get her into bed first. She's very resistant and stubborn."

"Why first? That's a little out of order, isn't it?"

"Says the man who's getting married to his pregnant fiancée with whom he has been cohabitating for the past year and a half," Marvin said, smiling wryly.

Shadow grinned. "Touché. But in all fairness, Ronni's broken societal rules just by being in your household when she's a single woman."

Marvin frowned. "I couldn't give two shits about societal rules and you know it. Since when did you start caring about them?"

"Since I found out I'm going to be a father. If it were just myself, I wouldn't care, but I don't want my transgressions to cause our child any grief. I think you and Ronni would make a good match. She has Eva to worry about, you know," Shadow said.

The mere mention of Ronni's adorable thirteen-month-old baby was enough to make Marvin grin. Then he sobered. "I understand what you're saying Shadow, but Bree knows all about you and the things we've done and she completely accepts you. Ronni only knows about your childhood and that you were kept secret. She doesn't even know the full extent of that. Before I would consider marrying Ronni, I'd prefer that she knows the truth so that she can't say she didn't know she'd married a monster," Marvin said.

Shadow said. "I just want you to be happy."

"I am. Reasonably enough, anyway," Marvin said. "Bree is a special woman and you met under … unusual circumstances. Not so with Ronni. She's not a former captive criminal who can understand me the way Bree does you. So it's different."

Shadow frowned. "The longer you wait the worse it'll be, Marvy. If you explain it to her now before you've fallen in love with her, it won't hurt as much if she walks away. If she can't accept you now, she's not going to accept you later on."

Marvin smiled and patted Shadow's shoulder. "Let's not worry about all of this right now, Shadow. This is your wedding day—a day of celebration. I'd just as soon not ruin it with this sort of talk. Let's go downstairs to wait for your bride."

As Marvin walked to the door, Shadow said, "I know you're scared, but I think Ronni might surprise you."

Marvin froze and Shadow felt his twin's cold anger seep into his brain. "Scared? And just why would I be scared, Shadow?"

"Because you're afraid you'll fall in love with her and she'll reject you when she finds out the truth, and your heart will be broken again," Shadow said, even as he flinched slightly inside from the force of Marvin's anger.

Marvin laughed, a sound as frigid as the emotion he was giving off. "Of course I am! Wouldn't you be?" he asked, coming back to stand in front of Shadow. "And I'd not only be losing a woman, but also a child I've come to love. There's much at stake and I have to be sure that Ronni is sufficiently enamored of me before springing the fact that we—"

Someone knocked on Marvin's door and he growled in frustration. He took a deep breath, composing himself, and Shadow felt Marvin's anger recede.

Opening the door, Marvin saw Pauline Desmond standing in the hall. "Uncle Marvin, they're ready for you and Spider," she said with a smile.

Marvin laughed. "Well, we don't want to keep everyone waiting, do we?" he asked as Shadow came to stand by him.

Before Shadow's existence had been revealed, Marvin had forbidden Ronni from going into the basement, telling her that there were poisonous spiders down there. In reality, he hadn't wanted her to accidentally find Shadow's lair, which was essentially an underground house. He'd told Ronni about Shadow after his capture and she'd been amused that the fictional spiders were really Shadow. Ronni had started calling Shadow "Spider", and Pauline had picked it up from her.

Pauline was Marvin's ranch foreman's daughter. Travis, along with many people, hated Marvin for his ruthless, cruel ways, but Marvin loved animals and children dearly and had struck up a friendship with nine-year-old Pauline. Marvin paid Travis extra to bring Pauline to see him once or twice a week.

Shadow said, "You look very pretty, Miss Pauline."

The pretty brunette girl smiled. "Thanks, Spider."

Marvin stepped out into the hallway. "Yes, quite fetching. Come along, *Spider*, so we can get you married."

Shadow put his conversation with Marvin out of his mind as they went downstairs. He was about to marry the woman he was desperately in love with and he'd never imagined he'd be so happy. She was his salvation, the one person who took away the nightmares, and had brought so much light into his life of darkness.

As he entered the foyer and turned right into their huge parlor, Shadow took off his tinted glasses, grateful that the heavy gold brocade drapes had been drawn in one part of the room and a candelabra placed in the darkened corner. This allowed for enough light for everyone to see by without hurting Shadow's eyes. He didn't want to look at his bride through the dark glasses.

He looked around at the guests assembled and was surprised that some of them had actually come. He'd known that Evan, Josie, and Edna would, but he hadn't been sure about the others. Billy and Nina stood talking with Tansy and Reggie Temple, the owners of the general store. Lucky was trying to keep Otto from playing the baby grand piano that stood in one corner of the parlor. Erin wasn't feeling well and Win had stayed home with her.

Shadow was shocked to see Jerry Belker and his wife Sonya there, along with a few others to whom Shadow and Bree had extended invitations. He knew that many people had come simply to satisfy their curiosity. Pauline's mother, Jenny, looked around, her discomfort at being there showing clearly on her face.

Otto saw Marvin and ran over to him. "Marvy, hi!" he said.

Much to Lucky's displeasure, Otto also liked Marvin and Shadow and always wanted to talk with the twins. Marvin grinned and bent down. "Hi, yourself, Master Quinn. What kind of trouble are you causing?"

"I want to hear some music, please?" Otto asked, giving Marvin a coaxing smile.

"I promise to play you a song after the wedding, all right?" Marvin asked.

Otto nodded. "Ok."

Marvin stood straight again and caught Shadow's worried glance. His brother was still concerned that he would hurt himself with certain movements. "I'm fine, Shadow."

The doorbell rang and Otto ran to answer it even though it wasn't his house. Prior to coming to Echo, he'd never heard a doorbell or knocked on a door. Now he rang bells and knocked on doors whenever he got the chance. He also liked answering the door.

He was fast and got to the door before Lucky could stop him, pulling it open.

"Thad!" he shouted happily.

A man in his late fifties stepped inside, sweeping Otto up into his arms. "Look at that little blond Indian!" Thad McIntyre said. "Did they put you to work answering the door?"

Otto shook his head. "No. I like it."

"Well, you're doing a good job," Thad said, carrying Otto into the parlor.

Thaddeus McIntyre, bounty hunter extraordinaire, was a close family friend of the Tafts. He'd followed Evan and Edna when they'd come to Echo six years ago. He was known throughout the Midwest for his ability to track down even the most cunning criminals and was often gone for a couple months at a time.

He'd become friends with a lot of people in Echo over the past couple of years. Surprisingly, he and Shadow had struck up a friendship, maybe because they shared the same sort of sense of humor. Despite who and what Shadow was, Thad couldn't help liking him. However, Marvin was a different story. They'd both been in love with the same woman, who had been sleeping with both men. Thad hadn't known Phoebe Stevens had been seeing Marvin, but Marvin had known about Thad. He'd taken great pleasure in knowing that Thad was being two-timed.

Marvin had been in love with Phoebe and had proposed to her several times, but she had kept refusing, and Marvin had ended the relationship. The situation had turned tragic when she'd discovered that she was pregnant with Thad's baby. Phoebe hadn't wanted the baby and had come to Marvin for help, which he'd refused her.

One night she'd come to Marvin's and tried to kill him. They'd struggled over the gun and she'd shot Marvin in the leg. Bree had come to Marvin's rescue, shooting and killing Phoebe. Thad had been devastated by the death of the woman he loved and that of his unborn child. Although daunted by the prospect of becoming a father at first, he'd started getting excited about it. Then the baby had been gone. Needing time to heal, he'd left Echo for several months. Eventually, he'd come back, his heart mended for the most part.

Shadow walked over to him. "I'm glad you came. I wasn't sure if you would."

Thad smiled. "Of course I came. I wasn't going to miss the entertainment."

"I'm sure there'll be some," Shadow said.

"Good," Thad said as Marvin approached and Thad's expression turned dark.

Marvin smiled a little. "I'm surprised to see you, Mr. McIntyre, given our history."

Thad half smiled. "Well, the reason I'm here is simple. You I hate, but him, I like. I'm going to take a seat. Good luck, Mayhem."

Marvin chuckled as Thad moved away and Sam came over to them. "I think we're all set, Shadow," Sam said, completely ignoring Marvin.

Sam's attitude towards Marvin was usually cool, but not downright rude. Marvin looked over at Evan and saw the sheriff's jaw clench as he glared at the preacher's back. Marvin smiled in dark pleasure. *It looks like Evan has had a chat with Pastor Watson. Very good. I'd like to know more about that, but not now. This is Bree and Shadow's day and I'll do nothing to ruin it for them.*

Sam saw Marvin's smug smile and wanted to smash his face in. Instead, he turned away and asked Bea to begin the Wedding March. Everyone took their places. Pauline had gone back upstairs and now came down ahead of Ronni, sprinkling rose petals as she came into the parlor. Marvin's brindle bulldog, Barkley, trotted beside her, carrying a small, decorated pouch that contained the wedding bands.

Ronni entered the parlor and hunger burned inside Marvin as his gaze roamed over the auburn-haired beauty's slim curves. The muted gold dress with slightly puffed sleeves showed off her fine figure and was the perfect complement to her coloring and pale skin. Ronni glanced at Marvin as he stood by Shadow and saw desire smoldering in his gorgeous blue eyes. Her pulse skipped a little in response as she walked down the short aisle between the small group of chairs.

Taking her place a little ways from Sam, she smiled over at Shadow, who smiled back. Her eyes shifted to Marvin then and she let him see her own appreciation of his appearance. He looked suave and incredibly handsome in the black tuxedo. Then everyone's eyes turned towards the parlor door again as Bree came through it on Spike's arm.

Since they'd started frequenting the bar, Bree had become friendly with the older man. He'd been thrilled when she'd asked him to give her away.

Shadow drank in his bride's beauty, feeling as though he was dreaming. The style of her off-the-shoulder, cream-colored dress hid her pregnancy, but Shadow wouldn't have cared if it hadn't. He found the changes in Bree's body very exciting. It made him feel manlier to know that he'd helped create new life. Bree worried that he wouldn't find her attractive as her waist grew, but that wasn't the case at all. Although more gentle, their lovemaking hadn't diminished, which reassured her that he still found her beautiful.

Her wavy brown hair had been piled in a mass of curls on top of her head. Shadow knew how soft her hair was and he wanted to take it down and run his fingers through it. She walked towards them and a little more of his terrible past fell away as his future looked at him with her beautiful brown eyes shining with love. Tears burned his eyes and he had to blink them away.

She smiled at him and its radiance blinded him to everyone and everything but her. Was it Fate or God, if there was one, trying to make up to him for all of the horror and pain he'd endured as a child? If that was true for him, it was certainly true for Bree. She'd been held against her will, subjected to sexual abuse, and forced to create counterfeit money. Two broken people had come together, mending each other's' wounds and finding unexpected love.

Reaching the altar, Bree couldn't take her eyes from the beautiful man before her. Others feared her fiancé, but he'd never given her a reason to be afraid of him. Every look, touch, and kiss was filled with tenderness and love and she trusted him implicitly. Many people would never understand him or Marvin, but she did. She knew how horrible treatment twisted and corrupted the psyche, and she thanked whatever higher power had brought not only her and Shadow together, but also Marvin.

In Marvin, she'd found an older brother, a protector, and a friend. Marvin had accepted her immediately upon meeting her and had shielded her as much as possible from the nasty gossip about her that had swirled through Echo. Although Marvin had his faults, Bree chose to ignore them and focus on his kindness, humor, and intelligence rather than the cruel, cold parts of his personality. And in doing so, she'd earned Marvin's devotion, respect, and brotherly affection.

"Who gives this woman to be married?" Sam asked.

Spike proudly announced, "I do." He looked at Shadow and narrowed his eyes. "You better take good care of her, Mayhem."

Shadow grinned. "I will."

Spike nodded, gave her a kiss, and went on his way. Shadow held out his hands to his bride and she gave hers to him. Bree couldn't believe that she was about to marry the man she'd come to love so intensely. His deep blue eyes stared into hers and she remembered telling him once that he was so handsome that it almost hurt to look at him. It was true; from head to toe, Shadow was sheer male perfection. However, it was what she'd discovered inside him that made her love him so much.

As their vows were exchanged, a few tears that were a mixture of joy and a little disbelief trickled from her eyes, and Shadow kept wiping them away even though he, too, had tears in his eyes. Evan watched the man he'd seen commit savage acts of violence tenderly wipe away his bride's tears and wondered if he was really the same man. It actually brought tears to his eyes to see the softer side of Shadow.

A sniff to his left made him turn to look at Josie, who blotted tears from her face. She wasn't the only one crying. Looking around him, Evan noticed that there was hardly anyone who didn't have tears in their eyes. Even Thad sniffed once or twice. Facing frontwards again, Evan's gaze met Marvin's and the two men shared a smile before Marvin's attention refocused on the couple being married.

When Sam pronounced them man and wife and told Shadow to kiss his bride, they took their time, savoring the moment by unspoken consent. As their lips met, Bree poured all of her love into that kiss, again giving herself completely to Shadow. He felt her love and returned it, his message one of promise and hope for their future together. Parting, they smiled at each other and then faced the guests so that Sam could present them.

The small group clapped and a couple of the guys whistled, which made Otto cover his ears and yell at them to be quiet. Lucky laughed along with everyone else.

Marvin said, "If I may have your attention, we sincerely hope you'll stay and celebrate with us. We have a lovely dinner planned and some entertainment afterwards."

His request was genuine. He wanted the wonderful day to continue for the newlyweds. He was surprised by how many people ended up staying for the meal. Marvin had hired a small wait staff who began serving the meal as soon as everyone was seated. Shadow hadn't wanted a best man's speech, saying that it would embarrass him. While Marvin had acquiesced at the time, he decided to make a short, impromptu one.

He stood up and tapped a fork on his wine glass. "At the risk of my brother murdering me, I'd like to make a toast to him and his lovely bride."

Bree could almost feel anger radiate off Shadow and put her hand on his thigh under the table, patting it. Shadow looked at her and she shook her head a little, giving him a smile. He relaxed and smiled back.

"You may all know him as Deputy Mayhem or some such thing, but I know him as a loyal, loving, humorous man who is supportive and kind. I couldn't be happier in his choice for a mate. Bree has quickly become the sister I never had. She brings out our better sides and has shown unconditional love to Shadow. She's courageous, intelligent, and fun. I wish the both of you many, many years of happiness together. To Shadow and Bree."

The guests clapped and clinked glasses together before drinking to the toast. The meal continued, and some of the guests were surprised that they were having such a good time. They saw a different side of Marvin, finding him to be a witty, attentive host. The food was excellent and the alcohol plentiful.

Evan remembered coming to parties that Marvin had thrown back when he had first come to Echo. They'd always been fun and he'd often left hoarse from laughing so much. Maybe that's why Marvin's betrayal had hurt so much. He'd genuinely liked Marvin and had thought they were friends. Combined with Louise's unfaithfulness, it had created the perfect storm of anger and pain that had solidified into a granite-hard hatred in Evan's heart.

As he ate, Evan thought of the way Marvin had protected Shadow. His deputy had told him that Marvin had taught him how to do simple, everyday things, the same way a parent taught a child. Essentially, Marvin had become the only parent Shadow had ever known. He tried to put himself in Marvin's shoes, imagining what it would be like to find out that your parents were monsters who had committed such atrocities on your brother, whom you'd never known had existed.

And then to find your brother in such a condition? It actually spoke to the depths of Marvin's devotion to Shadow that he hadn't contacted the sheriff or someone at the time and let them take Shadow away. Something suddenly clicked in Evan's mind, a question that hadn't come to him before. This was the way his mind often worked. Things might not always fall into place right away during an investigation, but they usually did at some point, often after coming up with wild theories.

If Marvin had found Shadow when they'd been sixteen and their parents had gone to Europe when they were sixteen, had their parents simply left Shadow to die in the cage or had Marvin found his brother before that? Not today, but at some point, he planned to ask. Something told him there was much more to that story, but would either brother reveal it? If not, why?

Josie noticed Evan's preoccupation and the familiar frown told her that he was running something law-enforcement related around in his brain. "Evan?"

"Hmm? I'm sorry, honey. Were you talking to me?"

She smiled at him. "No. Where are you?"

He leaned a little closer and said, "I'll tell you later."

"I'm going to hold you to that," she said.

He smiled into her blue eyes. "You can hold me to anything you want."

She almost giggled at his innuendo, but managed to keep it from bubbling forth. "We'll discuss that later, too."

"I hope so."

At the other end of the table, Lucky was telling Billy, Nina, and Thad about the letter he'd received from Leah's father.

"So, I'll be goin' to California just as soon as I can," Lucky said.

"You're kidding?" Billy said. "You're really going to go? You just got back home in April."

"I'm aware, lad, but if this is the only way to get her, then that's what I'll do," Lucky said.

Marvin had overheard the conversation. "Pardon me, but are you enamored of the young lady?"

Lucky didn't want to talk to Marvin, but the manners that had been drilled into him by his mother wouldn't allow him to be rude at a social function. "Not enamored exactly, but I admire her for becomin' so independent even though she's deaf. She's a cobbler and works with her father in their shop."

"Deaf? I had a friend in school who was deaf. He taught a bunch of us sign language. It came in useful for more than just talking to him," Marvin said. "I passed calculus because he could tell me the answers on tests that way. Not only that, when we snuck out of the dorm at night, we were all able to talk without making noise. The only problem was when our one friend, Slushy, long story about his name, was too drunk to see someone's hands clearly, he'd shout, 'What? I didn't catch that.' He did that one night and I knocked him out before he kept yelling. The rest of us were sober enough to get him upstairs without getting caught. I'm still not sure how, though."

The story would have been funny no matter who was telling it and Lucky and others laughed. Something occurred to him. "Was it American Sign Language?"

"Yes, actually."

"Do ya remember it?"

Marvin said, "I'm rusty, of course, but with some practice, I'd recall most of it."

Thinking of the greater good and how it would impress Leah's family if he knew some, Lucky asked, "Would ya be willin' to teach me?"

Marvin's eyes widened in surprise. "Am I to understand that you're asking me for a favor?"

Lucky's jaw clenched. "Aye. I am. I suppose ya want something in return."

Using the middle and index fingers and thumb of his right hand, Marvin closed them together much like the way someone shows a duck or bird talking. He did it twice quickly in a snapping motion while shaking his head slightly. "No. I don't want anything in return. There. Now you've had your first lesson. That's how you say 'no' if someone asks you something like, 'did it rain?' If you mean it as a command, it's done just once with a very definitive motion." He demonstrated. "So if Otto did something you didn't want him to, you'd do it that way."

Lucky practiced it. "Well, that one is simple enough, but if it's anything like Indian sign, I'm sure it gets more difficult."

Marvin smiled. "True, but you're an intelligent man. I'm sure you'll pick it up quickly."

Nina said, "You should teach us all so we can talk to her when she comes to marry Lucky."

Marvin looked at her and said, "I would certainly be willing. We could meet a couple nights a week and whomever wants to come is welcome."

"You actually want us in your home?" Billy asked incredulously.

Marvin looked around to see who all was paying attention to them before saying in a low voice, "The only reason I kept everyone away was because of Shadow. Since that's no longer an issue, I wholeheartedly welcome visitors. Well, certain visitors, anyway. Besides, I'm the one who owes all of you a favor since you've kept the circumstances of Shadow's past a secret. So, I'll teach you to show my appreciation."

Lucky pounced. "Done. You tell me what nights are good and I'll be here."

Marvin thought a moment. "Tuesdays and Thursdays. Does that suit?"

"Aye."

Marvin nodded. "Good. We can start this coming week. Six o'clock, and come hungry."

"What?"

"Come for supper. I'll cook," Marvin said. "You and Evan aren't the only men around here who are good in the kitchen. Unless you're afraid I'll poison you."

Lucky responded to the gleam of humor in Marvin's eyes. He laughed. "Only if I get to bring the soup and ya have to eat it."

"A challenge. Good. And whatever *I* make *you* have to eat."

"It's a deal," Lucky said.

Chapter Six

The entertainment consisted of Marvin playing piano so everyone could dance. Most people didn't know that he and Shadow played. Marvin had taken lessons from experts when he'd been away at school and had excelled at the instrument. He had taught Shadow and his twin had picked it up as easily as he had. That expertise showed and he played with flair.

At the end of one song, he said loudly, "If only we had a singer here," while looking at Josie.

The beautiful blonde had a lovely voice and played guitar, too. She'd taught Billy to play guitar and his baritone voice was a great complement to her soprano. They often performed at Spike's.

"Oh, no. I couldn't," she said, even though she'd been humming along with the songs he'd been playing.

"Why not? Do you suddenly have a frog in your throat, Mrs. Taft?"

Shadow said, "If you sing, Josie, I'll play along with Marvin."

Thad perked up at that. He'd never seen the brothers do a duet. He'd seen Shadow play a few times at the Burgundy House, the other saloon in Echo, but watching them play together would be entertaining.

"Go ahead, Josie," he said. "You know how much we love hearing you sing."

Josie's face turned pink and she smiled. "All right. You probably don't know the same songs I do."

"Try us. We play anything from classical to ragtime or even hymns," Shadow said, sitting down by Marvin on the piano bench. "You think of a song while I warm up."

He cracked his knuckles, which made Marvin flinch a little, and then they laughed together. He limbered up with a shortened version of a Beethoven number he liked. Bree loved hearing him play, thinking it ironic that the hands that caused so much pain could also create such beautiful music. When he finished, Josie gave them the name of a song and they decided who was going to do which part.

Marvin and Shadow began together in perfect unison and Josie came in on her cue. Everyone began dancing, not able to keep still during the fine performance. Lucky got Edna up and had her put her feet on top of his so that she could dance, too. His strong muscles were able to take a lot of the weight off her legs and still move gracefully across the floor.

For the next hour, the brothers Earnest and Josie regaled their guests with their musical ability before Shadow and Bree were ready to leave for their honeymoon. The guests began leaving, the newlyweds thanking them heartily for coming.

When everyone had gone, Marvin asked them, "Is there anything you've forgotten to pack or that you need?"

Bree smiled. "No, we have everything. I'm just going to change and I'll be ready."

"We'll both change. I'm ready to get out of this," Shadow said.

"You look so handsome in it," Bree told him.

Marvin gave Shadow a knowing smile, but remained silent.

Shadow said, "And you look absolutely ravishing."

"So you've told me," she replied. "Well, let's go so we can be on our way."

"Yes, dear," Shadow said, imitating an old man.

She giggled as they walked away.

Chapter Seven

On the first night of the sign language lessons, the group was surprised to see Shadow and Bree since they were supposed to be away on their honeymoon. They'd been halfway to Dickensville when Bree had made Shadow stop.

"What is it?" he'd asked. "The baby? Are you all right?"

"I'm fine. We're fine," she'd said. "I'm scared. I know it's been a long time, but what if any of those men are still around and see me? I don't want to disappoint you, but can we please go home?"

"You don't want to go on a honeymoon? We can go somewhere else," Shadow had replied.

Bree had shaken her head. "No. Please can we go home? Don't be angry."

He'd pulled her into his embrace, stroking her hair. "If you want to go home, then go home we shall. I'm not angry. When have I ever been angry with you?"

She'd smiled against his shoulder. "Never."

"And I'm not now, either. So, my little counterfeiter, let's go home," he'd said.

So that's how they came to be present on the first night of the sign language lessons.

After the unconventional meal of blood soup and *okonomiyaki*, a traditional Japanese dish, they went to the parlor where Marvin and Ronni had set up chairs in a large half-circle. He began teaching them simple words and phrases. When Lucky had trouble getting one of them, Marvin had taken his hands without thinking, so he could manipulate them the way they should go. Lucky had pulled his hands away.

Marvin laughed. "Do you want to do it right or embarrass yourself? You just told me that you like licking squirrels. Now, unless that's what you meant to say, I suggest you let me help you."

"Fine," Lucky said, giving him back his hands.

Marvin smiled and went on with the lesson, doing the same for anyone else who was having difficulty.

"Mayhem, why don't you ever have any trouble?" Thad asked Shadow.

"Marvy taught me long ago," he said.

"Why do you call him Marvy?" Edna asked.

To the shock of the group assembled, Shadow flushed beet red. Marvin stood stock still as he looked at his brother. When he would have jumped in to answer and spare Shadow more embarrassment, Shadow held up a hand. Bree took his other one in a gesture of support.

"Because of my speech impediment, I couldn't say Marvin correctly. It always came out as Marvy, and it became my pet name for him. Marvin had to teach me how to speak correctly since Father was the only one I'd ever heard talk before and we didn't exactly have productive conversations."

Evan's green eyes glittered with anger over Shadow's former plight. "Your father was a real evil bastard, wasn't he?"

"Yes," the brothers said in unison.

Edna asked, "How do you say 'bastard' in sign language?"

The room rang with laughter and Marvin had to sit down, holding a hand over his groin because he was laughing with such force over her remark. Shadow was relieved for the humor and also glad that the conversation didn't pick up there again. Instead, Marvin spent the remaining time of their lesson showing them vulgar language.

On the last day of their lessons before Lucky was to leave for California, he received a telegram from Leah and he could almost feel her frustration in the message.

Father will not let me come back with you unless we are married or we have a chaperone. As you know, Sofia was supposed to come with me, but she can't now because Gary proposed and their wedding plans are moving forward.

Lucky had growled his own frustration. The letters he and Leah had exchanged had only cemented his feelings that they would make a great match. Billy couldn't go with him this time because Nina was pregnant and he couldn't afford to take time away from their shop. Thad had gone on another job, Evan certainly couldn't go, nor could Win, Erin, or Josie. Edna had come down with the flu so Josie was taking care of her.

That night, after dinner, he thanked Marvin for all of his help.

"I appreciate all you've done, but I have to postpone the trip," Lucky said.

Marvin frowned. "Why?"

Lucky told him about Broderick's new demand. "I can understand, but I'd hoped by now he'd come to realize that I wouldn't harm Leah in any way. I'm not gettin' married without my best man and my friends, so I won't marry her out there. No one can go with me right now."

"What about Wild Wind?"

"Too much risk of him bein' taken by the military," Lucky said. "Besides, he's gonna be helpin' on the farm while I'm gone."

"I see." A sly smiled spread across Marvin's face. "Do you know what would be better than a single man or woman going with you?"

"What?"

"A family," Marvin said, looking across the room at Ronni and Eva, who were talking with Erin and Win.

Lucky followed his eyes. "What kind of nonsense are ya talkin'. Youse aren't married."

Marvin said, "I know that, but your bride's family doesn't."

Lucky could almost see Marvin's mind working. "What kind of crazy scheme are ya thinkin' up now?"

"You would be doing me as much of a favor as I would be you," Marvin said. "You see, as much as Ronni and I fight, I'm quite attracted to her and she to me, but she won't admit it. Perhaps if I could get her away from here, I might stand a better chance of making her see that we could make a go of it."

Lucky said, "But if we go away, ye'll hafta stay in the same room to make it look like yer married."

"I'll sleep on the floor," Marvin said. "The trick is to get her to agree to it."

"Now, look, I won't be a part of ya takin' advantage of her," Lucky said.

Marvin's gaze turned cold. "I won't be taking advantage of her. Trust me."

Lucky smirked at him. "That's funny coming from you."

"Do you want your bride or not?" Marvin asked. "If you do, this is the payment."

"I shoulda figured it was too good to last," Lucky said.

Marvin closed his eyes a moment. When he opened them, he said, "Lucky, I know that we have a bad history. Well, I have a bad history with almost everyone. That said, almost dying tends to make a man think about the way he's lived his life in the past. I'm not saying that I've seen some sort of light and now I'm a saint. However, I do see where I've made some mistakes and I'd rather not repeat them. So, in the spirit of altruism, whether or not Ronni goes with me, I'll come with you."

"Do ya really mean all that?" Lucky's gray eyes focused intently on Marvin's gaze. It was the Irishman's nature to see the good in people and he believed in forgiveness and repentance.

Marvin searched down deep inside, a place he rarely went. "Yes. I mean it. You're leaving on Monday, correct?"

"I am."

"Well, either way, you won't be going alone."

Lucky said, "If ya back out for any other reason than an emergency, I'll make ya sorry."

Marvin smiled. "I understand how important this is to you. I won't back out."

Lucky saw the way Marvin was staring at Ronni and thought that maybe he really did have feelings for her. "Thanks again."

Marvin nodded.

Marvin couldn't sleep that night because his brain kept working on how to convince Ronni to agree to his idea. While his plan behooved Lucky, and, for once, he wanted to do something to help someone besides his loved ones, he still had his own agenda.

Giving up, he went downstairs where he was greeted by Barkley, who liked to sleep on the sofa. Marvin was indulgent with the dog and let him up on the furniture. Pouring some scotch into a glass, he sat down on the sofa with the dog, who immediately scrambled onto his lap.

"Easy, Barkley. You're heavier than you think you are," he said, patting the dog's broad back.

Barkley panted happily and tried to lick Marvin's face.

Marvin laughed. "You're always happy to see me, aren't you? I'm always glad to see you, too. Sorry to wake you, but I know you don't mind. What kind of doggy dreams were you having? Pleasant ones I hope. I wasn't having any. You have to sleep to do that."

The dog whined as though he understood what Marvin was saying. Then he let out a soft woof that told Marvin that someone was moving around the house. He was expecting Shadow to come into the parlor since his brother's internal clock still wasn't adjusted to his new schedule and he was still awake some nights. He was surprised to see Ronni come into the room.

"Marvin? Are you all right?"

"Yes. Just couldn't sleep."

She walked towards him and Marvin's strong craving for her flooded through his body.

Ronni sat on the other end of the sofa and Barkley came over to say hello to her, too. His stubby tail wagged right along with his rear end, showing his happiness at seeing her. She hugged him and chuckled when he rolled over so she could scratch his belly.

"What's on your mind?" she asked.

"You."

She smiled and leaned her head back against the sofa. "Now you're teasing me."

"No, I'm not," he said, rubbing Barkley's head.

Looking at her, Marvin knew he'd never encountered a more beautiful woman. It wasn't only her physical beauty, but also her spirit, bravery, and kindness. She was a wonderful mother and he could see that she must have been an equally wonderful wife to her husband. He thought David had been a very lucky man.

"So what exactly are you thinking about me?"

Marvin could out-manipulate almost anyone, blackmail them, bend them to his will, intimidate them, or make them rue the day they ever crossed him, but revealing his true feelings was something he'd only ever done with Shadow. Not even Phoebe had ever seen past the blackened part of his heart to what light might lie underneath the hard outer shell. He'd hidden that part of himself away for many years. It was what he thought of as the Young Marvin. The boy who had believed in good and fun and who'd thought his parents were the most loving, generous people on Earth.

The day he'd found Shadow, his world had shattered and he'd come to believe that because he'd come from monstrous people, than he must be a monster, too. So he'd become that vile creature, not only to protect Shadow, but to protect himself as well. Being cold, cruel, and heartless had become second nature to him, but not showing his softer side. However, Shadow had begun doing it with Bree and it seemed to be working for him. Could it work for him, too?

He dug down deep and found courage and determination of a different nature.

"I've been trying to figure out a way to ask you for a favor, not only for myself, but for someone else. I'm a very convincing man, but not normally by kind methods. However, I can't seem to come up with anything devious at the moment, which is odd for me. Odder still, I find that I don't want to," he said, meeting her eyes. "So, I'm just going to ask."

Ronni's forehead puckered with puzzlement. "All right. Go ahead."

He explained Lucky's predicament in a straightforward manner, outlining the reasons why the subterfuge was necessary and then fell silent.

"So I would have to sleep in the same room as you?" she asked.

"Yes, but I would sleep on the floor."

"Would we wear wedding bands?"

"I suppose we'd have to. I can take care of that. I just need your ring size."

"How do I know that you wouldn't try to take advantage of me?" she asked.

Marvin laughed. "I've been trying to take advantage of you, but you're having none of it. I haven't even gotten a proper kiss out of you."

She turned towards him and drew her feet up underneath her. "I'll tell you why that is. I know that you're a womanizer and I don't want to be just a conquest to you. I believe in being married before being intimate with a man. I was a virgin on my wedding night and I never expected to be a widow. I thought that I would only ever be with David. I haven't been with anyone since and I won't be again without being married."

Marvin nodded. "I suspected as much, which is why I haven't offered marriage, Ronni. I'd like to, but it's really for your own good that I don't, or won't, until we've been intimate."

"I don't understand what you mean. Why is that a prerequisite to marriage?"

Marvin dug down for more courage. "My original injury left me incapable of fathering children. Everything worked, and worked very well, but I couldn't make a baby. However, since being reinjured and having a second surgery, I don't know if that's still the case. So I would never marry any woman without knowing if I could properly perform. I recognize that women have needs and urges of their own, and I would never trap a woman in a passionless marriage. It's bad enough I can't father children."

Ronni had come to know Marvin fairly well and she knew that there were very few subjects he would shy away from even if they were considered improper or scandalous. This conversation certainly fell into that category, but she actually appreciated his candor about the matter. Even though other people might not see it, he was actually being kind about his reasons for wanting intimacy before marriage.

Men were prideful, especially about something that showed their virility, and fathering children was one of the most important ways to do that. She could only imagine how much not being able to father a child must hurt, especially for a man like Marvin who loved children so much.

She saw it whenever he played with Eva and Pauline. Whenever he saw one of them, his eyes lit up and if he'd been in a bad mood, it instantly dissipated. He was also growing closer to Otto even though it was evident that Lucky hadn't been comfortable with that at first. However, during their sign language lessons she'd seen Lucky become more accepting of it.

Ronni wasn't blind to Marvin's faults. She'd heard people talk about him and some had asked her how she could stand working for Marvin and living with him. She had just smiled and said, "You don't really know him," and left it at that. Marvin had committed many transgressions over the years. She couldn't dispute that and neither did he. She knew he was often temperamental and cold with his employees, but she hadn't let herself be one of them. The secret to dealing with Marvin was pushing back when he came at you. He liked the challenge and respected courage.

Should he be like that? No. However, she'd seen him mellow a little since being hurt and being a hair's breadth away from death's door. Sometimes that's what it took to make people examine their lives and make changes for the better.

"Will you do it? The favor for Lucky?" he asked.

"I want to trust you, Marvin," she said. "I just don't know. I don't want to promise anything."

Marvin smiled a little. "I understand. It's ok. I had to try." He drained his glass and rose.

A crazy idea came to her as he walked away from her. "Marvin?"

"Yes?" he asked, looking back at her.

She got up and came to stand before him. "I propose a test."

One golden eyebrow lifted. "What kind of test?"

She squared her shoulders. "I will sleep with you tonight, just *sleep* in the same bed with you. If you can do that without trying anything, I'll go with you and Lucky."

Marvin remembered a conversation he'd had with Shadow the previous year about just this subject.

"Have you ever just slept with a woman, Marvin? Just slept, nothing more?" Shadow asked.

Marvin thought back through the women he'd been with. "No, I haven't. After we were intimate, there were times when we slept, but we never just slept."

Shadow laughed. "Neither did I until Bree came along. It's a beautiful experience. I hope you get the chance to do it sometime."

His mouth curved upwards. *I think I'll find out exactly what Shadow meant.* "I accept your challenge."

Chapter Eight

Ronni had been torn between wanting him to accept and hoping he'd refuse. She was trapped now, though. "Ok. I'll check on Eva and be right along."

As they climbed the stairs, Marvin couldn't help teasing her. "I sleep in the nude, just to let you know."

Ronni tripped up a step and Marvin slipped an arm around her waist to steady her. "Careful. Don't worry, I'll be decent when you come over."

He released her and she almost ran the rest of the way up them. Pride made her keep a slower pace. They turned in opposite directions at the top of the stairs. Eva slept peacefully, so Ronni went to her room for a moment to collect herself.

I must be insane! What was I thinking? I wasn't, I guess. Oh, what have I gotten myself into? I'm so stupid. If I back out now, though, he'll know I'm scared. I don't want him to know or think he's bested me. If anything happens, I'll just stop it. If only he weren't so damn handsome! Get ahold of yourself! It's just sleeping!

Her inner tirade over, she decided that the warm nightgown and underthings made her decent enough. She certainly wasn't going to put on a dress to sleep in. Ronni almost changed her mind as she walked down the hall. What if he really was nude? So what? She wasn't. He was only teasing, or so he said.

She knocked on his partially open door.

"No need to knock. Come in."

He still wore long underwear, which made him presentable enough, she supposed. "Which side do you prefer?" he asked. "It makes no difference to me since I'm usually all over the bed."

"Um, the right side."

"Ok." He blew out the lamp, lay down on the left side of the bed, and sighed as he relaxed. Ronni hadn't moved. "Are you waiting for an engraved invitation? Come on then. I won't bite. Unless you want me to."

She stomped around to the other side and sat down, looking at him over her shoulder to make sure he hadn't moved. Getting up the nerve, she lay down, pulling the covers up to her chin. She stayed as far away from Marvin as she could.

"Ronni?"

"Yes?" She didn't even look at him. Her heart pounded in her chest.

"Welcome to my bed."

His absurd statement made her giggle. He chuckled and her giggle turned into a laugh, which made him laugh harder. She felt him move and she knew he'd rolled over to face her. Ronni couldn't believe how shy she felt. She almost bolted from the bed, but her pride rose up again, insisting that she stay.

"Do you always sleep straight as a board?"

"No."

"That's good. I can't imagine that's very comfortable."

"No."

Marvin grew irritated. "Ronni, you can look at me for God's sake. I'm not going to accost you."

"I'm not afraid of you. I'm afraid of myself."

"Why?"

"In case you don't know, which is impossible, you're an extremely handsome man and very tempting to a lonely widow."

"You don't have to be lonely, Ronni. I guess I'll have to be the strong one, then," he said, chuckling. "That's something I'm not used to being in this area. But I do like the idea that I tempt you. However, I'm a little scared, too. As much as I want you, I'm afraid to start anything in case … well, you get the idea."

The uncertainty in his voice made her look at him and she saw his fear in the luminous depths of his eyes. Sympathy replaced her own fear. She rolled in his direction, feeling for his hand. She couldn't find it.

"What are you doing?" he asked.

"Well, I wanted to hold your hand. Where are they?"

He laughed. "I don't know why, but I sleep with them under my pillow."

"Hiding them on me, huh?"

"You'll have to forgive me. I wasn't expecting hand-holding. You shock me with your forwardness, madam."

She giggled as she felt him take her hand.

"Oh! How scandalous," he said. "Do you believe that some mothers tell their girls they can get pregnant just by kissing a boy? It's cruel, really. Scaring the poor girls to death like that. I understand the intent, but I still think it's mean."

"My mother didn't tell me anything at all," Ronni said.

"Really? She didn't explain anything to you so you knew what to expect on your wedding night?" Marvin asked.

"No. And you're right; I was terrified. All I knew what that it was a duty I had to perform and that it wasn't pleasant. David proved all of that wrong," Ronni said.

"Well, I'm glad for that at least."

Ronni decided to challenge him. "So if *you* had to explain things to a girl, how would you do it?"

Marvin didn't hesitate to answer. "I would explain the mechanics of it first and then tell her to wait at least until her body was fully mature, but that it was her choice if she waited for marriage or not. I would also tell her to make sure that any of her partners were gentlemen she felt comfortable with and not to let anyone pressure her into it."

"So that's what you would say to Eva if she were your daughter?"

"Yes, I would. I think it's terrible to put constraints on that sort of thing, girl or boy. Know the consequences of your actions, however. I realize that's worse for girls since boys can't get pregnant, but still. I also don't have time for all of the namby-pambies who are afraid to utter anything remotely sexual."

"You like shocking people, don't you?"

"Yes, I do. It's amusing, to say the least. Even the religious can't deny that some of the most famous men in the Bible were adulterers. I've had that argument with several pastors over the years and they can't refute it or get around it. I always end up saying something like, if God's people did it and it was overlooked, then why is it so wrong if I do it?"

"Marvin! That's terrible," she said even though she found it funny.

"I know. I'm very wicked." He sighed. "You have no idea how wicked I am."

Ronni sobered. "What do you mean?" A tingle of fear shot up her spine.

Marvin sighed. "Ronni, you are lying in a bed with a very vile individual and before you stay any longer tonight or agree to go to California with me, I'm going to confess some things to you because I respect you and care for you. They will significantly alter the way you see me. Do you want to hear these things or shall we just let it go?"

Curiosity made her say, "Tell me."

"As you already know, Shadow was kept caged until I found him. I'm grateful to you for not telling anyone the true circumstances of his childhood, if you could call it that," Marvin said.

"Yes."

"When I found out that my parents had been keeping my twin from me, I was livid. I was beyond furious at the state in which I found him...."

Marvin struck a match and lit the candle he'd brought with him. He found himself looking at a large cage, much like one that a circus tiger would be kept in. He judged it to be about eight by eight feet. Something moved and he jumped. Then he saw that it was what looked like a human, but it scurried away from the light.

"Hello? Who are you?" Marvin asked. "Why are you down here?"

The person glanced at him briefly and Marvin could tell that he was afraid. He thought it was a boy, judging by the clothing on him. It was hard to tell because long, dark, matted hair hid their face so much.

"It's ok. I won't hurt you, I promise. It's all right. Come here so I can help you," Marvin said.

The boy shuffled a little closer and then looked at him and Marvin's blood froze in his veins. His own face looked back at him. The boy's hair might be dark, but the blue eyes were the same and the bone structure was identical to his. Marvin touched his own face a moment.

"Who are you?" he asked softly. "I'm Marvin. I think you're my brother. You look like me, but you're dead. They told me you'd died."

The boy came a little closer again, but squinted in the candlelight. "Marvee? Brodder?"

Marvin grinned, excited that he'd gotten through to the other boy. He'd noticed the way that he'd spoken. It occurred to him that his brother had been down there for as many days as he himself had drawn breath. He saw the horrible conditions his brother lived in. A stained mattress laid in one corner with a couple of blankets piled near it. There was one chair in the enclosure and a chamber pot sat in one corner. A fetid odor hung in the air.

Near the bed sat a stand with a few children's books on it. He noticed that a candle sat on the stand. Was that the boy's only source of light? Looking around, Marvin confirmed his suspicion that it was. How could his parents do this? What kind of people were they?

"What's your name?" he asked.

The boy came a little closer.

"That's it. It's ok. I'm your brother. I won't hurt you. Come here," Marvin said.

Finally his brother came over to the bars and Marvin reached his hand through them. The boy flinched away, but Marvin kept his hand there, smiling at the boy.

"It's ok. I won't hurt you. Take my hand."

The boy slowly reached out and slipped his hand into Marvin's. In that moment a connection was made—one so strong, so powerful that both of them knew that nothing but death would ever break it. Marvin smiled at the boy again and was rewarded by the boy returning it.

"What's your name?" Marvin asked again. "Your name?"

"Thadow."

Marvin asked, "Thadow?"

The boy pointed at the shadow the candlelight made on the wall. "Thadow."

"Shadow? Your name is Shadow?" Marvin couldn't believe it. Who in their right mind would name their son Shadow? Then he realized that everything he thought he knew about his parents and his life had been false. His parents were strangers to him. Complete, insane, cruel-beyond-belief strangers.

There was a noise from back the way Marvin had come and Marvin knew his father, their *father, was coming. He gripped Shadow's hand tighter. "Don't tell him I was here. I'll come back, ok? I'll come back for you. It's ok. You're not alone anymore."*

Then he gave Shadow's hand a last squeeze and went back out to the first part of the cellar, hiding under the stairs as his father walked to the secret door and went through it. Hot rage flowed through him and he vowed to get Shadow out of that cage if it was the last thing he did. He hurried from the cellar, running outside and into the woods. He kept running until he had a stitch in his side.

Then he sank down on the ground and cried for his brother and for himself. He let out screams of anger and grief. There in those woods a powerful hatred for his parents was born inside his heart. He made another vow to avenge the wrong that had been done, mainly to Shadow by their parents, but also to himself by them keeping Shadow from him. The first cruel smile Marvin had ever made settled on his face and his keen mind began formulating a plan.

Ronni watched his face and listened in horror to Marvin's recounting of the terrifying ordeal the brothers had undergone. Marvin's countenance underwent so many changes and his story was so eloquent that Ronni felt as though she were experiencing it along with him. Anger, joy, disbelief, and hate showed so plainly that Ronni felt dazed by all of the emotions that coursed through her.

Marvin's own emotions overcame him and he couldn't continue. He'd never told another soul these things. Who could he tell since he'd had to keep Shadow's existence a secret for so long? There'd been no one to confide in, no one to whom he could unburden himself. The recounting was painful, but yet it also felt good. Tears ran down his face and he covered it with his hands.

The kind, motherly side of Ronni rose to the fore and she moved so that she could put her arms around Marvin. His arms closed around her and he clung tightly to her. She stroked his hair and whispered reassurances to him.

"It's ok now, Marvin. Shh. Everything's all right," she said as he sobbed against her.

Marvin tried to stop crying, but he couldn't for a long while. The boy, who had been forced to bury it all down deep inside him, needed to be released from his own cage. The boy who'd found his brother, freed him, and secured their safety, surged up out of Marvin's dark heart and demanded to finally be heard.

Eventually, he cleared his throat and said, "That's not the worst of it. I've never told anyone any of this. No one but you. I don't know why, but I trust you enough to tell you. I didn't just make sure Shadow got out of that cage; we made sure he'd never be put back in one. I was damned if I would ever let anyone hurt him again and they needed to pay, and they did. Trust me when I tell you that they paid dearly."

Ronni drew back a little from him, brushing hair from his forehead. "What happened?"

Marvin's eyes met hers. "We killed them, Ronni. We killed them and I'll never regret it. Neither of us do."

Her breath caught in her throat. "You murdered them?"

"Yes. On the last night that Shadow ever spent in that cage, I let him out and together, we killed them, but not right away. I'd slipped some laudanum in their nightcaps and they slept soundly while we dragged them downstairs and put them in that cage."

Marvin had stopped crying now and he said, "And when they woke up and realized where they were, the looks on their faces was one of the greatest things I've ever seen. And they soon realized that they had entered their own personal hell." The look of rapture on his face made her tremble.

Marvin felt it and looked into her eyes. "I told you I was wicked. Do you believe me now?"

Ronni nodded. "Yes," she whispered.

"Are you going to turn us in?" he asked.

"No."

"Why? Because you're afraid of what we'll do to you if you do?"

"No," she said, her expression turning furious. "Because I'd have killed them, too! I don't want to know what you did to them, but I am so glad you made them suffer. They deserved it. If I had been there, I would have helped you. How does a parent do such unspeakable things to a child?"

She hugged Marvin and he returned her embrace even though he was in shock. He'd expected revulsion, fear, and rejection, but instead Ronni had offered him sympathy and comfort. Stunned wasn't a strong enough word to describe what he felt at that moment. He also felt lighter and freer than he had in a very long time.

He heaved a shuddering sigh. "Why aren't you running for your life and taking Eva with you?"

"Because if you'd wanted to harm us you'd have done it long ago. I know that we have nothing to fear from you. In fact, after hearing your story, I would hate to be anyone who ever did anything to us."

Marvin took her by the arms and pushed her away so he could look into her eyes. "I promise that no harm will come to you or that sweet baby as long as you are in my household. I don't care who it was or what they did to me, I would die before I'd let anyone harm you. And if anyone did, they would die the worst death imaginable. I promise you that here and now, Ronni."

His grip was firm but he wasn't hurting her. The fierce expression on his beautiful features was so intense that she forgot to breathe as she looked at him. "I believe you," she said, tracing his jawline with her fingertips.

Marvin moved swiftly, capturing her lips as he pulled her hard against him. Ronni was shocked and pushed against him, but then his kiss gentled and he loosened his arms from around her somewhat.

He abruptly broke the kiss. "I'm sorry. I shouldn't have done that. My emotions are all over the place. Forgive me. I honestly didn't intend to seduce you. I'm rambling and I need to shut up and I can't."

Rolling away from her, he sat up on the side of the bed, and plowed his hands through his hair. "Go on back to your own bed, Ronni. You don't have to come with me and Lucky."

Hunger rose in Ronni as she looked at his strong back, but she curbed it somewhat. She reached over and ran a hand over it. "Marvin, I'm not going anywhere. Come back."

He turned to her, uncertainty showing on his face. "Are you sure? I just want to hold you."

She motioned for him to come to her. He slid back into bed and stretched out beside her. Then they put their arms around each other and Marvin hugged Ronni to him. As she listened to his heartbeat under her ear, his warmth seeped into her and after a while and her eyelids grew heavy. Marvin felt her breathing change and her arms relax a little.

He smiled and kissed her forehead. "Sweet dreams, Ronni," he whispered and closed his eyes.

Chapter Nine

Lucky smiled down at his sleeping son as they neared their destination. His hair was even curlier with it shorter and it surrounded his head like a halo. He certainly hadn't been angelic about getting it cut. Otto's hair had been down to his shoulders and wild since he'd never had a haircut before. Win had cut about four inches off it and shaped it so that it was a little more presentable for meeting Leah and her family. In the end, he'd had to promise to buy Otto a pony so he'd sit still for Win.

Win's mother had taught him how to cut hair and it was a service that many in Echo now sought out. When Erin and he had first met, he'd had to cut her hair because she'd been attacked by a thief who'd torn out a large chunk of her hair. That was on the day Win had picked her up in Cheyenne. Win had fixed it for her as best he could and she'd looked attractive with her rich brown hair in the short cut. The style had grown on her and she had Win keep it that way now.

The conductor signaled that they had about ten minutes until they reached Glendale. Lucky shifted Otto and shook him a little. "Time to wake up, lad," he said. "We're almost there." Otto groaned a little and buried his face against Lucky. "I know. It's been a long trip, but I'll let ya have a nap after we get settled at the hotel. All right?"

Otto sat straight again and gave a huge yawn before wiping sleep from his eyes. "Da, I'm hungry."

Lucky smiled. "You always wake up that way. Yer like me. I have some wasna. Will that do for now?"

Otto's eyes lit up. "Yes!"

Lucky opened the sack he'd brought with them and gave Otto a strip of the jerky, which the boy immediately began gnawing on. He couldn't quiet the nerves in his stomach as his anticipation grew. Mentally he went over the correct hand gestures with which to greet Leah, wanting it to be perfect. In their last letters to each other, they'd sent pictures, and Lucky pulled Leah's out of the inner pocket of his suit jacket to look at it again.

She was smiling in the picture and her pretty dark eyes shone with good humor. Her black hair was done up in a Gibson-Girl style and the dress she wore hinted at lush curves. She was a beautiful woman.

"Da, where are we?" Otto asked.

"Glendale, California," he replied.

"Where is that?"

Lucky smiled. His son was curious about everything. "I'll show ya on the map later."

Otto nodded as he finished his treat. Lucky looked across the aisle at Marvin and Ronni. Marvin held Eva up so that she was standing on his thigh. Lucky looked at the ring on Marvin's left hand and smiled. He didn't know how he'd convinced Ronni to go with them, but he was grateful, which he'd told the both of them a couple of times.

Who would have ever thought that he'd be depending on Marvin for anything? Life sure was strange, he thought. That was one of many things Lucky had learned in his lifetime. Another was to plan on things changing because they always did. Life wasn't static; it was fluid and one had to either meet the challenges that arose and be victorious over them or shy away from them and be left behind, miserable and broken. He always chose the former and not the latter.

The train slowed as it rolled into the station and stopped. Otto jerked a little at the loud hissing sound of steam releasing from the train. Then he laughed.

"This train animal is loud," he said. "Is it hungry?"

Lucky laughed. Otto insisted that the train was alive and he didn't bother arguing with him. "Well, it does sorta eat, so ya might say it's hungry. Put yer coat on. It's cold out there."

"Ok." Otto plopped the last piece of wasna into his mouth, stuck his arms in the little warm dress coat, and stood still while Lucky buttoned it.

"There." He took Otto's face in his hands and said, "What a handsome fella ya are. Just wait 'til yer older. All the girls will chase ya."

Otto grinned. "I'll just keep runnin'."

"When ya find the right one, stop runnin', though."

"Ok."

Lucky stood and picked Otto up. Marvin, and Ronni, who now held Eva, also moved into the aisle with them.

"Don't be nervous, Lucky," Ronni said. "She'll take one look at you and fall in love."

Lucky smiled. "I'm not worried so much about Leah; it's her parents, her father especially."

"You'll do just fine. Just put on that Irish charm of yours and none of them will be able to resist you," Marvin said.

Lucky couldn't figure out what was different about Marvin, but he was somehow ... happier maybe? "Thanks."

When they disembarked from the train, Otto reached over and patted it. "Good train. Bye."

Lucky chuckled and followed the "Earnests" to get his luggage. Upon fetching it, he looked at his pocket watch and concluded that Leah should be along shortly.

"Hurry, Papa!" Leah signed and walked ahead of her father.

He drew even with her and signed. "I'm right here. We're on time, Leah."

"I can't believe he came even after the way you kept changing things on him," Leah said.

Broderick knew she was still angry with him. "At least you know he's serious about you. I wish you'd wait to leave until after the New Year."

She gave him a steady look. "I've waited long enough."

He pursed his lips, but stayed silent. His headstrong, impulsive daughter was a trial to him, but also a great joy.

Leah caught sight of the man she thought was Lucky. He wore a very nice black woolen coat and a matching bowler hat. A little blond boy walked beside him, holding onto the man's coat. The little boy's blond hair was curly and his dark eyes were wide as he looked around at everything. The man looked up, saw them, and smiled. Leah was spellbound by his grin.

He was bigger than she'd anticipated and only became more so the closer he came. She could imagine how strong he was. His broad shoulders looked like he could easily carry a sheep or haul hay or anything else, for that matter. He moved with grace and confidence. As he and the boy drew nearer, she saw the way his gray eyes twinkled and she couldn't keep from smiling.

He took off his gloves and she wondered why until he signed, "Hello. You must be Leah, but yer even more beautiful in person. Yer picture didn't do ya justice, lass."

She was so surprised that he'd signed as he'd spoken that she didn't respond right away. Then she grinned up at him. "Hello. You didn't tell me you signed."

Lucky motioned to the blond man and redheaded woman standing beside him. "Well, allow me to introduce Marvin and Ronni Earnest, my good friends. This is their daughter, Eva. Marvin taught me American Sign Language since you don't know Indian sign."

Leah turned her attention to the Earnests. "Hello. It's so nice to meet you. Lucky said you would be coming with him."

"It's a pleasure to meet you as well," Marvin signed. "Lucky's right. You're quite the attractive young lady."

Leah blushed. "This is my father, Broderick."

Broderick smiled and shook hands with the other three adults.

Lucky said, "This is my son, Otto. Otto, this is Leah and Mr. Carter. Can you say hello?"

Otto hid behind Lucky a little, but he signed, "Hello."

Leah smiled. "You taught him, too?"

"We did," Lucky said. "He needed to be able to sign, too. He knows Indian sign, too."

"Will you teach me?" she asked.

"Aye."

Leah noticed that his spoken words didn't quite match his signed words, but he'd explained that he spoke differently than Americans and the British. The Irish rarely said, "yes" or "no" unless they were being very emphatic. He said either, "aye" or some variation of "I will" or "I won't", "she will" or "she won't". Lucky had also told her that he rarely pronounced the "th" sound, so "think" came out as "tink" and so on.

She was glad that he'd told her and was impressed by his thoughtfulness in general. That would limit confusion if he didn't sign something to her. She'd still understand what he was saying.

Broderick said, "Well, let's get you to your hotel and then go over to our house. Constance and Sofia are making a nice dinner for us."

Lucky nodded. "All right."

He could see where Leah got her looks. Broderick might have an English given name, but his Spanish heritage was plain to see in his black hair, dark eyes, slightly dusky skin, and aquiline nose. He was a handsome man and Leah looked very much like him, only in female form with more delicate features. Broderick was slightly shorter than Lucky's six-foot-two height, but he was strong and his hands were calloused from all the work he did with them.

As they walked to the area where taxis congregated, Lucky fell into step with Leah.

"How was your trip?" she asked.

"It was fine. Otto likes the train—he thinks it's alive. I'm glad he wasn't afraid of it. He's been curious about everything. He's never seen a train since he lived on the reservation all of his life."

Leah met Lucky's eyes and said, "I'm sorry for everything you had to go through. I know it had to be hard."

Her kindness touched him. "Thanks." Then he smiled at her and nudged her a little with his elbow. "But I'd say that things are lookin' up."

She grinned. "I'm glad you feel that way." She took his arm and squeezed it a little. It amazed her that she felt comfortable enough to do that. His large bicep was hard, confirming her perception that he was very strong. Then she let him go. "I can't wait to see the pictures of the house. I'm so impressed by the idea of a different doorbell and that you would be so thoughtful."

Lucky smiled down at her, noting that she had very pretty lips. Stifling the urge to kiss her, he said, "Well, I wanted ya to have a nice house and made it so that ya can keep bein' independent. I meant it when I said that I admire yer determination. Some people would whine about bein' deaf or blind and just sit back and let others do things for them, but not you. Yer a brave woman and I'm lucky to find someone like that."

His praise made her feel shy, yet pleased. "You're the first man who's ever told me that outside of my father."

Lucky laughed. "I guess it's a good thing for me that other men are idiots for not appreciatin' ya for the strong, beautiful woman ya are."

"Stop it. You're making me blush. You'll make my head swell," she said.

"All right, but I mean it," he replied.

Broderick watched them but didn't stare, wanting to give them a little privacy. He liked the easy way Lucky talked to Leah. He was also impressed that Lucky and his friends signed and that Lucky had taken the time to learn. It showed Broderick that Lucky truly was a kind, thoughtful person and that he didn't view Leah's deafness negatively.

Arriving at the hotel, they checked in and went to their rooms. Lucky decided to change into something a little more casual. He kept on his gray dress pants, white shirt, and gray tie, but put on a black, cable-knit sweater that Edna had made for him out of the yarn that another woman in town had made out of some wool that Lucky had paid her to process into yarn.

It wasn't really the style at the time, but it was comfortable and warm and he wanted to show the Carters one of the products of the farm.

"Da, can I wear mine?" Otto asked.

Lucky knew that his son didn't like the formal attire after wearing the looser, more comfortable Cheyenne clothing all his life. He smiled. "I don't see why not."

He got it out while Otto took off his blue suit jacket and began taking off his tie. "Do I have to wear it?"

"You don't. Go ahead and take it off," Lucky said.

He couldn't see the boy being uncomfortable. Leah's father had already seen that Otto was suitably dressed and he'd rather Otto not become cranky because he felt constrained by his clothing. Otto smiled and took it off, giving it to Lucky. Once Otto was changed, Lucky combed his son's hair since it stood up from static electricity.

"There. That's better. Now you're presentable again," Lucky said.

"What's that mean?"

"You look handsome again."

Otto nodded seriously. "So the girls will chase me?"

Lucky laughed. "Right. But right now, we're gonna go see *my* girl again. Ready?"

"Aye," Otto said mimicking him.

"Come on, ya Irish Indian."

They left their room, went across the hall to Marvin's room, and knocked. Ronni answered the door and Lucky saw that she'd also changed out of her traveling clothes and freshened up a little.

"Well, don't you look handsome in your sweaters?" She felt Lucky's sleeve. "That's so soft. I'd love a cardigan."

He smiled. "Consider it done. Where's himself?"

This was how Lucky spoke about people he considered pompous. In this case, he said it half-jokingly.

Ronni smiled. "Himself is changing Eva's diaper."

"Really?"

"Yes. He does it quite a bit and talks to her the whole time. It's so funny. He's good at it, too." She motioned him closer. "Listen."

Lucky poked his head in the door so he could hear.

"That'll feel better, sweet Eva. We can't have you in a squishy, dirty diaper, now can we? No. We don't want you to be stinky."

Eva babbled back to him, reaching her little hands for his face while she smiled.

"That's right. There. All better. Now we'll get you all put back together," Marvin said.

Lucky barely held back a laugh and Ronni muffled a giggle on a sleeve of her blouse.

"We'll be right out here," Lucky said, withdrawing his head.

They didn't have long to wait until the others joined them. Marvin eyed Lucky's sweater critically and then grinned. "Well, it certainly shows off your strong physique, which I'm guessing is one reason you wore it."

"Possibly," Lucky agreed. "Well, let's not keep them waitin'."

Chapter Ten

Dinner was going very well, with one exception: Gary Hossler. Lucky wanted to punch him in the head in the worst way, but he tried to ignore the man as much as possible. He noticed the way Gary avoided talking directly to Leah, relying on others to translate for him. Marvin had come to know the Irishman and could see the anger simmering close the surface by the slightly brighter color of Lucky's eyes.

Having dealt with Shadow's hotter temper over the years, Marvin knew how to intervene so that Lucky didn't cause a scene. He tried to keep Gary's attention so that the boorish man's conversations didn't involve Leah very much.

Constance was an observant woman and could also see Lucky's irritation. Her opinion of Lucky went up upon seeing his protectiveness of Leah. She liked the way Lucky signed everything, no matter who he was talking to, so that Leah could follow the conversation. His signing was very good, but occasionally he made mistakes that amused those who were fluent. Instead of getting angry or giving up, Lucky just laughed and asked for help so he did it correctly.

"At least I didn't say I enjoy lickin' squirrels," he said, making everyone laugh.

He related a few stories of some of the mistakes he and their friends had made while learning to sign.

"Where did you learn, Marvin?" Leah asked.

"What did she say?" Gary asked.

Marvin didn't bother answering him, instead signing while saying, "At boarding school. My friend Rich was deaf and he taught a bunch of us. He was a good fellow and very mischievous. Of course, the rest of us liked being able to talk to each other while other people didn't know what we were saying since they were too inconsiderate to learn so they could communicate with him. He was very intelligent and passed all of his exams with ease. In fact, he helped me pass a test or two because he was sharper than me at several subjects."

For once, Lucky was glad for Marvin's sadistic side and silently applauded the smooth way in which he'd pointed out what a jackass Gary was.

Lucky followed that up with, "Sometimes people just give up on somethin' because it's hard instead of keepin' at it. I wanted to learn so I could talk to Leah, even though she reads lips. A bunch of us learned and we're not perfect at it, but we get by and we'll get better as time goes on. Determination is the key to succeeding at a lot of things. If I'd have quit the first time someone told me I was just a dumb Irishman, I wouldn't have even made it to America, let alone started a sheep farm."

"Which has quickly become a success," Ronni said.

Lucky just smiled while he felt satisfaction upon seeing Gary's red face. Obviously his point had been made. He said no more along that vein because he didn't want to further embarrass Sofia, whose face was a little pink.

The conversation turned to the sheep farm and after dessert was eaten, Lucky took out the pictures of the farm he'd brought. He showed them to Leah first, explaining what they were of, and then she passed them on to the rest. Their house was mostly done now, but Lucky had gotten Dan, a young photographer in Echo, to take pictures of the different stages of construction.

Lucky showed them the pulley system that Adam had helped perfect. "It won't matter what room yer in, ye'll be able to see that someone's at the door."

Constance asked, "But won't you be around most of the time?"

"Aye, but if I'm in one of the barns or in town, someone might come then. Leah doesn't need to be constantly watched anyhow."

"What about safety? It's a ways out of town," Broderick said.

"It is, but there's the dogs and Sugar," Lucky said.

"Sugar?" Broderick asked.

"Aye. Win's burro. She's bigger than a dog, but smaller than most ponies. Don't let her size fool ya, though. She's protective of her loved ones and won't tolerate any funny business," Lucky said.

Marvin chuckled. "Yes, as my brother found out on one occasion. He encountered her rather unexpectedly and she charged him. She still doesn't like him. It's best to stay on her good side. She's quite strong and very quick."

"Besides, if I'm not home, usually someone else is around. Win is home in the mornings, and Billy and Nina are always poppin' round. Nina likes to help feed and milk the goats. Josie comes out with Julia. All kinds of people."

Gary said, "Once children come along, how will she know that the baby is crying if she's in another room?"

Leah's face flushed and Lucky wanted to do bodily harm to the man. "I've already thought of a solution to that, but I think that's a private conversation for later once Leah and I are married."

"Yes, I think that's a discussion best left to them," Broderick said coldly.

He wasn't overly fond of his future son-in-law and still didn't understand what Sofia saw in him. With her blonde hair and blue eyes, Sofia favored her mother, and was a very beautiful woman. Gary's inconsiderate treatment of Leah in the past hadn't left her parents with a favorable impression of the young man and his insensitive question didn't help improve it any.

Lucky saw Otto yawn and said, "I guess it's time for someone to go beddy-bye."

Otto shook his head. "No, Da. Not sleepy," he said on another yawn.

"Sure and yer not," Lucky said, chuckling.

The photographs were gathered and put back in the large envelope in which Lucky had brought them. Leah handed it to Lucky, but he gave it back to her. "Those are yers, so ya can really get an idea of things."

"Thank you." Her smile was captivating.

"Mr. and Mrs. Carter, thank ya for having us. It was lovely meetin' ya and I'm lookin' forward to spendin' more time with ya," Lucky said. "And that goes for you, too, Sofia."

"Thank you, Lucky," she said. "Leah and I should be going, too. We both have work in the morning."

"Oh. Are ya far away, then?" Lucky asked. "We'd be glad to drop ya off."

Gary said, "I can see them home. I have my buggy out back."

Lucky didn't like his haughty tone, but reined in his irritation.

Leah signed, "If it's not too much trouble, I wouldn't mind a ride home."

"No trouble at all," Lucky said, helping her on with her coat.

When Gary made no move to help Sofia with hers, Lucky took her coat and held it for her. Gary's face turned red again.

What a complete plonker, Lucky thought. *He's got a good-lookin' gal like Sofia and treats her like that. Shame on him.* He noticed Constance's small smile and looked away before he laughed.

Leah kissed her parents and Sofia goodnight and followed the others out into the night. Lucky tucked her hand into the crook of his elbow and led her to the carriage they'd rented for the next few days until they went back to Echo. As soon as they were in the carriage, Leah began laughing silently. She'd long ago curbed her desire to laugh out loud because it wasn't like other people's. In school, someone had commented that it sounded like the bray of a mule and ever since she'd tried not to laugh out loud.

Lucky wasn't sure what she was laughing at, but he had a good idea, and so did Marvin and Ronni. They laughed with her. It felt great to see Gary put in his place, not once, but twice in one night. Sofia tried to make excuses for Gary's shortcomings, but Leah had no time for him. She'd found his embarrassment funny and satisfying and didn't feel guilty about it.

It did Lucky's heart good to see her laugh and he joined her, his robust laugh mingling with Marvin and Ronni's.

Leah tried to compose herself. "He never expected you two to come off with those veiled putdowns. You're both very smooth."

Lucky signed, "I've come across his kind before and I can't stand them. How does yer sister? I'm sorry. I shouldn't have said that."

Leah said, "It's all right. I feel the same way. I hate the thought of him being my brother-in-law someday."

"So I was right in thinkin' he always acts like that around ya?" Lucky asked.

She nodded. "He thinks I'm stupid. A lot of people assume that about the deaf."

"They're the stupid ones," Lucky said. "It's easy to judge people without botherin' to get to know them."

"That's right," Ronni said. "People aren't always what they seem to be."

If he didn't know any better, Lucky would have sworn that Marvin's smile was bashful. *What's goin' on there?*

They fell silent when the street darkened for a moment and then their conversation resumed. Leah asked all kinds of questions about Echo and she and Lucky set up a time for him to come to the shop in the morning so she could show him around. When the carriage pulled up in front of Leah's apartment building, Otto was asleep.

"I'll take him," Marvin said, holding out his arms.

Lucky gave Otto to him and alighted from the carriage, holding the door for Leah while helping her down. He gave her his arm and led her to the building.

"I'll be all right from here," she said.

"While I'm sure ya will, a gentleman always walks a lady to her door," Lucky said.

She smiled at his gallant manner and unlocked the door to the building. They walked down a hallway to the last door on the left.

Lucky said, "Well, Miss Leah, sleep well. I'll see ya tomorrow mornin'. Thanks for a wonderful time."

"Thank you, too. You're a very thoughtful man, Lucky Quinn, and not bad on the eyes, either." She blushed a little, but wasn't sorry about saying it.

"Aw, go on with ye," Lucky said, grinning. "Yer the one who's easy on the eyes." He kissed her cheek and said, "Go in so I know yer safe. I'll sleep better that way." Then he winked at her, making her laugh.

She tried the door, but it was still locked. Sofia must not be home yet. She unlocked it, said goodnight to Lucky and went in, closing the door behind her. Then she leaned against it, smiling to herself. Allowing herself what felt like a quiet laugh, she hung up her coat and went into the kitchen to put on water for tea. She liked to drink chamomile tea before bed.

Just as she sat down to drink it, the door opened and Sofia came in. She shut and locked the door and joined Leah in the kitchen.

"There's enough hot water if you wanted some tea," Leah said.

Sofia shook her head and sat down. "No, I'm fine. So your Lucky is quite the fellow."

Leah grinned and signed, "I know! He's like a dream, isn't he? And so handsome! Those eyes of his! And he insisted on walking me right to our door."

Sofia forced a smile as she thought about the way Gary always just dropped her off. He rarely even got out of the buggy. She had let him know that she hadn't appreciated his behavior at dinner that evening, which had put him in a bad mood. Sofia didn't care.

"I'm so happy for you," she said.

"I'm happy for me, too," Leah said, finishing her tea. "I'd better get some sleep so that I'm not falling asleep at the shop tomorrow."

"Goodnight," Sofia said.

Ronni sat in their hotel room after putting Eva down for the night. Marvin was in the washroom changing. She looked at the gold band on the ring finger of her left hand and thought about the conversation she'd had with Marvin several nights ago. What would it be like to really be married to Marvin? She and Eva would certainly never want for anything, nor would anyone dare do harm to them. If he offered, she thought she would accept, but he'd said he wouldn't without knowing if certain things worked. She could understand his position, but what if they tried and it was a disaster? Where did they go from there?

She looked at the bed and thought about the way they'd held each other at night ever since the night of their "test". They hadn't intended for it to keep occurring, but the next night, she'd woken up to find Marvin's arms wrapped around her. Although shocked, she was nevertheless happy he was there. Instead of throwing him out, which she should have, she'd snuggled closer and gone back to sleep.

The next night, he'd playfully asked, "Your bed or mine?" and held out a hand.

His smile had been too much for her to refuse and she'd said, "Yours."

He'd never tried anything more than holding her. He hadn't even kissed her, which had surprised her. Her thoughts were interrupted when he came out of the washroom. Going over to the crib, he looked down at Eva, smiling down at her.

"Angelic, isn't she?"

"Yes, she is," Ronni agreed. "Are you her guardian angel?"

He nodded. "Yes. I'll kill anyone who ever tries to harm a single silky hair on that pretty little head of hers. And if anyone ever did harm her, I'd swiftly turn into her avenging angel. That goes for you, too, Ronni. I meant that the other night, and we both know that I have it in me to do it."

Ronni said, "I know you do, but I hope you never have to do that again, Marvin."

"So do I. Although I like making people suffer, it's usually in more cerebral ways. Shadow's the one who enjoys physical violence," Marvin said. "Coming to bed?"

"Yes."

"Am I sleeping on the floor or on the bed?" he asked.

"Get in the bed, Marvin," she responded.

"God, I love it when you're bossy," he said, pulling the covers down.

Ronni chuckled and climbed in while Marvin turned out the light. "It's strange having electricity after having to always use candles and oil lamps."

Marvin lay down. "Yes, it is. Someday we'll have electricity, but there's something warmer about a flame, and I don't mean that as a pun."

They pulled up the covers and then Ronni let out a little squeak when Marvin unexpectedly yanked her to him. He laughed quietly. "You're better than any teddy bear, Veronica. You feel better, you smell heavenly, and you taste divine, although the small tastes I've had make it hard to know for sure."

She giggled, put her arms around him, and squeezed his midsection until he grunted. "You're a very nice teddy bear, too."

"Thank you," he said, grunting again.

Ronni giggled and eased her grasp. She laid her head on his chest and smiled. "I like Leah. I think she's a good match for Lucky. Don't you?"

"Yes, actually. She's sweet and feisty and no dummy. I think they'll do well together. Lucky wanted to punch Gary. He reminds me of Shadow that way. He has a lot of patience, but he won't tolerate any ill treatment of women."

"You like him, don't you?" she said, looking at him in the moonlight.

"Yes. He's a good man—and very smart. I respect his business savvy."

"Have you ever plotted against him?"

Marvin chuckled. "My dear, I've plotted against everyone at one time or another."

"But that was because you needed to. What about now?"

"I'll do what I need to in business, but I won't plot against people personally unless I don't like them. Are you asking if I'll turn over a new leaf?"

"I guess I am."

"Ronni, a leopard doesn't change its spots, or at least not right away."

"But maybe with some time, those spots might fade somewhat."

Marvin considered that for a moment. "They might, with the right incentive."

She smiled. "Are you talking about me?"

"You know I am."

"And we're back at the same stalemate," she said.

"So we are."

"Kiss me."

"What?"

She ran a hand over his pajama-clad chest. "You heard me."

"Is this a test?"

"No. Just do it."

"Well, that's not very romantic," Marvin said.

Ronnie hooked a hand around the back of his neck and pressed her lips to his. Marvin never resisted pressing an advantage and he kissed her back, holding her tighter. Ronni deepened the kiss and Marvin willing followed along, running a hand through her hair and rolling her over.

Finding herself pinned under him, Ronni panicked for a moment, but then relaxed when he ended the kiss. "I can't," he said. "I want you so badly, but I just can't."

"Why?" Ronni said, stroking his cheek.

"It's Eva. I've never been intimate with a baby present," Marvin said.

Ronni hadn't meant to laugh, but a snort escaped her.

"Why is that funny?" he asked.

"Because if you can't now, what will you…?" Her question trailed away when she realized what she'd been about to say.

She saw his face tighten and he moved away.

"I'm so sorry, Marvin. I wasn't thinking. I'm sorry."

He sighed and asked, "Ronni, do you want more children?"

Quietly she said, "Yes."

Marvin reached down inside for a bucket of courage. "And would you be willing to adopt?"

Ronni smiled. "Yes."

"Really? Please don't tease me. Not about this."

She moved closer again and said, "I would never tease you about this subject. Yes, really. I wouldn't mind adopting at all. Orphanages are overrun with children needing good homes."

"They are?"

"Yes."

"I didn't know that. Of course, I never had a reason to know before."

Ronni said, "It's such a shame. It wouldn't have to be a baby, either."

"I'll keep that in mind, but Ronni, that doesn't solve the other problem," Marvin said.

"If I'm willing to take a chance on that, why aren't you?" she asked.

"Because you're not the one with a possible problem," he said. "Besides, what do you mean you're willing to take a chance?"

Ronni bit her lip a moment and then said, "I mean, if you should ever ask, I would accept."

He grinned. "Trying to make an honest man out of me, hmm?"

"I guess so."

Marvin yawned. "I'll keep that in mind." He pulled her close again and she let him. "For now, this will do, but don't think for a moment that this is the end of it."

Ronni smiled. "I didn't think it was."

"Go to sleep, Ronni."

"Goodnight."

Chapter Eleven

Leah kept watching the clock as she worked the next morning. Lucky had said he'd come at ten and the clock hands seemed like they were frozen. There was a lot of repair work that had come in and she worked quickly, putting on new soles and replacing heels. Knowing how important good footwear was, she paid close attention to detail and double-checked her work to make sure the repairs were topnotch.

When she worked, she wore older dresses because it wasn't uncommon to catch them on nails, get glue stuck to them, or get shoe polish on her clothes even though she wore an apron, too. She'd thought about wearing something nicer, but then decided against it, figuring that Lucky wouldn't really care what she was wearing. She still wanted to look pretty, so she'd done her hair nicely and worn pearl earrings.

She became caught up in a particularly difficult repair on a worn tongue and didn't notice Lucky come in. He saw Broderick dealing with a customer and just watched Leah for a moment. She sat behind a work bench at the far end of the shop, hard at work on something. Her glossy, black hair was pulled back in a simpler style that he thought very becoming to her. Pearl earrings winked in the light and her dark brows were drawn together as she concentrated. Everything about her spoke to his maleness: her face, her figure, and the way she smelled.

He'd had a good opportunity to be close to her last night in the carriage and he'd subtly inhaled it then and when he'd kissed her cheek. He hadn't wanted to kiss a woman other than Avasa in a long time. There had been a girl back in Ireland whom he'd left behind when he'd come to America, but they hadn't been in love. He'd been in love with a girl in New York, but her family wouldn't hear of her marrying him since he was Irish.

Avasa had been the last woman he'd wanted to kiss passionately and that had been four years ago. Thad had told him that was one hell of a dry spell and he was right. However, Lucky just couldn't engage in casual relationships, so being intimate with someone outside the bounds of marriage just wasn't an option for him. But as he looked at Leah, the urge to kiss her came over him again. There were a couple of women around Echo who had shown interest in him, but his heart had still belonged to Avasa, so he hadn't been receptive to them.

Besides, they weren't exactly the faithful kind of women and that was something of the utmost importance to him. He'd always been faithful and he expected his mate to be the same. He didn't sense that Leah was a cheater, especially because she'd said that other men hadn't shown interest in her once they learned she was deaf. Idiots.

Not wanting her father to catch him staring, he began walking back towards the work area. Leah must have caught his movement because she looked up and the beautiful smile she sent him caused his heart to beat in triple-time.

He signed, "Good morning, Leah. How are you today?"

"Good morning. I'm fine, thanks. Did you get some rest?"

Lucky nodded. "Aye. I slept like a rock. Otto, too."

"Good. Where is he?" she asked.

"With Marvin and Ronni. I was wonderin' if ya might like to get some lunch after a bit," he said.

She smiled. "Yes. That would be very nice."

"Good. What are ya workin' on here?" He indicated the shoe with the worn tongue.

Leah picked up the men's dress shoe and showed him what needed to be repaired. "I have to remove it carefully so I don't ruin the other parts of the shoe. I'll use the old tongue to make a pattern for the new one, which I'll make out of matching leather. Then I have to put the new tongue back into the shoe."

Lucky looked over the shoe and saw all of the work that had to be done just for that one shoe alone. It gave him a new appreciation for what cobblers did. "Can't ya just glue it back in?"

She saw the teasing light in his eyes and laughed. "No, silly. You wouldn't want to walk around with a glued tongue, would you?"

"I wouldn't, but some of my friends wish my tongue was glued. They always tell me I talk too much," he said, laughing.

She shook her head. "It sounds like your friends are funny."

"Ye've no idea. They're all a mess in one way or another, but good messes."

"I can't wait to meet them," Leah said.

"They can't wait to meet you, either. I'm certainly glad I met ya."

His meaning was clear and so was the appreciation in his gray eyes. She blushed and looked down while signing, "I'm glad you put that ad in the paper."

He smiled at her shy behavior. When she looked back up at him, he signed, "Me, too."

Broderick finished up with his customer and came over to greet Lucky. "Leah said you'd be stopping by to take a look around. How are you?"

"Good, sir, thanks. Ya have a fine shop here. Leah was showin' me the work that goes into just replacin' a tongue. I know it's hard work, but she knows what she's doin'," Lucky said.

"Leah is such a smart girl and she took an interest in my work when she was just little. I caught her taking apart one of her shoes just so she could try to put it back together and I knew that she'd make a fine cobbler," Broderick said proudly.

Leah grinned. "He was so happy about it, but Mama was mad because Papa had just made the shoes for me."

"Yes, she was. She forbade Leah from taking any of her own shoes apart again," Broderick said. "Leah, why don't you show Lucky all of the equipment you'll need so he knows what it actually looks like? I'm happy that she found a man who isn't threatened by the fact that she has a brain in her head and who appreciates her skill. If only Sofia had. Well, I'll leave you to it."

Broderick knew that the couple wouldn't want him following them all over, so he went back behind the counter and began doing some paperwork. He could see them while Leah showed him around, but he knew that even if he couldn't, Lucky could be trusted with Leah. He knew the look of a womanizer and Lucky wasn't it. He'd been surprised to see that Marvin was married with a child. He seemed more the sort to carouse. There was also something slightly menacing about the man. He'd enjoyed the way he and Lucky had embarrassed Gary. Broderick figured he must be wrong about Marvin, but he knew his instincts about Lucky were spot on.

Leah enjoyed showing Lucky her craft because he was genuinely interested, even pulling out a small notepad so he could jot things down. She appreciated the way he mostly always signed even while speaking to her and how he looked her in the eyes. The woman in her also appreciated the way he looked.

He'd taken off his coat and casual suit jacket and his white shirt and black dress pants showed off his trim waist, broad shoulders, wide chest, and long legs very nicely. His nice-looking hands were slightly work-roughened from all of the farm work he did, and his skin was still tanned from the long hours he spent outdoors. Sometimes as she showed him something, their heads were close together and he smelled very nice.

Broderick watched them off and on, not because he was trying to be nosy, but because he liked how serious Lucky was about the things Leah was showing him. He saw Lucky writing things down and he'd caught a few of the questions he'd asked her and thought them pertinent to setting up a business. All of this reassured him about Lucky's character and he would feel better about Leah going to Echo with him in a few days.

Near noon, the younger people came to the counter and Leah said,

"Lucky is taking me to lunch now. We're going to Grover's, just so you know. Would you like me to bring anything back for you?"

Broderick smiled. "No, thanks. Your mother packed me a nice lunch. Have a good time."

Lucky held Leah's coat for her and said, "Don't worry, I'll bring her back safe and sound, Mr. Carter."

"You can call me Broderick, Lucky."

"All right then, Broderick. I'll take good care of yer girl," Lucky assured him.

Walking to Grover's, a nice little diner a couple of blocks away, Leah pointed things out to Lucky and he asked about places they passed. Once at the restaurant, they chose a table near the back of the place that offered them more privacy.

After they ordered, Leah said, "Last night at dinner you made a remark that made me think that getting to America had been hard for you."

Lucky pursed his lips and nodded. "Aye. The reason I came here isn't a pleasant one."

"You don't have to talk about it if you don't want to."

"It's all right. Ya should know my history," Lucky said. "See, some people don't know that a couple centuries ago, the British used to kidnap the Irish and bring them to America as slaves. I'm not speakin' ill about the British because it wasn't all of 'em that did it. I don't hate the British or anything, I'm just statin' facts. Like any country, there's good and bad people.

"Anyhow, hundreds of thousands were brought here and sold as slaves and we were cheaper than the Negro slaves. Some of the Irish were purposely bred with colored slaves to create lighter skinned people."

"You mean bred like cattle?" Leah asked, horrified at the idea.

"Aye. Just like that. That's mostly stopped now, but there are some pirates who are still doing it, I guess you'd call them. My sister, Becky, was kidnapped and brought here like that. So me and my brothers, Ian, Mick, and Duncan, and our sister Corrine, followed her trail. It wasn't the only reason we came here, though. After Ma and Da passed on, no one but Corrine and me wanted to run the sheep farm there and we couldn't handle it on our own. We started losin' too much money and we had to sell the farm. I guess it was meant to be, because we needed that money to track Becky down and make the trip here."

"Lucky, that's terrible! All of it," Leah said, sympathy filling her eyes.

"Aye." Lucky was quiet for a few moments as he gathered himself for the next part of the story. "Mick was only a little older than me and we were very close. The trip over was horrible. There was hardly any room, barely any food or water, and such dirty conditions. Mick got bit by a rat and the wound became infected. The infection went through his body and he died from it."

Leah's eyes filled with tears and she saw them welling in his eyes, too. "I'm so sorry," she signed and then held one of his hands for several moments.

Her touch was comforting to Lucky and he was able to compose himself. "Once we got here, we buried him in a cemetery in New York. The Lord was lookin' out for Becky and we were able to find her. Ian, Duncan, and I took care of her kidnappers. They'll never kidnap anyone ever again, if you get my meaning."

A chill ran through Leah. "You mean…?"

"I do. It was that or we'd have wound up dead. Those chancers didn't take kindly to us showin' up there, and they weren't gonna give her up easily because Becky's a beautiful woman and would have brought a good price," Lucky said, a fierce light in his eyes.

"So it was in defense of Becky and yourselves?"

"It was. We'd have never done such a thing otherwise," Lucky assured her.

Leah said, "In that case, I don't blame you."

"I've prayed for forgiveness a lot," Lucky said. "Becky got married last year, but I couldn't make it to her weddin'. She's happy and healthy, though, and they're lookin' forward to havin' some wee bairns."

"Some what?" Leah asked.

Lucky laughed. "Babies. We often call them bairns."

Leah watched him spell and say the word and tucked it away for future reference. "I'm so glad you were able to rescue her and that she's doing so well."

"Us, too."

"Where are your other siblings?"

"Corinne got married and moved to California, Ian moved to Toronto and married a Canadian lass, and Duncan is traveling around somewhere. He has a bad case of wanderlust and I'm not sure where he's at right now. Last I knew he was in Texas, accordin' to the post card he sent me. That was last year sometime. I'd told a buddy of his where I was goin' so that Duncan knew and he must have told him," Lucky said.

"So you're all pretty far flung."

"Aye. Someday I'd like to visit them," Lucky said.

"That would be nice."

Their food came and they spent the rest of lunch talking about the farm and all they wanted to do with the house.

Sofia walked along on the chilly October day, heading to Gary's office to surprise him with a lunch she'd packed. She did things like that for him, trying to show her appreciation for him. She wasn't in love with him, but she cared for him and he would make a good husband.

She went into the accounting firm and greeted their secretary Edward. "Is Gary in his office?" she asked.

Edward nodded. "Yes. He'll be glad to see you," he said, smiling.

"Thanks, Edward," Sofia said and went back the hall to Gary's office. She knocked lightly and then entered his office. "Guess who…?"

Her question trailed off into stunned silence when she saw Gary in a passionate embrace with a brunette woman.

"Sofia," Gary said, practically shoving the woman away from him. "I wasn't expecting you."

Sofia found her voice as rage took hold of her. "Obviously. Is this what you do at lunchtime every day?"

"Of course not," Gary said.

Sofia looked at the other woman who stared brazenly back at her. Sofia dropped the basket of food, forcefully removed her engagement ring and threw it at Gary. It bounced off his forehead and landed at his feet. "We're through," Sofia said.

"Sofia, please listen," Gary said.

"Go to hell!" Sofia said before angrily exiting the office and quickly leaving the building.

Leah looked over at her sister, who gazed out the window. It was raining as though the world outside wept with Sofia. Leah could tell that her sister was crying, even though she couldn't see her face. She felt a tap on her shoulder and looked to her right across the aisle of the train car in which they rode.

"Is she all right?" Lucky asked only in sign, his gray eyes full of concern.

"No," Leah sent back, frowning.

Their conversation continued in sign.

"Damn that man!" Lucky said. "I'm glad I paid him a little visit last night."

Leah's eyes widened. "What did you do?"

Lucky's grin was half-cocky, half-angry. "Let's just say that he never knew what hit him and that he doesn't look very pretty right now."

Leah grinned. "You're quite the hero."

"I just wanted him to feel some pain and I made sure he did," Lucky said.

"Bravo, Mr. Quinn," Marvin signed. "I applaud you taking revenge on Sofia's behalf."

"I figured it was owed to him," Lucky said. "She'll be all right with some help. She'll have a fresh start in Echo, and God knows there's plenty of men to choose from when her heart's healed enough."

Leah said, "I don't think that will happen very soon."

Ronni signed, "I agree. She'll have plenty of friends, though."

Leah nodded and turned back to Sofia. She put her arms around her sister from the back and Sofia leaned her head on Leah's shoulder. The others exchanged sympathetic glances and Lucky felt the desire to go back to Glendale and mete out more justice on Gary.

Sofia let Leah comfort her. She felt bereft and empty. Her mother and Leah had helped her immediately start to send out notes informing the guests that the wedding had been canceled. As they had worked, Sofia had decided that she couldn't stay in Glendale and put up with the whispering and sympathy from so many people. She was crushed and embarrassed and couldn't deal with all of the gossip.

Sofia had asked if Lucky and company would mind if she accompanied them to Echo so she could have some time to clear her head without enduring a scandal. Lucky, being the tender- hearted, generous man he was, had immediately acquiesced to her request. Leah was thrilled to have her sister going with her, but hated the reason why Sofia was coming along.

Although Broderick and Constance were doubly sad to be left without both daughters, they agreed that it was probably best for Sofia to have a change of scenery. They'd began getting Sofia ready for the trip. Ronni had also helped with the packing.

Lucky said that instead of the girls paying to stay at Hanover House, the boarding house in Echo, they might as well just live in his and Leah's house and save money. He asked Broderick and Constance about it first, however. They agreed that since the two sisters would be together, there wouldn't be any impropriety in living so close to Lucky, who would continue to live in his tipi until he and Leah were married. Broderick had warned Lucky to be respectful of Leah, but it was more for show.

Sofia's self-esteem had taken a severe blow and she was very withdrawn as they traveled. Everyone tried to make her smile, but those were few and far between. Her appetite dwindled and she mostly just pushed her food around whenever they went to the dining car for meals.

Outside of Leah, Otto and Eva were the greatest sources of comfort to her.

The kids made her smile and Otto had a crush on her. He kissed her a lot and told her she was pretty, which made her feel good.

"I see he has your personality, Lucky," Sofia said, smiling as Otto hugged her good morning on the day they were due to arrive in Billings.

Lucky grinned. "Aye. I always liked kissin' pretty girls, too."

Leah had almost signed, "The only girl you better kiss from now on is me," but caught herself in time. Not only would that have been forward, it would have upset Sofia. Instead, she said, "Behave."

"Uh oh. I'm in trouble now," Lucky said.

Sofia hugged Otto and then smiled into his dark eyes. "You are such a handsome boy and your da is going to have a hard time keeping the girls away from you."

Otto nodded. "Yep."

The adults laughed at him and settled in for breakfast. Sofia ate more that morning, mainly because Otto wanted her to clean her plate or else he wasn't going to marry her. Lucky and the rest from Echo were glad when they arrived in Billings. Win and Billy had brought two wagons so they could haul all of the luggage.

They kept hoping that the railroad would come to Dickensville at some point soon, but although it was being discussed between the town council of Dickensville and the railroad company, nothing had been decided yet. It would be a lot closer to Echo and cut down on travel time.

When they alighted from the train, Billy and Win were already there, along with someone unexpected. Adam had accompanied them with a closed-in carriage that he'd borrowed from Jerry so that the ladies and children could ride in it to be out of the cold weather. It was better for Adam, too, although his asthma had subsided like it always did once all of the plants were dead or dormant for winter.

Lucky introduced everyone and there was a party atmosphere as the travelers were welcomed home. Lucky thought the way Adam blushed around Sofia was cute. At twenty-four, she was much too old for him, but who could blame the boy for liking the beautiful woman? Leah also noticed it. She and Lucky exchanged amused glances over it.

Adam's instant crush on her was also apparent to Sofia and, while he was too young for her, it boosted her morale to have a handsome boy feel that way about her. His attentiveness to her lifted her spirits. He helped her into the carriage and gave her a lap afghan to keep her warm. They made a train with Billy and Lucky leading the way. Win wasn't happy about being stuck with Marvin, but he knew he could ignore him.

Billy smiled at Lucky. "Leah's a beautiful girl."

"Aye, she is. And smart, too. She's a miracle worker with shoes. Ye'll see."

The excited expression on Lucky's face warmed Billy's heart. Lucky had suffered enough and he wanted his friend to be happy. It seemed like he was. "It's a shame about Sofia. I'm glad you gave that guy a good lickin'."

Lucky nodded. "It felt good, too. I've never understood cheatin'. If yer not ready to get married or ya can't commit to any one woman, then don't get married and don't lead the woman to believe she's the only one. The same goes for the woman. Ya know, I don't approve of what Phoebe did for so many reasons, but at least she didn't commit to either Thad or Marvin. She didn't make them think that she was either one of theirs alone."

Billy shook his head as he thought about the woman both Marvin and Thad had been seeing. "I'll never understand it, either. I mean, I'm no angel, but I never led anyone on and I never went all that far with them, either. When I was with Shelby, I didn't see anyone but her."

Lucky said, "I know. I think things worked out the way they were meant to, though."

Billy grinned. "You're right. I couldn't love Nina any more if I tried. And our little one will be here around Christmas. I can't wait. I hope she has Nina's eyes. They're the most beautiful eyes I've ever seen."

Lucky chuckled. "Listen to ya. This from the man who thought he'd never find someone to marry and have kids with."

"I know." Billy's smile was sheepish. "I had to go all the way to Oklahoma to find her, but it was worth it. The only regret I have is that my family and friends, outside of you and Wild Wind, couldn't be there."

"Well, I'm glad I could be there for ya. So now it's yer turn to be there for me. Will ya be my best man?" Lucky asked.

Billy's eyes grew bigger and he grabbed Lucky, hugging him tight, and almost dropping the reins in the process. "Yes! Of course I will and I'll throw you the best bachelor party and give you the rings right and everything!"

Lucky laughed. "Ok, lad. Watch the horses. Yer jerkin' 'em off the road."

Billy let him go and straightened out the wagon again. "Sorry I got so excited, but I didn't think you'd ask me to be your best man."

"Of course I would. Who else would I ask?"

"I thought maybe Evan."

Lucky said, "Well, now, Evan and I are great friends, but you and I have been through some stuff together that's created a stronger bond, more like brothers. Like me and Wild Wind, but only different. Do ya know what I mean?"

"Yeah. I know what you mean," Billy said. "I feel the same way."

"Good. All right. Enough with the mushy stuff. Tell me what's been goin' on since we were gone," Lucky said.

Chapter Twelve

Lucky watched Leah closely as they toured through the house the day after their arrival back in Echo. Not only to gauge her reaction to everything, but just simply because she was so beautiful that it was hard to take his eyes away from her. Her shining dark eyes, glossy black hair, and full lips drew his gaze again and again. He ached to kiss her and bury his hands in her gorgeous mane of hair. He could just imagine how soft and silky it was. He shook those thoughts from his head so he could pay attention to what she was saying.

"This is a wonderful house. I can't believe you did all this." Her eyes glowed with happiness.

Pride welled inside Lucky. "I'm glad ya like it. I wanted it to be the place where we would raise our family and be happy."

Leah's smile captivated him. "I know we will be."

Lucky fidgeted a little. He was glad that they were alone. "Speakin' of raisin' a family, I have an idea for whenever a baby comes along and it's cryin'."

Leah only blushed slightly. "Ok."

"Well, a gent here in town, Glen Robbins, has a dog that had a litter a few weeks back. She's some sort of little terrier mix and the father was a smaller dog, too. I was wonderin' how you'd feel about havin' a house dog. We could train it to let ya know when the baby was cryin'. What do ya think?" He was startled by the sudden tears in her eyes. "What's wrong?"

She shook her head a little. "Nothing. I think you're the most amazing man I've ever met. You're so thoughtful and kind. And funny. I don't know how I got so lucky in finding you, Lucky." She brushed away her tears and smiled.

He said, "Thanks, lass. I feel the same way about you. Yer smart, sweet, and beautiful."

"And deaf. Why do you want me when I'm … defective?" she asked.

Lucky frowned. "Leah, I don't think about ya being deaf except that we made a few modifications to the house. Yer not defective at all. I'm sorry if other people have made ya feel that way, but yer not. Please don't say that about yerself."

His kindness touched a place deep inside where all of her frustration and hurtful things people said about her had been locked up. She took a deep breath, determined to keep it shut up, but the door opened a little and more tears spilled from her eyes.

Lucky couldn't stand seeing her cry. He put his arms around her, pulling her close. Leah rested her head against his chest and let the tears come. She held on to him, feeling anchored and safe in his embrace. She felt him stroke her hair and she could feel the vibration of his voice under her ear. How she wished she could hear his Irish brogue and his laugh. Most of the time, she didn't think much about her deafness since she was so used to it now, but every so often, she became upset by it.

"I know ya can't hear me, but I hope ya can feel what I'm tellin' ya. Yer such a wonderful woman and I know the Great Spirit sent ya to me and Otto. There's nothin' wrong with ya, nothin' at all. No one'll ever make fun of ya again, lass. I swear that to ya." He drew back a little, tipping up her chin so she could see him talk. "I know it hasn't always been easy for ya, but look at all ye've done with your life. Yer a skilled cobbler, you read lips, and do anything else. Well, maybe not sing, but I can't sing, either, so we're matched there."

Leah smiled as Lucky took out a handkerchief and blotted her tears away.

"There. That's better."

She took his hand and kissed it. "Thank you," she mouthed.

He smiled. "I didn't know ya could do that," he said trying to stifle the desire just the touch of her lips on his skin set off.

She signed. "I don't like doing it. I sound stupid."

He frowned. "There ain't nothin' stupid about ya. What'd I just tell ya?"

"Ok, ok," she signed. Her eyes collided with his before her gaze dipped to his mouth. Then she looked into his eyes again.

He'd seen her eye movement and his eyes held hers for several moments before he lowered his head to take a taste of her lips. Leah wasn't sure what to do at first. She'd only been kissed by a boy once, but that had been when she was thirteen and it had barely been a kiss at all. Lucky sensed her confusion, but just pressed his lips more firmly to hers while he cupped the back of her head and tilted it slightly.

Leah followed his lead and kissed him back a little, laying her hands on his chest. A very nice, muscular chest, she couldn't help noting. Suddenly, she found herself wanting to run her hands over his shoulders, but she kept them where they were. By degrees, his kiss grew more insistent and it was the most exciting thing she'd ever felt. Her hands slid upwards until she could encircle his neck with her arms. Just when she was really getting the hang of it, he suddenly broke away from her and set her slightly away from him.

She saw a middle-aged man come into the parlor and knew that this was the reason Lucky had ended the kiss. She'd been afraid at first that she'd done something wrong. Even as her heartbeat throbbed inside her chest, she smiled at the man and tried to look like she hadn't just been kissing Lucky.

Lucky was having a similar problem. She'd felt so good and tasted better than he'd imagined and she had picked up the idea of kissing pretty well already. It was a good thing Thad had called out before he'd come into the parlor or it would have been a very awkward moment for him and Leah.

"Hi, there!" Thad said, his brown eyes taking in the slightly uncomfortable expressions on their faces and the slight flush on Leah's pretty face. *Oh boy. Looks like I interrupted. Crap. Sorry about that, kids.* "It's good to see you, Irish. You gonna introduce me to your fine lookin' filly here?"

Lucky chuckled. "Leah, this is my good friend, Thad McIntyre. Thad, this is Leah Carter, a very special lass."

Thad's signing was a little shaky, but he spoke while he signed, "It's a pleasure to meet you, Leah. We've heard a lot of good things about you. You're going to be a very busy woman. There's a lot of people around here who need shoes repaired."

Leah smiled. "Nice to meet you, too. I'm glad to hear that. You're the bounty hunter. That must be exciting."

Thad had picked up her meaning well enough. "It has its moments. I'll tell you all about it sometime."

"Good," she said. "I look forward to it."

She thought he was a very handsome man with his salt-and-pepper hair, strong jaw, close-cropped beard, and brown eyes. He looked like he was very fit, which made sense given his occupation.

Thad smiled and looked around at the house. "I haven't had a chance to see the place since you completely finished it now. Mind if I take a look-see?"

"Of course not," Lucky said.

Leah became excited about the house all over again. "I'll be your tour guide, ok?"

Thad grinned. "Fine by me. You're a lot prettier to look at than he is."

Leah laughed silently. "Follow me, Mr. McIntyre. Since we're in the parlor, I guess you've already seen it, but I'll show you the bedrooms."

"Lead on," Thad said.

He followed her down a long hallway with two windows on the right side. All of the bedrooms and the washroom were on the left side of the hallway. The washroom was big enough for a large metal tub, commode, and dry sink. The next room was one of the smaller bedrooms, but it was still a nice size. Thad smiled when Leah shyly told him that the second bedroom they came to was most likely the one they'd use for the nursery. It took grinding his teeth together to keep from laughing and embarrassing her.

Like they had with Win's cabin, they made sure that there was plenty of closet space and there would be a lot of natural light due the placement of the windows. As Leah showed Thad around, she couldn't believe how thoughtful Lucky had been in the design of the house. In his letters, he'd asked her about the sorts of things she'd like in a home and he'd incorporated many of them in the house. It was just one more way that made her see how much he paid attention to her and valued her opinions.

She loved all of the pine-paneled walls and she was eager to hang curtains. Sofia and several of Lucky's women friends were going to help her make braided rugs for the house and she couldn't wait to lay in food and start cooking for Lucky. However, she was very curious about the way he cooked.

They went out to the kitchen and she showed Thad the pantry. He looked over the new stove and commented on the large fireplace in both the kitchen and parlor. He couldn't help chuckling at how excited she was and he thought she was a good match for Lucky. They would certainly never lack for conversation.

Lucky was equal parts amused and proud as he watched Leah show everything to Thad. He was proud of the job they'd all done on the house, but more than that, he was proud of Leah. She was everything a man could want in a wife and he was looking forward to getting to know her better. He also couldn't deny that she excited his senses. That short kiss they'd shared had reignited a passion inside him that had lain dormant for quite some time.

Thad didn't let on, but he saw the way Lucky watched Leah and it was the look of a hungry man. He understood that particular hunger. He hadn't been able to bring himself to satisfy it with another woman since Phoebe.

He'd tried, but he just couldn't. Thad shoved those thoughts aside.

"Lucky, it's a great house and I'm sure you two kids will be happy here," Thad said.

"Thanks," Lucky said. "I appreciate all yer help."

"So do I," Leah signed. "I'll make you something nice to show my appreciation."

Thad smiled. "Well, I never turn down food or money, so you won't get any objection from me. Well, I'm off to go see what's going on at Evan's place and visit with Julia. Are you cooking tomorrow night?"

Lucky nodded. "I am. Are ya comin' to supper then?"

"Yep. I hear you're gonna make mutton stew."

"Ya heard right," Lucky said. "I have to make sure to have all the butcherin' done by the time Billy arrives."

Thad chuckled. "I still can't believe how touchy he is about that. Anyway, I'll see you folks tomorrow night then. Leah, it was good to meet you. Take care."

"You, too," Leah responded. Once Thad was gone, she signed to Lucky, "I like him. He's funny."

"Aye," Lucky said. "He's a very good friend. He's had a bad time of it, but it's gettin' better for him. I hope he can find some happiness."

Leah said, "I hope so, too."

Lucky said, "Well, Miss Carter, let's go get that furniture. Billy's gonna meet up with us and help me unload it. Wild Wind should be back by then and he'll help, too."

Wild Wind still went hunting every morning and he hadn't returned yet.

"That sounds like a good plan," Leah said.

Lucky impulsively pressed a quick kiss to her lips while no one was around before taking her hand and leading her out the door. Leah smiled the whole time they walked hand-in-hand to the barn. Win came out of his cabin and saw them. A grin lit up his face at the sight and he was filled with happiness for his friend. "Irish deserves some good luck," he mumbled to himself before heading to the barn himself to get his horse.

Chapter Thirteen

Travis Desmond sat awkwardly in one of the chairs in Marvin's office, his brown eyes filled with trepidation. He hated his boss and was always on edge when Marvin asked him to come to his office.

Marvin shut the door and walked around to sit behind his desk. He watched Travis for a moment and then tilted his head a little. "Why haven't you and Jenny had another baby yet?"

Travis blinked a few times at the abrupt question. "What?"

"As I recall, you were going to try to have a baby. It's been a couple of years, but still no baby. That was one of the reasons I gave you a raise."

"I know, but I can't help it that Jenny hasn't conceived and it's really none of your business," Travis said irritably.

Marvin's blue eyes narrowed and Travis swallowed because that look usually meant trouble. "Perhaps not, but you stabbing me in the back is my business."

"What are you talking about?" Travis asked, his heart kicking into a faster rhythm.

The malevolent grin Marvin gave him made the hair on Travis' neck stand up.

"Well, it seems funny to me that Mr. Quinn and his friends were able to get their sheep across my land without being noticed. Now, if I didn't know any better, I'd say you helped them since you know the ranch and I never heard our cattle dogs bark at all. They know you and they wouldn't make any noise if you were with them."

Travis' face suffused with color and he couldn't respond.

Marvin let out a cold laugh. "I see that I'm right. I'm sure they paid you to do that. Do you or do you not work for me?"

The foreman was still silent.

Marvin pounded the desk. "Answer me! Do you or don't you work for me?"

"Yes!" Travis responded.

Marvin's eyes turned ice blue. "Then why wouldn't you protect my interests? There's only one reason: you're in on their business."

Travis knew he was trapped. He wasn't the kind of man who could bluff his way out of situations. Quietly he said, "Yes, I am."

Marvin nodded. "At least you're being honest—now anyway."

"Are you firing me?" Travis asked. The sheep farm was doing very well, but he wasn't making quite enough to allow him to quit his job.

"No, but I am going to reduce your wages by five dollars per week," Marvin said.

Travis' temper simmered. "Now, look, Marvin, it didn't hurt the ranch none to have those sheep come across that pasture."

"That's not the point! If you're doing that behind my back, what else are you doing?" Marvin said. "It's a matter of trust. I thought things were better between us lately. Didn't you?"

Travis had to admit they had been. Marvin hadn't been snarky with him and had actually complimented him on a job well done. "Yeah."

"Then why would you do that and put your job in jeopardy?"

"I still needed more money to make the house payment and there were some other things we needed," Travis said. "The extra money helped us."

"All right. I'm going to forgive you, but I'm still reducing your wages. I think you need to ask your wife some questions. Remember I said that to you a couple of years ago? You've done nothing about it," Marvin said.

"I don't know what you mean. What do you want me to ask her?" Travis asked.

"You need to ask her about what happened with Louise and you need to ask her why she hasn't gotten pregnant," Marvin said.

Travis shook his head. "Are you sayin' that she's not gettin' pregnant on purpose? How is that even possible?" His face flushed. "I don't use anything."

Marvin sighed. "There are other ways. There are devices for females, Travis. Do you only make love at certain times of the month?"

Travis thought about it and he began to see what Marvin was getting at. "Why would she do that?"

"I think you need to ask her that," Marvin said.

"How do you know all of this?" Travis asked.

Marvin spread his hands wide. "I know everything, Travis. You should know that by now."

"It's that creepy brother of yours. I'll bet he's the one that gets this information somehow," Travis said.

Marvin leaned forward, his eyes boring into Travis'. "If you disparage my brother to me one more time, I'll cut your pay even more. You don't know anything about him. He's had a difficult time of things. Understand?"

"Yeah. Sure," Travis said. He just wanted to get away from Marvin. He was furious over losing money, too.

"Good. You may go. Remember to talk to Jenny. You'll be thanking me once you do."

Travis just glared at Marvin before leaving the office. Marvin leaned back, chuckling over the situation. "This will be glorious."

The next thing he knew, Ronni stormed into his office. "What did you do to him?" she demanded.

Marvin merely lifted an eyebrow. "Do to him? Nothing that concerns you."

She came around the desk to stand glowering down at him. "I know that part of you is a sadist, but why do you have to be cruel?"

"Ronni, I like that you're willing to challenge me, believe me, I do, but he has been helping Lucky and the rest behind my back. They have the easement now, but before that, Travis was helping them get their sheep across our land and he's working with them. So not only is he drawing pay from me, he's making money with them while betraying me. Now, I would say that is cause for me being angry and punishing him. I could have fired him, but I didn't. I cut his wages, but he still has his job. I know for a fact that Mr. Terranova would have fired him for such an offense, but I allowed him to retain his position. Now, do you still think I'm being cruel?"

"Oh. I didn't know that," she said. She could see why he'd taken such action.

"I know," he said, smiling. "I must say, though, you looked quite beautiful rushing in here like that. Your eyes blazing fire and your cheeks flushed with anger. It's very exciting when you look like that."

She tried not to smile but failed. How was it that the man who could be such a bastard could also be funny and tender? He held her every night, but hadn't tried to seduce her even though she knew he wanted to. "You are so bad."

He grabbed her, pulling her down onto his lap.

"Marvin! Be careful!" Ronni said.

"I'm fine," Marvin assured her. "Do you understand what torture it is to wrap my arms around you every night but yet not be able to quench my desire for you? Sheer torture, but yet the sweetest torture and I don't want to stop what we're doing. How long are you going to hang on to this silly notion of not giving in to what we both feel?"

Ronni's eyes grew moist. "My silly notion is protection for me and Eva. I don't know that once you get what you want from me, that you'll be through with me."

His jaw clenched. "Through with you? I think not, Ronni. I've told you all of my deepest, darkest secrets. Do you think I would do that if I were going to toss you aside once I'd had a taste of you? Oh, no. I have the feeling that I'll never get enough of you. I crave you now as it is."

Ronni's breathing became more rapid. "Craving isn't enough, Marvin. And it isn't marriage." His nearness was making it hard to resist him. His sensual mouth drew her gaze and his beautiful eyes looked her over, too.

"I know, but I've explained why I haven't proposed," Marvin said.

"Yes, you have, but what happens if things go well? What kind of assurance do I have that you won't throw me away," Ronni asked, her dark eyes locking on his.

He brought a hand up to caress her cheek. "Because my dear infuriating, beautiful, stubborn woman, I've fallen in love with you," he said softly. "After Phoebe, I never thought that would happen again, and I now realize that what I thought was love, wasn't. I'm not really sure what it was, but it wasn't love. But I love you and I love Eva. There's nothing I won't do for the both of you. Nothing."

Ronni was stunned into silence and Marvin took the opportunity to kiss her. It was a hungry embrace that stole her good sense and threw it out the window. Her own frustration at being so close to him every night rose to the surface and she kissed him back, matching his intensity.

Marvin growled and held her tighter. He wanted to sweep everything off his desk and take her right there, but anyone could walk in and he didn't want their first time to be somewhere like that. No, his newfound love for her demanded that he do things right. He allowed himself a few more moments of pleasure before gentling the kiss and ending it.

Ronni searched his eyes for the truth. "Do you mean that? Do you really love me? Please don't toy with me."

"I would never toss around such a statement lightly. I love you, Ronni. Really and truly, I do."

Suddenly, Ronni felt terrified and struggled off Marvin's lap. She put a hand over her mouth as she saw his confused expression. Then she did the only thing she could think of; she ran. Picking up her skirts, she mounted the stairs as quickly as she could and rushed down the hall to her room. She shut and locked the door behind her, her breathing ragged in her chest.

"Why am I afraid?" she whispered to herself before sitting down on the bed to examine her feelings.

Down in his office, Marvin still sat in his chair, thoroughly bewildered and embarrassed. He'd just bared his soul to her again and she'd run? Hadn't she wanted commitment from him? Wasn't an admission of love a form of commitment? He felt rebuffed and it made him angry, which was never good.

"I won't make that mistake again," he said, rising. He wrote a note on a piece of stationery and went to the kitchen where he used a mug to hold the note on the table. Then he quickly strode from the house, heading for the barn.

Chapter Fourteen

The next night, Leah and several others sat in Lucky's tipi eating mutton stew, fresh-baked bread, and coffee cake. He'd cooked the stew all day and it was delicious. The bread was perfect and the coffee cake the perfect ending to the meal.

She watched Billy eat, marveling at how he could shovel so much food into his mouth and not choke. It was amusing to watch Lucky berate him for his bad manners and have Billy just smile as he continued eating. It had taken her a little while to get used to eating without utensils, but she'd done it, determined to fit in.

However, that didn't seem to be hard to do since everyone talked to her, sometimes two people at once. It made her feel accepted and she didn't feel self-conscious about being deaf since they all signed. Some were better than others at it, but they got their point across or laughed at their blunders when someone else told them what they'd said. Once in a while, Wild Wind would forget and use Indian sign, which confused the heck out of Leah.

She signed to him, "What sign is that?"

"Sorry. It was Indian sign," he said, smiling.

Grinning, she said, "In my sign language you just told me that you saw a moose mount a stump."

The group burst into laughter and Billy almost choked on the mouthful of bread he was eating, which made everyone laugh even harder. Evan pounded him on the back and Billy was able to get the bread down.

"You almost killed me, Leah," he signed.

"Sorry."

Billy smiled. "You don't look sorry."

She schooled her face into a serious mask. "Is that better?"

"No, because you still don't mean it," he teased.

"You're right."

Everyone laughed again, even Sofia. Leah had continued to be worried about her sister's lackluster disposition, but she saw a little spark in her that night, for which she was grateful.

Leah signed, "This is a big tipi."

"Aye." Lucky motioned around at all the people present. "This is why. I had to make it bigger so that I could get everyone in here whenever I cook. Technically, it's almost the size of a lodge, but not quite."

"Your food is so good, it's no wonder they want you to cook," Leah said.

"I'm glad ya like it," Lucky said.

Thad let out a belch and said, "Amen!"

"Yer as bad as Billy," Lucky said, frowning.

"You're just lucky it didn't come out the other end," Thad said, grinning.

This tickled Leah so much that she laughed out loud with everyone else and then promptly clapped a hand over her mouth. She looked around, but no one seemed to notice except Lucky, who had a pleased grin on his face.

"It's good to hear ya laugh, lass," he said. "Ya should do it more often."

Leah shook her head. "I sound like a donkey."

Win had caught her statement. "Leah, you don't sound like a donkey. Sugar sounds like a donkey. There's nothing wrong with your laugh."

Josie asked, "Did someone tell you that you did?"

Leah nodded shyly.

Lucky said, "Well, they were just being nasty. There's not a damn thing wrong with yer laugh."

Sofia caught Leah's attention and said, "I told you so."

Leah smiled. "Ok. If you're sure."

"Aye. We are."

Edna drank her willow bark tea that Wild Wind had made for her. It did help with her pain and she was very grateful for Lucky's thoughtfulness in making her a high cushion she could sit on so she'd be comfortable. Evan had mentioned to Lucky that he hated leaving his aunt at home whenever they came out to supper and Lucky had told him he'd fix that problem. The higher cushion was his solution, as well as a small cushion for Edna to put her feet on.

"Reb would have loved this," she said out of the blue. She'd been thinking about her husband for some reason. "It's very peaceful and fun out here, isn't it?"

"Yeah, it is," Billy agreed. "When he first told me he was gonna build a tipi, I thought he was kidding me. Then when I realized he was serious, I thought he was crazy. You're not gonna take it down, are you?"

"I'm not," Lucky said. "Everyone enjoys it too much, me included."

"I'm glad," Leah said. "I really like it. I'm like Billy; when you told me in your letter that you lived in a tipi, I thought you were pulling my leg. The picture of an Irishman living in a tipi was so funny, but it somehow suits you."

Wild Wind said, "It didn't always. When we first brought him to our village and I told him he would have to sleep in a tipi, he didn't like that idea. He stayed with me and I don't think he slept that night."

"Well, first off, I didn't know if ya were gonna kill me or not and secondly, it seemed like the thing would fall down if a good wind came up. I know better now, of course, but I didn't at the time," Lucky said.

"You caught on fast," Wild Wind said.

"That's because he's so smart," Josie said. "My hero."

Lucky smiled. "I don't know about that, but my good luck certainly saved us that day."

Josie said, "It sure did. You didn't have to help me, you know. Why did you?"

"I wasn't gonna leave ya to the likes of that chancer across the aisle and ya were gonna get squeezed out into the aisle by the other thing you were sitting by. I ain't got nothin' against larger people, but she was offended when ya asked her to move over. The best thing was for ya to sit with me. And then when the train started goin' haywire, somethin', most likely the Great Spirit, told me to grab ya and hang on for dear life. I don't have any other explanation for it."

Evan hugged Josie. "I'll never be able to thank you enough for saving her for me. I was worried sick when we heard that your train had derailed, so when that telegram came through, it was a huge relief."

She hugged him back and noticed that Edna looked tired. Julia, who was sitting with Sofia, looked sleepy, too. "I see a little girl who looks like she needs to go to bed."

Evan looked over at their daughter and smiled when she yawned. "I'd say that's about right."

Billy yawned and Nina laughed. "I think you're ready for bed, too. You're always sleepy after you eat."

He smiled. "I'm like a snake that way. They get their belly full and then can't move. If you guys are leaving, that means I get to take Edna out to the buggy."

Thad said, "I thought it was my turn. I'm number three."

Since Edna had been going out more often again, there were times when it was just easier for her to be carried, especially over rough ground, so they'd come up with a numbering system, but the men always argued over who got to carry her.

Edna chuckled, not self-conscious in the least. "Ladies do like it when men fight over them. Actually, it's Wild Wind's turn. I keep careful track, boys."

Evan grunted. "Of course you do."

She laughed as Wild Wind stood up, looking proud to do the honor of taking her to the buggy. She put on her coat and gloves. "Lucky, the meal was superb as always, and everyone, the company was delightful. Leah and Sofia, if we haven't already told you since you got here, we're all very happy to have you with us, especially a certain Irishman we know."

Thad said, "Yep. I'm real pleased to have the both of you here."

"Not you, the *blond* Irishman," Edna said as Wild Wind picked her up. "My goodness. Just feel that muscle," she said, squeezing his bicep.

Evan was holding the tipi flap open. "Quit squeezing the Indian, old woman."

"He doesn't seem to mind. Do you mind?" she asked Wild Wind.

"No. Squeeze away," Wild Wind said, playing along.

"How many times do I have to tell you to not encourage her?" Evan responded.

Wild Wind said, "What? I not English speak good. Understand not."

"Shut up and put her in the buggy," Evan groused good-naturedly.

Everyone listened, amused by the bantering. This was something that went on nightly in the Taft household. Bedtime was normally delayed for about ten or twenty minutes while the adults bickered like this. The later in the evening it got, the more scandalous Edna's remarks became. Finally Wild Wind had her settled comfortably and she kissed his cheek and thanked him.

Then Lucky handed her Otto.

"Goodnight, Grandma," he said, hugging her. "I love you."

"I love you, too, sweetheart. You get some sleep," she said.

"Ok," he responded before hugging everyone else, too.

Leah watched all of this going on as she said her goodbyes, too. It was wonderful to see people so close to each other. She was happy to have the chance to become friends with them. It was obvious that they had become Lucky's family over the past couple of years. As everyone left, the farm grew quiet. Win and Erin had gone to their cabin and Wild Wind had gone to his tipi. Lucky walked with Leah and Sofia to the new house. They were spending their first night there.

Lucky watched Sofia's face in the moonlight and felt badly for her when he saw the slightly dejected look on her face. He could only imagine what she was going through. Of course, he'd known a similar heartache. His gaze swung to Leah, who smiled at him. Smiling back, he felt his heart waking up and knew his pain was greatly easing thanks to her.

Just as they were going to walk up the porch steps, Lucky said, "Go say goodnight to Sugar, lad. Ya know she'll be mad if ya don't."

"Ok, Da," Otto said. "Goodnight, Sofia. Goodnight, Leah."

Both women hugged him goodnight. Leah was surprised how much she already cared for the little boy. He was so sweet and cute that it would be only the most cold-hearted person who couldn't love him. Otto's curly hair bounced as he ran off to Sugar's little shed to say goodnight to her.

Going up onto the porch, Sofia said, "Goodnight, Lucky. Thank you for supper. It really was delicious."

"Thanks. Sleep well," Lucky said.

Leah saw the concern in his eyes and was grateful for his kindness where Sofia was concerned. Sofia went inside and soon lamplight showed in the kitchen.

Lucky said, "If ya need anything, come get me, all right?"

"Yes. I will, but we'll be fine," she said.

He nodded as he slipped an arm around her waist. "I'm not gonna sleep without a little goodnight kiss."

She smiled at his mischievous expression. "You won't?"

"I won't. Just one little kiss," he said, looking in her eyes.

"Well, I guess one would be all right," she signed. The thought of kissing Lucky made her feel a little giddy.

Lucky brushed his lips against hers and the slight contact made his stomach clench. He'd only meant to give her a light kiss, but the inner male demanded more. He pressed his lips firmly to hers, drawing her harder against him. Leah didn't mind. Even though she was new to kissing, she was eager to learn; as Lucky deepened the kiss, she sighed. Although, she couldn't hear his low, answering growl, she felt it and it made her feel a little weak in the knees.

A giggle interrupted them. They broke apart and Lucky laughed.

"You were smoochin'," Otto said. "Uncle Billy and Aunt Nina smooch, too."

Lucky signed, "They taught him that word when he caught them at it one day. Go on home, ya rascal. I'll be right there."

Otto laughed and ran off.

Leah laughed against Lucky's chest. He tapped her shoulder and she looked up at him.

"Ye'll have to get used to that," Lucky said. "Kids interrupt at the darnedest times. He'll be tellin' everyone tomorrow. Just givin' ya a heads-up."

"Oh, boy," she said.

He smiled and pressed another kiss to her mouth. "Goodnight, lass."

"Goodnight, Lucky," she said, going up the porch steps.

Lucky watched her go inside. Then he took a huge breath of cold air and let it out while grinning. The grin stayed on his face the whole way to his tipi.

As the Tafts neared their home, Evan saw a figure up ahead. It looked like the person was running and Evan had the sinking feeling in his stomach that usually told him that trouble was afoot. As they drew abreast of the person, Evan saw that it was Adam.

"Hey, Adam! Stop running, son. What's wrong?"

Adam leaned against the buggy, trying to catch his breath. Evan opened the door and got out of the buggy. "Ok, slow and easy." He was concerned firstly about Adam passing out because he couldn't breathe, but also because he needed to know what was wrong.

"Were you coming to get me?" he asked.

Adam nodded. "Church. Gunshots. Mr. Desmond, Pastor Watson."

Evan asked, "How long ago?"

"Not long. Came as soon as I saw what was going on," Adam said.

"Ok. I need you to come to my house and get Aunt Edna in the house," Evan said. They weren't far away.

"Ok," Adam said.

Evan climbed back in the buggy and put his horse, Smitty, into a fast trot to get them home quickly. Once they were near the house, he stopped the horse and got out. Immediately, he began undoing Smitty's harness until the only tack he had on was the bridle. Going back to the buggy, he picked up his gun belt from the floor and put it on.

He kissed his three women. "Don't wait up for me. Who knows when I'll be home?"

"Be careful," Josie said.

"I will. Adam, you saddle Josie's horse and ride for the Earnest ranch and get Shadow up. What am I saying? He's most likely up. Anyway, tell him to meet me at the church," Evan said, hauling himself up on Smitty's back and thundering off.

Adam helped Josie get Edna and Julia in the house and went to do as Evan had directed.

Chapter Fifteen

As Evan rode Smitty into the church lot, he quickly dismounted, dropping Smitty's reins and hurrying to the door. He heard shouting from inside. Slipping in the door, he crept towards the sanctuary.

"You lyin', cheatin', bastard!" he heard Travis shout.

"Travis, you're drunk," Sam said. "Let's talk about this tomorrow when you're more clear-headed."

"No! You're not gonna live to see tomorrow!" Travis said.

Looking inside the sanctuary, Evan saw Travis holding a gun on Sam, who was down on his knees by the altar.

"Travis," Evan said. "Put down the gun."

Travis whirled in Evan's direction. "Stay out of this, Evan. I'm doin' this and no one's stopping me."

Evan walked slowly towards his friend. "Travis, what's going on? Talk to me."

Travis let out a sarcastic laugh. "Tell him what's going on, Sam. Go ahead."

Sam's jaw clenched, but he didn't say anything.

Travis squeezed off a shot that slammed into the floor. "Tell him!"

Evan reached for his gun, but he didn't want to have to shoot Travis. "Travis, listen to me. Whatever's happening, it's not worth going to jail over. You have a wife and daughter who need you."

He saw such rage on Travis' face that it was a little scary. "A wife? She can go to hell, right along with the good pastor here!"

Evan understood immediately what Travis was saying. Looking at Sam, he asked, "You and Jenny?"

Sam looked down at the floor and didn't say anything.

Evan was sorely tempted to let Travis shoot Sam. "Travis, I understand, believe me, I do. He's the one who slept with Louise. Looks like his philandering didn't stop after all. So I know what you're feeling, but you still have a daughter who needs her pa. Please don't make me put you in jail."

Travis' shoulders shook as he began crying. "She ain't mine. She's his. That's how long this has been going on. Jenny finally told me the truth when I cornered her about it tonight. Earnest—Marvin—told me I should talk to her and now I know why!"

Sam's gaze grew hot. "He's the one who needs to be shot. He needs to stop meddling in people's business!"

Travis said, "I'd agree with you, but not in this case. He did this so I knew what a lyin' whore I was married to! I won't be married to her for long!"

Evan shoved his shock down so he could do his job. "Travis, it doesn't matter if Pauline is yours biologically or not. You're her father no matter what, and she needs to have you around, not locked up in jail somewhere."

Travis said, "You don't get it, Evan. She's not mine and I have no say over whether I get to see her anymore or not when we get divorced. She's gonna take my little girl away from me. I have nothing left to live for. So I'm gonna take care of him and then take myself out of the picture."

Evan had been creeping closer and when he was within striking distance, he jumped on Travis and they wrestled for the gun. Evan slugged Travis a couple of times, almost knocking him out. He was able to get the gun off him and he rolled him over so he could put handcuffs on him. Just as he was finishing, Evan saw Sam grab for Travis' revolver. Evan jumped, slamming his shoulder into Sam's huge bulk. It was enough to knock the much bigger man off kilter so that he could snatch the gun away.

"Oh, no, you don't, you worthless piece of shit!" Evan said.

Sam swung at him, but Evan was able to duck in time to avoid the big fist. He used Travis' gun to shoot Sam in the foot. The preacher howled in pain and fell down. Evan got Travis up, sat him in a pew, and sat down behind him.

Sam sat on the floor, panting in pain. "Aren't you going to help me?" he asked Evan.

Evan's grin was malicious. "Yep. Right into a jail cell. Attempted murder of an officer."

"What about him? He tried to kill me!" Sam said.

"If Travis had had the guts to shoot you, he would have instead of talking to you all that time," Evan said. "He's going to jail for the night to dry out and calm down."

The church doors opened and Shadow came in, gun drawn. He swiftly took in the situation and holstered his gun again. "Well, it seems as though you've had all the fun, Evan. You could have left me have a little."

Evan smiled. "I did. You get to cuff asshole over there and help me get both of them to the office." He saw that Adam had accompanied Shadow inside. "What's he doing here?"

"I came with him to see if I could help," Adam said.

Shadow startled Adam by handing him a gun. "You can. If he moves while I'm cuffing him, shoot him."

"Don't tell him that!" Evan said. "He's …" He didn't want to hurt Adam's feelings, so he said, "He's not used to doing anything like this and he's not even a deputy."

Adam said, "I can do it. Go ahead, Mr. Earnest."

Evan's jaw clenched and he wanted to smack Shadow. "Get him cuffed, Shadow."

Stepping over to Sam, Shadow said, "Well, putting a man of God in jail is going to be fun. Paying for your past transgressions, hmm?"

Sam looked up at Shadow. "You know?"

Shadow smiled. "I know everything, Pastor Watson. Now put your hands behind your back. No funny business or else you'll wind up shot full of lead. Or I'll snap your neck. I haven't had the pleasure of doing that lately, so if that's what it boils down to, I won't mind too much."

Sam's fury grew. "You and your meddling brother—"

Shadow cuffed him upside the head hard. "Shut your mouth. You're in no position to judge anyone. Your own actions are what got you into this mess, not my brother or me." Roughly, Shadow yanked Sam's arms behind his back and put the cuffs on the preacher. "Now get up!"

Evan enjoyed watching Shadow smack Sam around a little bit. "All right, Travis, let's go. Adam, give Shadow his gun back, son, and go on home. I appreciate your help."

Adam nodded. "Sure, Evan. Happy to."

Shadow nudged Sam forward and Sam grunted in pain and stopped. "Sucks, doesn't it?" the deputy said, grinning. "Move!"

Sam limped along on the injured foot; his progress was slow.

"Adam, can you do me one last favor?" Evan asked.

"Sure."

"Once we're outside, blow out all the lamps in the church. I don't want the place to burn down. Ok, two things. Also, get your ma and go to parsonage and help her tell Bea that we had to take Sam to jail. Stay there with her until I can come to talk to Bea, ok?" Evan said.

"You got it," Adam said. Helping thc sheriff on official business made him feel more grownup.

Evan and Shadow took their prisoners to the office, which wasn't too far from the church, thankfully. However, some curious people had come out of their houses and they watched the two lawmen guide both prisoners along. They had heard the gunshots. One of them was Sam's oldest boy, Keith.

"Where are you taking Pa? What happened?" he asked.

Sam said, "Keith, go on back home to your ma and the rest. Go on. You're the man of the house for now. Understand?"

Keith nodded. "Ok, Pa."

Evan said, "I'll be along to talk to your ma, Keith. Let her know."

"Ok. I will, Sheriff," Keith said and jogged back to the parsonage.

"Adam, you still go get Charlene. I don't want Bea to be alone after I talk to her, ok?"

"Yes, sir. I'll go right away.

Evan told the onlookers to go back home and not to interfere with their job. Slowly, the small crowd dispersed and the lawmen and prisoners continued on their way. They put Sam in the first cell and Travis in the one on the other end so that there was a cell in between them. That way, they couldn't fight with each other. Then they sat down at their respective desks. Evan pulled his bottom drawer open and took out a bottle of scotch. He pulled off the lid, drank a swallow, and then looked at Shadow.

"Come outside, deputy. There's something I'd like to talk to you about," Evan said.

Shadow rose and followed Evan out into the cold night.

Evan turned towards him. "Just how is it that you know what Sam did?"

Shadow said, "Remember our agreement. You see, Evan, I'm a master at gathering information and I know everyone's dirty laundry, so to speak."

Evan ground his teeth together. "How long have you known about Jenny and Sam?"

"Long enough. I gather that Marvin thought it was the right time to dispense this information."

"You gather?"

"Yes. Marvin went to Dickensville on business. He won't be back until tomorrow."

Evan said, "How convenient for him."

Shadow said, "Marvin left for another reason. Otherwise, he'd have enjoyed the show."

Evan shook his head. "You're both a couple of sadists. So Pauline really isn't Travis'?"

"No, she's not." Shadow said. "It's very sad, really. It's one reason we haven't said anything. You know how much Marvin cares for Pauline. He didn't want her to suffer, but Travis has wanted more children and Jenny hadn't conceived yet. I guess Marvin wanted Travis to know why and what kind of woman he was married to."

"Are you saying that Jenny was preventing pregnancy?"

"Yes. She didn't want to have another baby at all," Shadow said.

Evan's heart went out to Travis. He'd not only been betrayed by his wife, who supposedly loved him, but also by Echo's pastor, whom everyone had trusted. He also felt sorry for Bea and her kids and Pauline. "What a screwed up, terrible situation."

"Yes."

"You stay with our prisoners. I'm going to talk Bea."

Shadow nodded and went back inside.

As Evan explained the circumstances to Bea, Charlene sat close to the preacher's wife. Bea's face went white and then became suffused with blood as fury and pain filled her breaking heart.

"How could he do this to me? To our children? I thought he loved me and only me. How could I be so blind? So stupid?"

Charlene put an arm around her. "You're not stupid. He's just really good at hiding things and lying. It's not your fault, Bea. You're a wonderful wife and mother."

"What am I going to do? I can't stay married to him after this, but I don't make enough money working at the diner to make it on my own," she said.

They had all been so wrapped up in their conversation that they didn't notice Keith come into the room. He had been listening at the door and heard the whole thing.

"I'll go to work, Ma. I'm the man of the house now. I'd like to kill him for this. He's not the man I thought he was," he said.

Bea jerked. "Keith! You shouldn't be in here."

"I'm seventeen, Ma. Old enough to understand what's going on." He sat down on the other side of Bea. Tears stood out in his eyes. "It'll be all right. I'll find work and we'll find a place to live. We'll have to move out of here."

Evan rubbed his chin. "Don't worry about moving out right away. You've got other worries at the moment. I'm gonna keep Sam in jail for a month. That'll give you some time to figure out what you want to do."

Bea nodded. "I'll talk to a lawyer right away. I have plenty of grounds for a divorce."

"Yes, you do," Evan agreed. "I'm so sorry about this, Bea." He reached over and squeezed her hand.

"Thank you, Evan." Her blue eyes filled with tears. "I loved him so much. I never imagined he'd ever betray me like this. I never thought I'd be a divorced woman, either."

She burst into tears and Keith pulled her into his arms. Rage shone in the boy's brown eyes. Keith was a younger version of his father and was on his way to rivaling Sam's size. He was already Evan's height and growing all the time. "It'll be ok, Ma. You'll see."

Evan respected Keith for supporting his mother, but it was a heck of a burden to put on a seventeen-year-old boy whose heart was surely breaking as badly as Bea's. Evan decided it was time for him to go. He knew that Bea was in good hands with Charlene and Keith. Adam was also there and he would help support Keith.

"Bea, if you need anything, you just say the word, ok? You're not alone."

Bea just nodded as she sobbed against Keith's shoulder. Evan pursed his lips and ground his teeth in anger as he left the parsonage.

Chapter Sixteen

Unaware of the scandal that had erupted in town, Lucky sat in the kitchen of the new house the next morning, drinking coffee with Leah and Sofia when Callie Carlisle showed up at the farm. She had originally come to Echo from Mississippi as Billy's mail-order bride, but Billy had fallen in love with Nina and Callie had developed feelings for Ross Ryder. She was vivacious and made friends easily.

She knocked on the door and Lucky answered it. "Callie, it's good to see ya, lass. C'mon in."

She came in the kitchen and said, "Hello, ladies. I haven't had the pleasure of meeting you yet, but I heard about your arrival."

Lucky made introductions.

"Thank you for the welcome," Leah signed; Lucky translated for her.

Callie smiled. "Of course."

Sofia asked, "Would you like some coffee?"

"Don't mind if I do," Callie said and sat down at the table. "Ross sent me out with your share of the profits for last week. Sales were great, especially the goat cheese, so he wants to know if you have any more ready."

Lucky nodded. "Aye. Did ya bring a buggy?"

"I brought a wagon," Callie said. "Are there any sheep butchered? He said for me to bring them if there are."

"We did a few yesterday," Lucky said. "I'll get things loaded once we're done here."

"Ok. Well, I have very sad news to tell you," Callie said, turning serious.

Sofia gave Callie coffee and sat down with the rest of them. They were shocked at the news of Jenny and Sam's infidelity and felt terrible for Bea and the children. Travis' plight also grieved them. Callie finished by saying, "Travis is still in the jail, I think. I haven't heard any different."

"I better go see Travis," Lucky said. "I can't even imagine what he's goin' through."

"What'll happen to little Pauline? I can't imagine Travis and Jenny will stay together now, and if Jenny tries to keep Pauline from Travis, there's not much he's going to be able to do about it," Sofia said.

Lucky shook his head. "Damn her hide and Sam's, too. I'll never understand it. How could they do that to the people who love them, but mostly to the kids? They're gonna be the ones to suffer the most."

Sofia nodded. "You're right. They must be so devastated. I was and I wasn't even married to Gary."

Lucky stood up. "I'm so sorry about that. He doesn't deserve you. Well, I'll get that stuff loaded and visit Travis."

Leah nodded. "Will you please hitch up the buggy? I'd like to go get some more groceries."

"Aye. Just put whatever ya buy on my account," Lucky said.

"I have money," Leah responded. "I can buy it."

Lucky saw that she wasn't going to change her mind about it and smiled. "As ye like it. I'll get the buggy ready."

When he and Callie went out the door, Sofia said, "Leah, I was wrong. Lucky is a rare find. Hold on to him."

Sofia's wistful expression made Leah feel bad for her sister. "You'll find someone, too, when the time is right."

"I doubt it. I don't think I'll ever trust another man. It seems as though most of them are the same," Sofia said and went to get her cloak.

Once again, Leah cursed Gary for hurting Sofia so much. Then she put on her coat, grabbed her purse, and went out to the barn. Lucky was almost done hitching up the buggy and Leah watched him. Although his coat hid his muscles from her view, she knew how firm his chest was and could imagine the way they flexed as he moved.

She'd never experienced desire before and it was intoxicating. However, she knew that it had more to do with Lucky himself. His blond hair and gray eyes were a very attractive combination. Add to that his impressive physique and fun-loving personality and it became almost a lethal mixture.

Lucky finished and patted the horse. He caught sight of Leah and saw the way she was looking at him. When she saw him looking at her, she smiled and came towards him. But for that split second, he'd seen appreciation in her eyes. He thought about the way they'd kissed the night before and he felt that hunger for her again.

Leah noted that his gray eyes had darkened and knew that he was having the same thoughts she was. He came to stand before her and her heartbeat's pace picked up. She couldn't keep her eyes away from his firm-yet-soft mouth and almost shivered as she remembered how delicious kissing him was.

Sofia came into the barn and Lucky put a smile on his face. "Well, there ya are. All set," he said to both women.

Sofia said, "Thank you, Lucky," before climbing into the buggy.

"Yer welcome." As he turned away, Lucky winked at Leah, as though in promise.

She smiled and let him help her up into the buggy. When she was situated, she winked back at him and he chuckled softly.

"Now you ladies be careful," Lucky said.

Sofia picked up the reins. "We will."

Lucky waved at them as they drove off and sobered. Then he saddled his horse and took off, heading for the sheriff's office.

Ronni was cleaning up from breakfast when Marvin came in the kitchen door. Anxiety flowed through her as she looked at him. He was sure to be furious with her after yesterday. She was prepared to talk to him and explain why she'd run away.

Marvin smiled pleasantly at her. "Good morning," he said, removing his coat and hanging it on the rack by the door. "I smell pancakes."

"Yes. Would you like some?" she asked.

"No, thanks. Is there still coffee?"

"Yes."

"Oh, good. It's cold out and something hot would be great. So how are things around the place?" he asked.

Ronni glanced at him before pouring him a cup of coffee. "You haven't heard?"

"Heard what? I just arrived back from Dickensville and I didn't stop anywhere in town," Marvin said.

"Travis won't be here today and I'm not sure when he will be," Ronni said.

Marvin said, "Come to my office and tell me what's happened."

She followed him, wondering why he wasn't angry. He sat behind his desk and she took a seat in a chair. As she related Shadow's story, Marvin sipped his coffee. When she was done, he smiled.

"Splendid."

"What do you mean 'splendid'? There's nothing splendid about the situation. It's horrible."

"Well, you see, I told Travis that he needed to talk to his wife because I knew about the affair between Sam and Jenny. I had actually told Travis to talk to Jenny about it a couple of years ago, but he didn't," Marvin said. "He should have."

"So you told him about it?" Ronni asked.

"No. I just told him that there was something very important he needed to speak with her about."

The wry twist of his lips angered her. "This isn't some game, Marvin. These are real people with feelings, or are you incapable of understanding that?"

His eyes turned an icy blue that chilled her blood. "Oh, no, Ronni. I understand people having feelings all too well. I understand emotional pain perhaps better than most other people. I told Travis because he wanted to have children, but Jenny wasn't getting pregnant. I wanted him to know why and to know what kind of woman he was married to. It was also better that everyone knows what kind of man was leading their congregation. The man who was supposed to be morally superior to everyone was the biggest liar and sinner of all. I may be many things, but I have never pretended to be anything other than what I am."

Ronni chewed on her lip as she digested his statements. Like Evan saw Shadow's twisted logic in things, Ronni saw Marvin's. "So you were doing this for altruistic reasons?"

He trapped her gaze. "Somewhat, I suppose. I try not to do that because it usually ends up backfiring on me."

He was talking about her. "Marvin, we need to talk about yesterday."

"No, we don't. You made your position clear and I think it's best if we go back to the way we were before I bared my soul to you. That way, I won't be trying to push myself on you when I'm obviously not wanted and I won't waste my time. I would appreciate it if you would keep the things I told you to yourself."

"You know I won't tell anyone, Marvin. Please let me explain," she said.

The kitchen door banged open right then. "Uncle Marvin!" Pauline called out.

"Pauline?" Marvin responded.

Pauline ran into the office, making a beeline for Marvin. She threw herself into his arms so hard that his chair almost went over backward. Marvin caught her with one arm and prevented them from winding up on the floor by gripping the edge of the desk with the other.

"Ma is going away and taking me with her. Someone said Pa isn't my real pa, that Pastor Sam is. It's not true, is it? Please say it isn't! I don't want to go. I love Pa! I don't want to go." She lapsed into loud sobs, and Marvin pulled her onto his lap. He held her and rocked her.

"Pauline, you know how much I love you, don't you?" Marvin asked after a little while.

She nodded against his shoulder. "Yes."

"Good. And because I love you so much, I'm going to be truthful with you." He gave her a handkerchief and she dried her eyes and blew her nose.

Her dark eyes were puffy from crying and Marvin wanted to slap both Jenny and Sam for the pain they were causing Pauline.

"Sweetie, grownups sometimes make very bad decisions and I'm afraid that's what's happened here. Your mother and Sam made some very bad decisions."

"So Pastor Sam really is my pa?" she asked.

"I'm afraid so, but not in the true sense of the word. I know all of this is a lot for you to understand, but I'll try to make it as simple as I can for you, ok?"

She nodded.

"Travis is your true father. He loves you more than life itself. He protects you, he makes you laugh, has fun with you, and takes good care of you, doesn't he?" Marvin asked.

"Yeah. I love Pa and I know he loves me. But how can they both be my pa?" Pauline asked.

"Well, part of this you're not old enough to understand, but you know it takes a woman and a man to make a baby, correct?"

"Like a boy horse and a girl horse make a baby?"

"Sort of, but not exactly. But even though Sam and your mother made you, Sam isn't the man who loves you the way Travis does. It's like with Eva. Her pa is dead, but if another man were to marry Ronni, I'm sure he would love Eva as much as if he was the one who had helped make her. He would make her laugh and protect and take care of her just like any good father takes care of his child," Marvin said. "Travis is, and will always be, your true father, Pauline. You must remember that, no matter what. Travis loves you more than anything. Do you promise to never forget that?"

Pauline sniffed. "Yes, I promise. But Ma is gonna take me away. Why was she bad? Doesn't she love Pa?"

Marvin sighed and kissed her forehead. "Again, I love you too much to lie to you. I'm not sure. I can't see into her heart, so I can't tell you one way or another. What I can tell you is that your pa has always loved your ma."

Pauline frowned. "Then if Pa loved Ma so much, why was she mean?"

"I don't know, but people who love each other should stick together no matter what. That's what I do. When I love someone who loves me back, I stick by them regardless of how hard things are. But, again, I can't speak for other people, so I can't answer that question," Marvin said.

Ronni's face grew hot and anger filled her chest. His remarks were somewhat aimed at her, punishing her for what she was sure he saw as her rejection of him. He wasn't giving her a chance to explain.

"Ok," Pauline said. "What do I do?"

Marvin asked, "How did you get here?"

"I ran," she said.

His expression became alarmed. "You ran all the way here from town? Pauline! You can't run around like that in this weather. You'll catch a chill. Ronni, will you please make Pauline some hot cocoa?"

"Yes, of course." She rose and went to the kitchen.

"Thank you. Now, you stay here with Ronni. I'm going to go talk with your pa and see if there's anything I can do to help," Marvin said, kissing Pauline's cheek.

She got off his lap and walked to the kitchen with him. He put his coat back on, kissed the top of her head, and left.

Evan planned to release Travis around noon to make sure he was in better control of his emotions. When Lucky had arrived to visit him, he'd barely given Sam a glance, his righteous anger at the preacher strong within him. Instead he'd gone right to Travis' cell.

"Why don't ya come stay at the farm when Evan lets ya out? That way ya can make some decisions in privacy," Lucky said, quietly.

Travis nodded. "That's a good idea. Thanks."

"That's what friends are for, lad. Now, when ya do get out, don't start no trouble with the likes of himself down there. He ain't worth it," Lucky said. "Yer daughter is gonna need ya."

Travis' eyes filled with tears. "Have you seen her? I need to see her and know that she's all right. I don't think she heard us arguing. We kept our voices down, but it was still a terrible argument. I need to see my little girl."

Lucky was glad to hear Travis talk about Pauline that way even though he wasn't the girl's biological father. "Ya will. Don't worry."

"But Jenny is gonna take her away from me," Travis said.

"No, we'll figure something out. We'll hire a good lawyer so ya can get part custody," Lucky said. He was surprised to see Leah come around the corner into the cell room. She carried a basket of some sort of baked goods with her. "What are ya doin' here?" he signed, not happy that she had come there.

She smiled and was about to respond to him when Sam reached through the bars of his cell, grabbed her hair, and yanked her back against the bars. She let out a hoarse cry of pain and shock, which was then cut off by Sam's huge hand wrapping around her throat.

"Let me out of here and I'll let her live!" Sam shouted, squeezing Leah's throat and cutting off her airway.

Lucky reacted with split-second reaction time. He leaped towards the cell, drawing the knife he carried. He didn't bother trying to dislodge Leah's neck from Sam's hand. Instead, he slashed his knife across Sam's forearm. The blade cut deep into Sam's flesh, severing the tendons that gave Sam control over his hand and his grip on Leah loosened as he screamed in pain.

Leah fell to the floor, dazed and coughing as she sucked in air again. Looking back up at Lucky, she didn't recognize the man. Gone was the affable, kind-hearted Irishman, and in his place was an infuriated warrior. Lucky didn't let Sam go. Instead, he reached through the bars, grasped the collar of Sam's shirt, and pulled him against bars, slamming Sam's face into them. He'd just been about to plunge his knife into Sam's heart when Evan grabbed his arm.

"Drop it, Lucky! Let the knife go!" Evan shouted. "Lucky, that's enough." He exerted his own considerable strength on Lucky's wrist, forcing Lucky to relinquish the weapon. "Let his shirt go! Lucky, let his shirt go. Please?"

Evan got through to the reasonable part of Lucky's brain and he released Sam's shirt, stepping back from the cell. He looked down at the floor and saw that Leah had scooted back from the men. Her eyes were wild with fear.

Lucky asked, "Are ya all right?"

Leah had never witnessed any sort of violence before and couldn't answer Lucky. He stepped towards her, but she moved further away. The life had just almost been choked out of her and she had witnessed him almost kill a man. Her shock made her scared of him. Lucky understood and sat down on the floor. It would be better if he wasn't looming over her.

"Leah, yer safe now. I won't hurt ya. I couldn't let him keep hurtin' ya like that. I'm sorry ya had to see that. So sorry. But I'm not gonna hurt ya. I promise. I only did it to save ya. I couldn't bear it if ya were hurt. Are you hurt? Is yer neck hurt?" he asked.

Suddenly he was the man she'd come to know again. His eyes were filled with fear and worry for her welfare. She put a hand to her bruised throat and then signed, "I'm ok."

Lucky asked, "Can I come to ya? I'm not gonna hurt ya, love."

Incredibly, she smiled. That was the first time he'd ever called her that. "Yes."

Lucky quickly crawled across the floor, but stopped when he saw blood on his shirt and hands. Quickly he took the shirt off and wiped away the blood from his hands before continuing to her. She held out her arms to him and he wrapped his around her, holding her close. Leah tried to control the tremors inside and be strong, but she shivered involuntarily against him.

His chest vibrated against her body and under her hands, which rested on his back, and she felt comforted by the sensation. Although she couldn't hear him, she knew he was telling her everything would be all right and that she was safe. She soon stopped shaking and raised her head from his shoulder.

"Are ya all right now?" he asked.

Leah smiled slightly and nodded.

"Good. I'll take ya home," Lucky said. "Where's Sofia?"

"Outside," Leah mouthed and pointed.

"Ok," Lucky said. He rose, pulling her with him. "Now, don't look at the cells. You just look right at me."

Leah nodded and let him guide her from the cell room. He kept her as close to the wall as possible, making sure she didn't step in any blood.

Evan said, "Get her in the buggy and come back in here, Lucky."

"I'm takin' her and Sofia home," Lucky said.

"Fine, but before you do, get back in here," Evan said in an iron-hard tone.

Lucky's jaw clenched, but he said, "I will." His blood was still running so hot that he never felt the cold air on his exposed skin when they exited the building.

Sofia's eyes widened when she saw Lucky's bare torso and the way he walked protectively with Leah. "What happened?"

Lucky picked up Leah and placed her in the buggy before telling Sofia.

"Are you all right?" Sofia asked Leah right away.

"Yes. I'm fine. Thanks to Lucky. He saved me," Leah responded, looking at him. "It seems like you do that for people a lot."

He smiled wryly. "I guess so. Now, I have to go back in and talk to Evan, but you ladies go straight home so you can rest. I'll be right along. Do ya promise me ya will?"

Leah read the worry in his eyes and wanted to allay his fears. "I'll be fine now. I'll have a couple swallows of whiskey and that'll steady me."

Lucky smiled and shook his head. "That sounds like a fine idea. Save some for me."

Sofia clicked to the horse and they pulled away from the sheriff's office.

Leah held her shivering at bay until they were out of Lucky's eyesight and then it came on her full force as her shock returned.

Sofia noticed her shaking and put an arm around her sister. Leah leaned against Sofia for a short while before straightening again. "I'll be ok. Just drive faster. That whiskey is sounding really good right now."

Chapter Seventeen

Erin stitched up Sam's arm, but it took a while. They'd had to sedate him in his cell; they couldn't get him to her office due to his injured foot and also because they couldn't handcuff him now. Win had assisted her, as he often did. The two of them made an excellent medical team as well as husband and wife.

Win loved watching Erin work. He admired her concentration and skill in patching up people. She was gentle and caring with all of her patients—most of them, anyhow. Win saw her anger in the set of her jaw and her hand movements as she sutured Sam's arm. Erin performed her job well, but Win knew that she wasn't being as gentle as she could have been and it amused him.

The doctor exacted just a little bit of revenge on Sam in her own way. She'd become fond of Leah and Sofia since they'd come to Echo and the thought of anyone hurting them made her furious. Secretly, she was glad that Lucky had caused so much damage to Sam's arm. It might make him think twice about grabbing someone like that again. As she finished up, she looked at the inert man and wanted to punch him. She didn't, of course.

"Finished," she said and started packing up her bag. "I'll check it tomorrow. No sudden movements. No hurting anyone else, because if you do and you get hurt, I'm not treating you again."

Sam didn't respond, just kept his eyes closed even though he was semi-awake. That suited Erin just fine. Win had her leave the cell first, just in case Sam tried anything. He wasn't taking any chance of something happening to his wife and child.

Leaving the cell room, Erin said, "All done, Evan. I already told him if he attacks anyone else again and gets hurt, I'm not fixing him again. He tried to shoot you last night and you shot his foot. He attacked Leah today and got his arm sliced. I hope he's learned his lesson. If something else happens, don't bother coming to get me unless someone besides him is hurt."

Evan saw she meant what she said and nodded. "Ok. Thanks."

Erin's moods had been volatile lately and she asked, "Why was Leah in here? She shouldn't have been in here. Where were you when she came in? Why weren't you watching her better?"

Evan was taken aback by her angry questions. "Well, like I told Lucky, Shadow had to go out on another emergency and I just went out back long enough to take a leak. I came in, saw her heading in there and yelled, but she couldn't hear me, of course. That's when everything happened."

"Ok. That's all right then," Erin said.

Win grinned from where he stood slightly behind his wife and Evan had difficulty keeping a straight face.

"Thank you," Evan said. "Was it ok that I let Lucky go?"

"Yeah, but you should have just let him finish the job," Erin said.

Evan laughed then. "You know I can't do that. He's just lucky that he did it in defense of someone else, or I'd have had to arrest him."

"If you had, I'd have broken him out. You can't lock everyone up, Evan," Erin said. "Ok, I have to get back to my office. See you later." She kissed Evan's forehead and walked out of the office.

Win grinned at Evan again and the sheriff gave him a questioning look. The veterinarian signed, "pregnancy insanity" to Evan. Evan nodded, remembering the way Josie had been when she'd been carrying Julia. Then Win followed Erin out the door.

Jenny blanched when she saw Marvin standing on her porch. "What do you want? Haven't you caused enough trouble? Are you here to gloat?"

Marvin pushed his way inside and slammed the door behind him. "I warned you what would happen if you didn't end things with Sam, but you didn't listen to me. People who don't listen to me end up regretting it. You've hurt Travis—a very good man, when he's not stabbing me in the back—and that sweet girl. You're no kind of mother and you don't deserve her."

"Don't you talk to me like that!" Jenny said, her dark eyes flashing.

"I'll talk to you any way I like, you whore!"

"Who are you to judge? It's not like you're innocent or anything!" Jenny shot back.

"You're right. I'm not, but I've never slept with a married woman or made any excuses for who I am. But you? Acting the pious little housewife while you're screwing the preacher behind your husband's back? I don't call that being an upstanding citizen, which is exactly what I'll tell the court when Travis sues you for custody of Pauline."

Jenny's mouth dropped open. "He can't do that! She's not his!"

Marvin's hand shot out and he slapped Jenny hard across the face. "She's his in all the ways that count, you stupid twit! He has been there from the beginning, supporting you, loving you, loving her from the moment she was born. He endured working for me just so he could put food on the table and keep a roof over your heads. On every level, he sacrificed just to take care of you, and how do you repay him? You keep on with your perverted, deceitful actions. I warned you when Louise left that you had to end it with Sam! Didn't I?"

Jenny held her face and nodded, scared that he was going to kill her.

"You know I always make good on my threats and promises, Jenny. It's bad enough that you've hurt Travis, but your actions have hurt Pauline and that I can't abide. You have a choice to make. I'll help Travis rake you over the coals in court when I testify against you and have you deemed an unfit mother or you can take this money and get the hell out of Echo, never to return. If you do come back, I'll make your life a living hell. Do you now believe that I'll make good on that threat?" he asked, pulling money out of his inner coat pocket.

Jenny took a step back from him. "Yes."

Marvin threw the two packs of bills at her. "There's five thousand dollars. Be gone by six o'clock tonight or else."

"But I want to say goodbye to Pauline," Jenny said. "I'm her mother."

In a deadly quiet voice, Marvin said, "Not anymore. The fact that you're not willing to fight for her in court tells me that you care more for yourself than you ever cared about her. You will never set eyes on her again. Make sure you write a goodbye note. Remember, six o'clock and no later."

His icy gaze held hers and Jenny shivered. "Ok," she whispered.

Marvin nodded curtly and left the house. Jenny stood for a few minutes before snatching up the money and running upstairs to pack.

When Lucky arrived at the farm, Wild Wind had returned with Otto from hunting and the boy was riding one of the sheep around the pasture while he giggled.

"You need to get that pony for him pretty soon," Wild Wind said, smiling. Then he noticed that Lucky was tense. "What happened?"

Lucky filled him in on the situation. "So I'm goin' to check on Leah. Can ya watch Otto just a little longer?"

"Sure. Go ahead," Wild Wind said. "Too bad you didn't kill him."

"No, it's better I didn't. Evan would have locked me up and he'd have been right to," Lucky said. "Harmin' Leah was wrong, but me killin' him once I'd sufficiently disarmed him would have been even worse. I'm glad he stopped me in time."

Wild Wind shrugged. "If you say so."

Lucky sometimes forgot how bloodthirsty Wild Wind was in battle. The brave didn't believe in giving an enemy the chance to offend again, and his adversaries usually ended up being gravely wounded or paying the ultimate price for their actions. Lucky just shook his head a little before going to his tipi to put on a shirt. He'd thrown the other one away, not wanting to keep the reminder that he'd almost murdered a man.

Once he'd changed, he jogged over to the house and pulled on the braided rope that hung close to the door, ringing the unusual doorbell. He wanted Leah to get used to answering it. Soon she opened the door and smiled at him. He opened the screen door, took her in his arms, and kissed her, not caring if anyone saw or not.

Leah didn't resist him, feeling a rush of relief that he was there. Relief gave way to desire and she responded to him, reveling in his strength and his warm lips on hers. Lucky heard someone clear their throat and he broke the kiss to see Sofia staring at them with a small smile on her face.

"Ye'll have to forgive me, Sofia. It's been one hell of a mornin'," he said to her.

He and Leah moved into the house and Lucky shut the door against the cold.

Sofia said, "I know. I'll let it go just this once."

Leah grinned. "I think that's my decision to make."

"Are ya ok? How's yer neck?" Lucky asked.

Leah's smile faded and she touched her neck a little. "Sore. There's some bruising."

Lucky's countenance darkened. "I shoulda—"

Leah put her hand over his mouth and shook her head. "Don't," she mouthed. He nodded and she removed her hand. "Thank you."

"Sorry," Lucky said. "Evan let Travis go. He's goin' to check on Pauline and he'll come stay with us for a little. I think it'll be good for him to be among friends right now."

Sofia said, "That's a good idea. I feel so badly for him. I know how he feels, although his situation is much worse than mine. Being here is helping me a little because I'm away from the situation, but mainly because of the friendship everyone has extended to me."

"Well, we're glad yer here," Lucky said. "And a beautiful woman like you is sure to attract a fella. You'll see. Someone who'll appreciate ya."

Sofia smiled tightly. "I appreciate the sentiment, but I doubt I'll be ready for anything like that for a long time."

Lucky said, "Yer right to take yer time. Give yerself some time to heal." said he asked Leah, "Are ya sure yer all right?"

She nodded. "Yes. I'm fine."

Lucky sighed. "Ok. I have to go work on the milkin', but I'll be in the barn if ya need me."

"All right," Leah signed.

Once he'd left, Sofia said, "Shame on you for letting him kiss you like that."

Leah grinned. "I can't help it. Look at him. Who wouldn't want to kiss him? I've never been kissed before, so let me enjoy it. Besides, it's just kissing."

Sofia said, "That better be all it is."

Leah became angry. "I'm twenty-six years old and I make my own decisions. If I want to kiss Lucky, I will. It's none of your business. I'm sorry for what happened with Gary, but Lucky isn't like him. Just because you're miserable, doesn't mean I have to be, so I'd appreciate it if you don't try to spoil my happiness." With that, she turned and went into the pantry.

Sofia stood still for a moment. Tears began to threaten over her sister's angry words and she needed to get away. Donning her coat and gloves, she went outside and began walking towards where Lucky had told her was the beginning of a trail. A walk would allow her to clear her head and calm down.

As he milked goats, Lucky thought about Leah and how terrified he'd been when Sam had attacked her. She was so sweet, kind, and funny. He smiled to himself as he thought that his good luck had once again helped him. He had begun to think that the Lord had had Leah in mind for him all along. Although it still stung a little that he'd lost Avasa, his wounded heart was mending, thanks to Leah.

They hadn't really had a chance to get to know each other better even though they'd been on a train for a few days together. Leah's focus had been on Sofia much of the time because her sister's pain was so fresh and she'd been so worried about her. They also hadn't had much time alone to just talk. However, Lucky was going to rectify that now since the girls were situated. He decided to see if the gang wanted to go to Spike's the next night. He could probably con Josie and Billy into playing for them so they could dance.

Then he looked over at Otto, who was milking a goat next to him. He smiled at the look of concentration on the little boy's face. Who would he get to watch him? He thought about Adam and decided he'd ask him when he came to the farm that afternoon. Otto loved Adam, so he was sure he wouldn't mind staying with him.

His thoughts returned to Leah. He hadn't known her long, but he could easily picture being married to her. They got along well so far and there was definitely chemistry between them. Lucky firmly believed in no sex before marriage, and the fact that Leah hadn't known how to kiss told him that she was a virgin. He'd only ever been with Avasa and he would never be intimate with anyone unless he was married to them.

He would also never violate Leah that way, even though both of them might want to be lovers. Lucky might lie about some things or tell ribald jokes and so forth, but he believed in the sanctity of marriage and held a deep, abiding respect for women. His parents had instilled these beliefs in him and he couldn't go against their teachings.

"Da?"

Lucky's thoughts were interrupted by his son. "What?"

"Look," Otto pointed at another goat. "She's sick."

Finishing with the goat he'd been milking, Lucky moved the bucket away to that it didn't get kicked over. Walking over to the doe that was lying down in the straw, Lucky ran a hand over her swollen belly.

He smiled at Otto. "She's not sick, lad. She's gonna have a baby."

Otto's mouth dropped open. He'd seen some of the sheep give birth in the spring and the prospect of the goat having a kid excited him. "Will it be mine?"

Lucky laughed. "Sure." Something occurred to him. "Go tell Leah and Sofia."

"Ok." Otto patted the goat's neck. "Wait to have it until I get back."

Then he ran from the barn, his blond curls bouncing as he went. Lucky chuckled and examined the doe. He didn't think it would be too long until the kid came.

Just as Leah started peeling potatoes, Otto came bursting in the kitchen door. Leah smiled and saw that he was very excited about something.

Otto signed, "Come to the barn. A goat is having my baby!"

His remark amused her. "It is? It's your baby?"

He nodded. "Yes. Da said that I could have the baby, so it's mine."

"Oh, I see. Ok. I'll get my coat and be right along," Leah replied.

"Ok," Otto said, running back out the door.

Sofia hadn't come back from her walk. Leah frowned as she thought about her sharp words to her sister. She knew that Sofia was only looking out for her, but she didn't need looked after, especially not where Lucky was concerned. She trusted him completely and knew that he wouldn't do anything truly inappropriate. Leah didn't think that a little kissing here and there was anything very scandalous.

She hurried out to the barn and found Lucky and Otto. "Hi. I've never seen an animal born."

"Yer in for a treat then," Lucky said. "I'll never get tired of seein' it. Come sit down here. We're just waitin'."

Leah sat down on the straw near Lucky and Otto. He put his arm around her and Otto came over to sit on Lucky's lap. He looked over at Leah. "Are you going to be my new mother?"

His question startled Leah, but she knew the subject would come up at some point. "Well, I'll never try to take your mother's place, but I'd like my own place in your heart someday," she replied.

Otto grasped her meaning. He nodded and said, "Ok." His question answered, he turned back to the goat.

Leah looked at Lucky. "Was that all right?"

He nodded. "Perfect." He gave her a little squeeze and she rested her head on his shoulder. Quietly they awaited the birth of the kid.

Chapter Eighteen

Leah watched the tiny kid nurse from his mother for the first time. Tears filled her eyes. Seeing the little life be born was a wonderful experience and she was thankful to Lucky for making sure she'd had the opportunity to witness it.

"It's beautiful," she signed to him. "I've never seen anything like it."

Lucky said, "I've seen hundreds of animals born, but I love it. I don't care whether it's a human or an animal baby—they're all little miracles to me."

"I agree. I'm so glad I was able to be here." Meeting his gaze, she said, "I'm glad to be here, period."

An understanding passed between them and Lucky felt his heart heal a little more. He ached to kiss her, but not with Otto there. "I'm glad you're here, too."

"Oh! I need to go work on supper. You cooked last night, so I'm cooking tonight," she said, rising and brushing off her skirt.

"All right. I look forward to it," Lucky said, getting up also. He had some other work to do, so he figured he'd better get to it.

"I'll let you know when it's ready," she said, giving him a wink before leaving the barn.

Lucky chuckled and had Otto help him finish the milking.

Marvin tended to be a light sleeper, so it was very hard to sneak up on him. He heard furtive movements in his room and became alert instantly. No one should be coming into his room. Phoebe used to pay him late night visits, but she was dead. Shadow or Bree would have knocked, so it wasn't them. He usually slept on his stomach so it was easy to turn his head to see who it was.

Ronni moved towards the bed. He rose up quickly and she jumped. "What is it? Is there something wrong with Eva?" he asked.

"No, no. She's fine, but something is wrong," Ronni said. She went around the other side of the bed and crawled in it, unable to prevent her eyes from roaming over his naked torso. He was lean and strong and utterly delicious. She'd missed having him wrapped around her at night.

"What are you doing? I thought we agreed that this was a bad idea from now on," Marvin said, glaring at her.

Ronni moved right up to him and sat up on her knees so she could look him square in the eyes. "No, you said that, but you didn't give me a chance to agree or disagree. You won't let me explain about yesterday."

"I think—"

She clapped a hand over his mouth. "Shut up. You don't get to talk right now."

He continued to glower at her, but remained silent when she took her hand away. Marvin moved up in the bed so he could lean against the headboard and Ronni followed him, but stayed facing him.

"Marvin, I loved my husband very much. I still do, but it's different now. The romantic part of that love is gone, but I still love him. When he died, I was devastated. I lost the person I loved most in this world outside of Eva. David was a wonderful man. He was handsome, and kind, and funny. And he was such a good father. He was so excited when we found out I was pregnant. But then he was just gone and I was broken-hearted. I know you know what that's like.

"When you go through something like that, you don't really believe that you'll find someone to love again. Eva was my first concern, of course. I had to go on for her sake. You're not the first man to express interest in me, but I was too scared to even think about getting involved with someone again. What if I lost another man I loved again? Could I come back from it or would it crush me? And would any other man be a good father to Eva or even willing to take on a child who wasn't theirs? Some men wouldn't."

Marvin said, "I understand what you're saying, Ronni, but I fail to see how this ties into what happened yesterday. You already know that I love Eva and you already know that I love you. Why would you run from me after knowing all of that?"

"You scared me! My feelings for you scare me! I love you, but I hadn't told you yet, so there was no threat. But then when you told me that you love me, the threat became very real because I wanted to say it back to you. Once you say something, you can't take it back, not really. I was afraid that once I said it to you, it would make everything real. And once that happened, what if I lost you?

"You almost died, Marvin! I was so scared that you would and I'd have lost another man that I loved! I don't want to go through that again! It's why I didn't want to make love with you. I told you that it was because we weren't married, but that's not the real reason. What if I hurt you and kill you? Just holding you at night and fighting with you during the day was much better than making love with you and killing you by reinjuring you. At least you'd be around for me to keep loving."

Although her last couple of statements struck him funny, the tears trickling down her face didn't amuse him at all. Neither did the sentiment behind her rather disjointed explanation or the fact that she'd just told him that she loved him. "So you ran from me because you were scared of losing me, not because you don't love me. Am I correct?"

Ronni was relieved that he understood. "Yes."

"And the true reason you wouldn't sleep with me is because you're afraid of killing me." He sighed. "You must be *incredible* in bed if you're afraid of doing that."

She let out a snort of laughter and smacked his arm. "Stop! It's not funny! What if we're in the middle of … and you keel over?"

"Then I would have died a happy man. Of course, I'd prefer to keel over at the end, but a dying man has to take what he can get," Marvin said, grinning.

When she drew her arm back, he grabbed it and said, "You know, for a woman who's worried about me dying, you seem to have no problem causing me pain."

"Then be serious about this," she said, even though she still smiled.

"You're right. This *is* serious. The fact that you love me is very humbling because I know you mean it in the true sense of the word. You don't love me because my very twisted side feeds some equally twisted need in you. For whatever reason, you love *me*, not my character traits."

"Yes, I love you for you. I know you have a dark side, but I love you in spite of it because, no matter what you or others think, your good qualities outweigh the bad ones. You just need to let them shine through more," she said.

"I'm trying," Marvin said. "It's not easy, but I'm trying. No one ever made me want to try before, Ronni, but you do. You may be stubborn, difficult, opinionated, and shrewish, but you're also kind, fun, and so very beautiful. You're a wonderful mother, too. Just the sort of woman I need in my life. The sort of woman I never thought I would have in my life."

"Well, you're snobbish, harsh, infuriating, and condescending, but you're many of those other things, too. Enough so that I overlook all of that other stuff, so I guess you're the kind of man I need in my life," Ronni said.

His smile was almost bashful and in the moonlight there was a boyish quality to it. "I'm glad you think so." Then the boyish look was gone, replaced by a very hungry male appreciation of her. It always amazed Ronni how fast his expressions could change. "I'm just letting you know that I've already talked to Dr. Avery about resuming sexual activity, and she said that there should be no problem in doing so. I can't swing from the chandelier or anything, but there is no problem with making love, except that I don't know if things work or not."

"No, I wouldn't advise you to swing from a chandelier," Ronni said.

He smiled and then sobered. "Tell me again."

"About the chandelier?"

"No. About your feelings for me. Tell me again," Marvin said.

Hearing the plea in his voice, Ronni moved even closer so she could take his face in her hands. "Marvin Earnest, I love you, all of you, the good and the bad. I love you."

She saw tears suddenly shimmer in his eyes before he leaned forward to press a demanding kiss to her lips. His arms wrapped around her, pinning her against his hard chest as he treated her to a sensual onslaught, the likes of which she'd never felt. One of his hands delved into her fiery hair while the other pressed her even harder to him.

The raw intensity of his kiss shook her to the core and she couldn't resist him. She ensnared his neck with her arms and kissed him back with full force. She ran her hands over his shoulders, squeezing the hard muscles. His kisses and caresses were driving her out of her mind and she felt like she was drowning in a sea of sensation. It was almost too much to bear and she broke the kiss.

"What are you doing?" Marvin asked. "Don't stop now! Things are working!"

Ronni giggled. "Let me check on Eva and I'll be right back."

He pursed his lips. "Fine. Yes. Make sure she's ok, but don't dawdle. I don't want things to fizzle. And be naked when you get back here."

She giggled again and scrambled off the bed. Quickly she pulled her nightgown up over her head and threw it at him. "There. Now things won't fizzle."

He laughed as she ran from the room even as the sight of her naked derriere heightened his desire for her. She was soon back and he was treated to the front view of her shapely body.

"You're not naked," she complained. "That's not fair."

"Who says I'm not?" he said pushing the covers away. "I told you I sleep naked."

She laughed as he embraced her and brought her down to the mattress with him. "You weren't lying about it."

His wicked grin flashed. "No. Now, woman whom I love, please make love with me."

She wiggled in his arms and he groaned. "You have very good manners when you want to, Marvin."

"So you like it when I'm polite?"

"Yes, but not right now," Ronni said.

Something else flashed in his expression, something dangerous, and Ronni shivered in anticipation. She pulled him down to her, fisting her hands in his hair. He growled and captured her mouth in a hard kiss that heated her from head to toe. Then she felt his embrace gentle and he slowly ended the kiss.

"I love you, Ronni, and I promise that I'll never make you regret giving me your heart," he said softly.

"I believe you," she replied. "I promise you the same thing."

He smiled and kissed her again, savoring the taste of her and the way she felt in his arms. Making love with Ronni was the sweetest, most powerful experience in his life; there was complete acceptance and unconditional love in Ronni's touch, kisses, and embraces. Now he understood what it was that Shadow had found with Bree. It was more important to him that he give instead of taking and throughout that night, Marvin gave himself over completely to Ronni.

Ronni fully discovered the man Marvin had never shown to anyone else before. There was nothing cold, cruel, sadistic, or sarcastic about him. Even during demanding moments, there was an underlying tenderness and warmth in his actions, and there was such love in his whispered words to her that they erased any last traces of doubt she had about his feelings for her.

Their two hearts joined, easing each other's fears and shining light into even the darkest corners that had once been filled with fear and grief. As their passion ebbed, they held each other. They knew that neither of them would ever be the same again and they were filled with a bright, shining joy.

Chapter Nineteen

Someone shook Thad and he let out a groan of protest. "Go away," he said.

"Mr. McIntyre, you gotta get up. The sheriff's here."

"Oh, God. What's he want? What time is it?" Thad asked.

"Six."

"Already? It feels like I just went to sleep. Ok, tell him I'll be right down. Hey, where's your mother?" Thad asked.

Eleven-year-old Porter Daughtry frowned. "She didn't come home last night."

Thad swore as he sat up on the side of the bed. "Where're your sisters?"

"Still sleeping," Porter said.

Thad coughed. "Ok. Go get the kitchen stove going while I talk to the sheriff, ok?"

"Ok," Porter said, preceding Thad out of his room.

Following the boy down the stairs, Thad yawned and then shook his head trying to clear his sleep-fuzzed mind. Padding into the parlor, Thad saw Evan sitting on the sofa.

"Good mornin', good-lookin'," he said, taking in Thad's untidy appearance.

His salt-and-pepper hair stood up at odd angles and there were pillow marks on his right cheek above his beard. "Go to hell. What do you want?"

Evan didn't take offense. Thad was always unpleasant until he'd had his first cigarette and cup of coffee in the morning. "I need you to help me take Sam to Helena today."

Thad coughed again. "Where's Mayhem?"

"Well, Bree went into labor, so he can't go," Evan said.

"Oh dear God. They're having their little bundle of mayhem, huh?" Thad said, smiling. "Why don't you just wait until tomorrow to go?"

"They're expecting him today. You know how cranky they get there if you don't arrive on the right day," Evan said.

Thad called them a nasty name. "Ok. Do we have to leave right this second? I gotta make sure the kids get off to school and they need breakfast, which you're cookin' since you're here," Thad said, getting up. "You do that while I get dressed and get the girls up." He didn't give Evan a chance to disagree with him. "Make the coffee stronger than that pansy-ass stuff you normally make, ok?"

Evan chuckled as Thad mounted the stairs again. Going out to the kitchen, Evan said, "Hey, Porter. How are you?"

"Fine. Ma didn't come home again last night," the boy said, his blue eyes meeting Evan's for a fleeting moment. His embarrassed expression told Evan that he knew why his mother hadn't come home.

"Oh." Evan frowned, but made no further comment. He didn't want to make Porter feel even worse. *What the hell is going on with this town? We don't have a pastor anymore because he's been cheating with the mother of his illegitimate daughter. Now his kids aren't gonna have a pa because he's going to jail. Jenny took off, leaving poor Travis and Pauline heartbroken. Dear Lord, we could use some help down here. Can you send us some?*

Porter opened their small pantry and said, "We have some eggs and bread. That's about it."

Evan cursed Darlene Daughtry for not making sure the kids had food to eat. If it wasn't for Thad, half the time they'd starve. Darlene had rented out a room to the bounty hunter and spent the money he paid her each month almost before she had it in her hand. She was a former dancing girl from the Burgundy House. She had no idea who any of their fathers were.

Evan said, "Ok. We can work with that. Do you have any milk?"

"Yeah." Porter went outside and retrieved a small pail from the porch. "It might have frozen a little."

"That's ok," Evan said.

There was enough milk that was still liquid for Evan to mix with the eggs. He beat them and added some cinnamon he'd found to the mixture. "Slice that bread," he instructed Porter.

By the time Porter's younger sisters, J.J., and Liz, came downstairs, Evan was just putting the first pieces of French toast on plates.

"Good morning, ladies," he said as they sat at the table.

Unfortunately, this routine was becoming familiar to them and to Thad and Evan. Darlene often didn't come home at night and the kids were left to fend for themselves. Ever since Thad had moved in, he'd almost immediately become a father figure to them. He paid a woman next door to wash the kids' clothes and fix their nightly meal if Darlene wasn't home. When he was in Echo, he made sure they were up for school on time and fixed them breakfast.

He argued with Darlene about her lack of motherly concern every time he saw her, but got nowhere. He could have moved out, but although Thad was often gruff and rough around the edges, he had a big heart and he couldn't leave the kids. Evan had noticed that Thad was taking jobs closer to home so that he didn't have to be gone so long, but hadn't mentioned it to his friend.

J.J. said, "Hi, Sheriff. That looks good. I'm hungry." The eight-year-old girl smiled at him, revealing a space where she'd recently lost a tooth.

"Me, too," nine-year-old Liz echoed. "We didn't have much for supper last night."

Porter looked like he wanted to slap his sister for revealing that fact. "We had beans and ham, Liz."

Evan knew that Porter was trying his best to fill the role of parent, but it was hard for a boy his age to do much about their circumstances. Thad came in the kitchen looking more put together and wider awake. "I'll be right back," he said, going outside on the porch to smoke a cigarette.

As he did, he tried to rein in his anger at Darlene for her wayward, callous behavior towards her kids. Taking a long drag, he blew out the smoke, trying to let his inner tension go out with it. Mentally, he went over his finances and knew that he was going to have to go out on a job soon. The kids needed new clothes, especially Porter, who was outgrowing his shoes again. He knew he could put a few things on his account at Temples', but he liked to keep his account paid up in case there was something he needed to get in an emergency.

"I guess that sort of qualifies as one. Looks like we're goin' shopping tomorrow after school," he said to himself. Going back inside, he pulled money out of his wallet and handed it to Porter. "After school, you take your sisters to the diner and have supper. Whatever change you have, hide it good so your mother doesn't get hold of it. I don't care if you gotta shove it where the sun don't shine to keep her hands off it. And you two, don't you mention it to her. Understand?"

All three heads nodded. "Yes, sir," Porter said. He had a huge case of hero worship where Thad was concerned. "I'll do that."

"Good boy. Now sit down and eat so we can get to school on time," Thad said, smiling at them.

Evan never interfered when Thad was dealing with the kids. He thought Thad's manner around the kids was a little rough, but then again, that was Thad. He didn't mince words, preferring to deal with things head on. The kids didn't seem to mind, though. He handed Thad a cup of coffee and caught the anger in Thad's dark eyes. Meeting his gaze, he shook his head in sympathy and Thad nodded his agreement before sighing and drinking his coffee.

It was a week since Ronni and Marvin had become lovers. During that week, Shadow had insisted that he and Bree move upstairs in case she needed help when he wasn't home. Down in his lair, there was no real way for her to get anyone's attention.

Now, as he paced outside their room, he thought he must have had a premonition about Bree going into labor. He couldn't remember a time when he'd been so scared, even when he'd been locked in that cage. His love for Bree and their baby was such that he was utterly terrified of losing either one of them.

He'd never envisioned falling in love, let alone becoming a father, but he was ecstatic about both. Ronni had been kind enough to show him how to diaper Eva so that he was ready for when his baby came along. He'd also gotten more comfortable holding and playing with her. He'd been afraid of hurting her, but Ronni and Marvin had reassured him that she wasn't as fragile as she seemed. Unlike Julia, who hated Shadow's glasses, Eva loved them and if he didn't have them on, she would ask, "Gasses?"

He winced every time Bree let out a groan or a sharp cry of pain. This was something Shadow couldn't help with and being so powerless was a terrible feeling. He trusted Erin to help bring their child into the world, but he couldn't help the anxiety that filled him. It made him want to punch a wall, but that wouldn't solve anything.

"Shadow, drink this," Marvin said, coming upstairs. He handed Shadow a tumbler of scotch.

Shadow didn't often drink, but he felt this was a special occasion and tossed the drink back without question. It burned down to his stomach and helped calm him a little.

"I'm going insane, Marvy. There's nothing I can do to help her. If there was, I'd do it, but there isn't. This is terrible," Shadow said.

"It's going to be all right," Marvin said, even though he was almost just as nervous. He'd never been present during a birthing before and his own nerves were stretched taut. "Dr. Avery is an excellent physician and because she's a woman, I believe it gives her even greater insight into women giving birth than a male doctor would have."

"You're right," Shadow said, trying to relax. "She's a very good doctor. I mean, she saved you, and if she can do that, she can certainly do this. She's also delivered other babies and they're all fine, so this will be, too, right? And Ronni's helping so it'll be fine, right?"

"Yes, of course," Marvin said.

The whole time they'd conversed, they'd both paced up and down the hall. They fell silent but kept pacing.

In the birthing room, Bree pushed, determined to get their baby delivered. Ronni held her hand as she gritted her teeth and worked on it while Erin urged her on.

"You're doing great, Bree," Erin said. "I don't think it'll be long until the baby crowns."

"Good," Bree said. "I can't wait to hold our baby." Her voice was strong and her face was set in a determined expression.

When the next contraction came, she pushed for all she was worth and Erin saw the head come into view. She was amazed by the strength Bree exhibited. She hadn't ever seen a mother so strong-minded before. Bree seemed untiring even though she was sweating profusely.

"Come on, my baby. Come out here so I can hold and kiss you," she grunted with the next contraction. "So your daddy can see you. We both love you so much."

Ronni smiled, remembering feeling the same way when Eva was being born. "You better listen to your mother, little Earnest."

Bree laughed a little and pushed harder. Erin urged her on and soon she held a tiny baby, who immediately squalled. Only then did Bree rest back, crying with joy. "What is it?" she asked.

Erin smiled as her eyes filled with tears. "A beautiful little girl, Bree."

Ronni hugged Bree. "I'm so happy for you and Shadow. Congratulations."

Bree laughed through her tears and then Erin gave Bree her daughter. Bree looked down at the pink little face and said, "Hello, Aurora. I'm your mommy." Suddenly, Bree was squeezed around her midsection again and she looked at Erin. "What was that?"

Erin's surprised eyes met hers. "Well, it looks like you've got another one in there."

"Twins?" Bree said, disbelievingly. Then she grinned. "Twins! Oh, how wonderful."

Ronni took Aurora from Bree and said, "I'll give her to Shadow and be right back. She's beautiful, Bree."

"Thank you," Bree said, getting back into position.

Shadow had heard the baby cry and had grabbed Marvin in a crushing hug. Marvin had hugged him back. "Congratulations, Daddy," he said, grinning.

The door opened and Ronni came out into the hall carrying the baby. "Shadow, would you like to meet your daughter?"

"Yes! A girl! We named her Aurora because it means light," Shadow said, holding his arms the way he'd been shown. Ronni placed the baby in them and grinned at the sight the big man and little baby made together.

"I'm so happy for you," Ronni said. "I have to get back in there so I can help with the next one."

Shadow's smile slipped. "Next one?"

Ronni laughed. "Twins, Shadow. You're having twins."

Shock made Shadow lightheaded and he leaned against the wall for support while Marvin let out shout of laughter and put a hand on his shoulder. "Twins. It never occurred to me that we might have twins. It should have. We need another crib and bassinet and everything. Oh, God."

Ronni said, "Don't worry about that right now."

"How is Bree?" Shadow asked. "Is she all right?"

"She's fine. She's a strong woman. She'll be tired, but fine. I have to go," Ronni said when Bree let out a groan.

Shadow said, "I want to see her. I *need* to see her."

Ronni's eyes widened. "I don't know—"

"I'm coming in." His stern tone told Ronni that he wasn't going to accept no for an answer.

He followed Ronni into the room and felt a rush of love as he looked at Bree.

"What are doing in here?" she asked, her eyes wide.

"I needed to see you," he said. "So we're having another one then?"

Bree grinned, "*Yeeesss!*" she groaned and pushed.

Shadow paled as he watched and then became caught up in the miracle unfolding before his eyes. "Aurora, you have a brother or sister. Isn't that wonderful?" he murmured to the baby in his arms. He kissed her forehead. "You'll play together and be best friends. You wait and see."

Even as she strained and pushed, Bree smiled at the tender way he spoke to their daughter.

Erin said, "Ok, Bree, give me a really good push."

Bree grunted and bore down, pushing their other baby out into the world. Ronni helped her lie back. A loud cry rang out and both Shadow and Bree wept with joy at the sound.

"Aurora has a brother," Erin said, laughing. "He's a handsome little guy, too."

Bree looked lovingly at Shadow. "Just like his father."

Shadow grinned as he watched Erin clean their son and then wrap him up. She handed him to Ronni, who gave him to Bree. "He's gorgeous," Bree said. "Shadow, I love you so much."

Shadow went to her, kissing her, not caring that she was sweaty. "I love you, too. Thank you for our children."

She smiled tiredly before kissing their son's forehead. "Why don't you take Lucas to meet Uncle Marvin?"

They'd chosen both a girl's and boy's name that meant light. "Of course," Shadow said. "We'll be back soon," Shadow said. "Dr. Avery, thank you. We're very grateful to you."

Erin smiled. "That's what I'm here for. Congratulations."

Shadow smiled, kissed Bree again, and then followed Ronni from the room. Ronni gave Lucas to Marvin, who grinned down at his nephew. "Well, aren't you the handsome little fellow?"

Ronni smiled. Marvin looked good with Eva and he looked equally good holding Lucas. She went back into the birthing room to help Erin with Bree.

Chapter Twenty

As Leah worked on putting new soles on a pair of work boots for one of ranchers in the area, she looked around at her shop. It was a nice little place, and she was grateful for Lucky's business expertise and all of the help from their friends in getting it set up over the past couple of weeks. They'd chosen the location for the shop on the corner of Main and Stratton Streets. Billy's art shop was down Main Street to her right, and Ross' butcher shop was down Stratton to her left.

She'd named the shop The Corner Cobbler, which Lucky had loved. It was catchy and told everyone exactly what she did. The shop had only been open a couple of days, but already she had work lined up. Just as she finished up with one of the boots, Jerry Belker came into the shop.

The tall, handsome black man smiled at her. "Hi, Leah. How are you today?"

Over the years, Leah had made up a stack of flashcards with common responses and questions on them so that she could communicate with people who didn't know sign language. She picked one up that said, "I'm good. And you?"

"Good, thanks." He held up a pair of dress shoes and asked, "Would you have some time this week to put new heels on these?"

She came over to the counter and took them from him. After looking them over, she nodded.

"Good. I appreciate it."

She wrote on a tablet, "Are you nervous about the election tomorrow?"

Jerry smiled. "Yep. Nervous I'll get elected. Just kidding. I'm most likely gonna win, according to Evan. My first order of business is to find us a new pastor." His smile had turned into a frown.

Leah shook her head sadly and wrote, "I feel so bad for Bea and her kids. How are they doing?"

Jerry sighed. "As well as can be expected, I guess. She's worried about finances, of course. Keith is looking for work."

Leah bit her lip a moment as she looked around at all of the work coming in. She was beginning to doubt that she was going to be able to handle it all herself. "Would you do me a favor and ask him to come see me? I might have some work for him."

Jerry's face lit up. "Really? You just opened."

She pointed to all of the shoes that needed repairs and spread her hands wide. "I could train him to do simple repairs and it would free me up to do the more difficult ones," she wrote.

Looking at all of the shoes, Jerry smiled. "Nothing like having plenty of work to do. We needed a cobbler. We're glad you're here. I'll stop by Bea's and ask him to come over right away."

Leah smiled. "Thanks," she mouthed.

"You bet," Jerry said. "Well, I'd better get back to my shop, too."

"Good luck tomorrow, not that you need it. You've got my vote."

"Thanks, Leah. Take care now," Jerry replied and left her store.

Keith walked quickly along Main Street, headed for the square. He kept his head down and didn't speak to anyone—he didn't want to see their pitying smiles or hear them whisper behind his back. His shame over his father's actions weighed heavily on his young shoulders. He had almost dropped out of school because he didn't want to be the target of snide remarks or gossiped about even more. However, his mother had convinced him to finish out the year. He would do it for her, but he'd made up his mind not to go back the next year.

His long legs swiftly brought him to the Corner Cobbler and he went inside the shop. Leah saw him, smiled, and gave him a little wave of greeting. He smiled back uneasily at her. He'd never met a deaf person before and he didn't know how he was going to communicate with her. He'd heard that she read lips, but how would he understand her responses? He needn't have worried.

She motioned for him to come around the counter and sit in an empty chair. She held up a card that said, "How are you doing?"

He looked at the floor and shrugged. "Ok, I guess."

She put her hand under his chin and raised it. Then made a motion that told him she needed him to look at her so she could read his lips.

Smiling, he repeated his answer.

Leah wrote, "I know you've had a hard time of it, but things will get better. One day at a time."

He frowned and shrugged again.

"It will. You'll see. In the meantime, you can work for me, if you want. I need help with repairing shoes. I'll train you if you're willing to learn. The pay won't be very high at first, but I'll give you raises whenever I can."

Keith was willing to do anything as long as he could bring in money for his family and make things easier on his mother. "Sure. I'll learn. I'm smart and I can carry heavy things and clean the store. Anything you want."

"Great! Can you give me three hours after school and on Saturdays?"

"Sure," Keith replied.

Leah ran some numbers through her head and wrote, "I can start you out at nine dollars a week."

It was more than he'd expected. "Ok. That's fine. Do you want me to start today?"

"Do you have time?"

"Yeah," Keith said. "It's better than hiding at home and I really need the money. Without *his* income, we don't have very much of one. Ma's job at the diner won't keep us going."

Leah wrote, "I understand. Come with me and I'll show you how to cut out some leather for me."

Keith smiled and felt a little better knowing that he was doing something to help his family.

"That was a very kind thing ya did, Leah," Lucky said that night during dinner. "I feel so bad for them all. I still can't believe it. Sam deserves to be in jail, and maybe it's a good thing that Jenny took off. She's not worthy of that little girl or Travis."

Sofia said, "You're right. I can't believe that she and Sam had been carrying on for so long. It's despicable."

Leah sighed. "I hope Jerry can find a new pastor soon."

"Me, too," Lucky said. "Well, let's get cleaned up here and go meet everyone at Spike's."

Wild Wind said, "I'm glad that Billy and Josie play for us. It's very nice of them."

Leah smiled. "Yes, it is. I'm looking forward to going. The last time was fun."

"Aye, t'was," Lucky agreed.

Sofia frowned. "I really don't feel like going."

"You can't stay holed up here forever," Leah said. "Come with us. A little fun is exactly what you need right now."

Lucky employed a little psychology on Sofia. "If ya keep lettin' yerself feel depressed, yer lettin' him win, Sofia."

Sofia's chin rose and her nostrils flared a little. Lucky was right. She could stay home and mope or start living again and feel better. "I'm not going to let that happen. I'll come with you."

Leah gave her a sideways hug. "Good. Let's get the dishes done."

Sofia rose and began scraping off the dishes into the dogs' bowl. Otto was good about taking his dishes to the sink. The only problem was that he was a little too short to get them up on the counter, but at least he took them over.

Working together, the two women had the kitchen quickly set to rights. Lucky had taken the scraps out to the dogs, who gobbled them up. Going back inside, Lucky watched Leah work and liked the graceful way she moved.

Her womanly form was a pleasure to see, as well as her beautiful face. He knew how soft her skin was from the few times he'd kissed her and she felt good in his arms. It was difficult, but he kept a firm grip on his desire for her. When he'd put his ad in the paper, he hadn't expected to meet someone like Leah, whom he not only liked and respected, but to whom he was intensely attracted.

Lucky was looking forward to going out that night. Opening her shop had created another intrusion into time for them to explore their relationship, but now that things were running smoothly there, nothing else should stand in their way. He looked away before she caught him staring at her.

Wild Wind smiled at him, letting him know that he'd seen Lucky admiring Leah. Lucky just frowned at him, but then smiled and, using Indian sign asked, "Can ya blame me?"

Wild Wind shook his head a little as he put his coat on. Soon the rest of them did the same and headed to town where they dropped Otto off at Charlene's house. They would pick him up when they were done at Spike's.

Lucky sat with Leah at a table as they watched other people dance. They talked about her shop and the farm, coming up with ideas for both. As they conversed, Lucky kept thinking how nice it would be to dance with her, but she couldn't hear the music. Then an idea came to him.

Giving her a smile, he said, "Leah, come dance with me."

Leah gave him a doubtful look. "I can't dance. I'm deaf."

"Sure ya can. I'll show ya how," Lucky said, standing up, and holding out a hand to her.

Reluctantly, she gave hers to him and let him lead her over to the dance floor.

Taking her in his arms, Lucky said, "Now, just let me guide ya and ye'll get a feel for the rhythm."

Leah didn't want to look like an idiot. "I don't know if I can, Lucky."

"Do ya trust me?" he asked.

"You know I do," she said.

"Then let me lead ya. I promise that it'll be all right."

Looking into his eyes, she saw his sincerity and couldn't resist him. "All right, but if I fall, you're going to be sorry."

He smiled. "I won't let ya fall."

Leah had never danced before and she was nervous as they started out. Her movements were awkward at first, but Lucky began tapping the beat on her back as they danced and she was able to pick up the rhythm just as he'd said she would. Soon they were stepping together perfectly and Leah felt as though she was in a dream.

"I'm dancing!" she mouthed to him. "I'm really dancing!"

Lucky had found that when she did that, it created a little whisper and it was easy to understand what she was saying. He wondered if she could actually speak aloud. She could laugh, so he knew that her voice box worked. Leah was still self-conscious about her laugh, but she needn't have been. While it had a throaty quality to it, it wasn't unpleasant and Lucky loved hearing it.

As they danced, he decided he was going to try to convince her to start speaking out loud, but he would be gentle about it. "Aye, yer dancin'. I'm proud of ya for tryin'." He leaned a little closer and mouthed, "I'm also enjoyin' havin' ya in my arms."

Leah blushed and smiled at him, letting him know that she felt the same way. One of the things she liked best about Lucky was the way he always looked her in the eyes. Now was no exception, and in his eyes she saw how much he cared for her and enjoyed being with her. Although she'd always hoped to meet someone who appreciated her, she'd never truly thought it would happen. And yet here he was—a big, handsome, funny, kind

Irishman who knew how to charm a lady and make her feel special.

As they danced, Lucky felt the happiest he had in a long time. Leah was everything he'd been looking for and more. He loved the way she played with Otto and helped take care of him now. The boy was becoming fonder of Leah every day, too. When they got up in the morning, Otto wanted to go see her right away, and he'd even stayed with her a few nights.

He also found himself wanting to see her right away in the morning and he hated leaving her at night. Her smile was one of the most beautiful sights he'd ever seen and he did everything he could to make her laugh. Suddenly Lucky felt a rush of a feeling he hadn't experienced since Avasa flow through him. He had fallen in love with Leah. She'd captured his heart with her gentle, sweet ways and he knew that he wanted to spend the rest of his life with her.

With his customary determination, he began mentally planning exactly how he was going to go about making sure that happened. Then he stopped planning and decided that he was just going to enjoy the moment and the feel of the woman in his arms.

Billy and Josie watched the couple dance and smiled at each other. As one song had ended, Billy leaned over to her and said, "I'm so glad to see him happy. He deserves it after everything he's been through."

Josie nodded as she looked at Lucky. He'd quickly become like a big brother to her. "I know. He's such a good man and I just love Leah. I think she's perfect for him."

"You're right. They'll be happy together," Billy said. "I don't ever want to see him look the way he did the night Avasa told him she'd remarried. It was the saddest thing I've ever seen. That and how heartbroken Otto was to leave his mother."

Josie said, "I couldn't let Julia go that way. I don't know how Avasa could give Otto up like that. I know why she did it, but she has much more strength than I would have."

Billy looked at Nina, who was close to eight months along now. "I know what you mean. There's no way I could ever give our baby away like that, either."

Josie nudged him. "And you thought you'd never find anyone."

He smiled at her. "Shut up about that. That's in the past where it belongs. I'm looking to the future now, and it's gonna be incredible."

"You're going to be a wonderful father, Billy. I can't wait for your baby to come along," she said.

Seeing that people were looking at them expectantly, Josie and Billy chose another song and resumed playing.

After they arrived home that night, Leah helped Lucky put Otto to bed. He was sleepy since it was late and she knew Lucky could do it by himself, but she'd come to love Otto and she enjoyed tucking him in. She knelt by his sleeping pallet and covered him up. Brushing his curly hair away from his forehead, she kissed his soft little cheek. He was already sound asleep and looked so sweet.

Lucky loved the tender way she always treated Otto. He could tell that she was going to be a wonderful mother to him. When she rose, he walked outside with her. It may seem silly, but he always walked her over to the house. It wasn't that he was afraid for her safety, he just wanted a little more time with her.

At the porch stairs, she turned to him and smiled. "I had a wonderful time tonight. Thank you for teaching me how to dance."

He could see her hand movements in the lamplight from inside the house. "Yer welcome. I had a great time, too."

Looking at Lucky, Leah drank in his handsome features and wanted to kiss him. Maybe it was the beer she'd had that night, but she felt bold. Moving closer, she grasped his coat lapels and pulled him down, pressing her mouth firmly to his. When he responded to her, she wound her arms around his neck, kissing him more urgently.

Although surprised, Lucky wasn't disappointed that the usually slightly shy Leah had suddenly become a temptress. He allowed himself to thoroughly taste her sweet, incredibly soft lips as he held her tightly. Her kisses grew even more insistent and Lucky couldn't find the strength to pull back from her right at that moment. She felt and tasted too good and everything in him wanted her. He wasn't quite ready to tell her of his love for her, but he tried to convey it with his kisses.

Leah had never felt anything so powerful and she wanted more. The urge became so strong that it scared her and she loosened her hold on Lucky. She broke the kiss, her breath coming in quick gasps. Lucky's breathing was just as rapid.

"I have to go to bed," she signed.

Lucky groaned. "Don't talk about bed. A man can only take so much."

She laughed. "I'm sorry. I don't know what came over me. I just couldn't help myself."

"That wasn't a complaint, lass. Just statin' a fact. I think it's a good idea for ya to go inside now before I haul ya off to the barn."

She gave him a saucy smile and said, "What would you do I if called your bluff on that?"

Lucky chuckled. "Tell ya to go inside. I think ya can tell that I want you, but I won't do that unless we're married. I won't disrespect ya that way."

Leah said, "I appreciate that. I'll try not to torture you too much."

"Ya can torture me. I really don't mind," Lucky said, giving her a rakish smile. "It's the best torture there is."

"I'll remember that," Leah said.

Lucky kissed her quickly and said, "Go on with ya then. Sleep well."

"Goodnight," she said.

He watched her go inside, blew out a breath, and mumbled, "Cold weather or not, I might have to take a dip in that stream now and then," before going to his tipi.

Chapter Twenty-One

Election Day was a busy time for Echo. People came from all over to cast their ballots for their candidate. Jerry's competition was Brock Parsons, an older gentleman who was set in his ways. The only real reason he was running was because he didn't want to have a black mayor, not because he was interested in helping Echo. Since September, he'd been spouting his racist remarks and had garnered some support for his cause.

Jerry hadn't gotten caught up in all of the name-calling and hyperbole. Instead, he'd focused on the issues and how he would resolve them. He talked to people wherever he went, finding out what their concerns were and trying to come up with solutions. The biggest problem was the town economy, which had gotten slightly better since he'd convinced Evan to start off his mail-order bride idea.

Since it had been a success thus far, people began paying attention to Jerry's ideas. Evan was one of Jerry's biggest supporters and whenever the subject came up around the sheriff, he extolled Jerry's virtues, which he firmly believed in. Josie, Win, and the rest did the same thing. The veterinarian told people, "If it wasn't for Jerry, I wouldn't be so happy and Echo wouldn't have a doctor."

While Jerry didn't waste his time getting into arguments with Brock, Lucky had no problem facing off with the man. On several occasions, Lucky had gotten right in the other man's face and yelled at him, telling him exactly what he thought about Brock's racist views.

"That's the only reason ya care about this election. Ya couldn't care less about Echo and ya have no idea how to help. Ya wouldn't know a good idea if one crawled up yer arse," he'd told Brock one time.

Jerry moved through the crowd around town, conversing easily with people. His laid back, genial attitude made him a very likable person. He had a good sense of humor and wasn't easily riled. He and Sonya thanked people for coming out to support him. By the time the polls closed, he and Sonya were tired. Evan and Josie invited them to the diner for dinner.

"I'll take you up on that," Jerry said. "I wonder how long it'll take them to count the ballots."

Evan said, "I don't know. There were a lot of people who came to vote."

"I just know that we're dining with the new first couple of Echo," Josie said. "I refuse to think otherwise. If Brock wins, we're moving."

Sonya laughed. "Us, too."

Jerry said, "Now, now, ladies. Let's not get ahead of ourselves. Even if I don't win, I'll still do whatever I can to help our town."

Sonya smiled at him and said, "That's why you're going to make such a fine mayor, honey. You truly care about other people."

Jerry put an arm around her. "That's what makes you such a great wife. You're always on my side."

Evan and Josie liked seeing their friends so happy. Their dinner was pleasant even though they were all eager to know the voting results. When they were finished, they went back to the town hall. The building hadn't really been used since the last time Echo had had a mayor and it had required some cleanup.

Going inside, they encountered Brock. He sneered at Jerry. "There's that ugly—"

He didn't get to finish his sentence because Evan said, "Don't say it or

I'll punch you in the mouth, Brock. Keep your filthy thoughts to yourself."

The hard glare Evan sent him and the anger glittering in his green eyes shut Brock up. He scowled at them, but said no more as they passed him to continue on into the town hall meeting room. They took some seats and waited. There were a lot of people awaiting the results.

Hank Winston had been chosen to head the poll workers and he stood up from the table at which he sat. "If I may have your attention, everyone! The votes have been tallied and I have the results here. The people have spoken and our new mayor is Jerry Belker!"

The big room was suddenly filled with both shouts of joy and cries of protest. Sonya hugged Jerry and they laughed together as they were congratulated by their friends and supporters.

"I told you that you'd win," Evan said, grinning.

Jerry laughed. "Yes, you did. I thought you were crazy when you told me I should run a couple of years ago."

"No more crazy than you sayin' I should advertise for a wife," Evan replied.

"I guess we both had some pretty good ideas," Jerry said. "We make a good team."

Evan nodded. "Yeah, we do."

Hank came over to them. "Jerry, people are waiting for you to speak."

"What? I have to talk?" Jerry asked.

Hank blinked a couple of times. "Yeah. You know that the winner of a political race gives a speech."

"I didn't write anything down," Jerry said.

Evan laughed. "Let me get this straight. You ran for mayor, but you didn't write a speech in case you won?"

Jerry shrugged. "Why do I have to say anything? I won, right?" At Evan's blank expression, he looked at Sonya and they started laughing. Jerry put his arm around his wife and said, "You're lookin' at the prettiest speech writer God ever made."

Sonya chuckled and pulled a couple of pieces of paper from her purse, handing them to Jerry.

The group around them laughed at the prank they'd pulled. Jerry went to the front of the room and stood behind the makeshift lectern there. Evan and Hank quieted the crowd.

Jerry wasn't used to speaking in front of large groups and he was nervous. He'd memorized the speech that he and Sonya had written, but he still wanted the speech in case he forgot his place.

"Dear friends and neighbors, I'd like to thank you for coming out to vote today, whether or not you voted for me. The right to vote isn't something to take lightly, and exercising that vote is crucial in shaping the future, whether it be the future of Echo or that of our nation. I'd also like to thank my beautiful wife, Sonya, for being right by my side during this campaign. I couldn't have done it without her love and support.

"I also want to thank everyone who did vote for me so that I could win. But I didn't want to win just for the sake of winning. This wasn't a popularity contest and I want you all to know that I take this job seriously. Recent events have shown us even more that Echo is a town in need. Yes, we need to improve our economy, but we also need to repair our town and turn it into a place we can all be proud of again.

"That's one of the reasons I took the advice I received from another mayor about finding mail-order brides. Let's face it: we need women, not just to repopulate the town, but to cut down on crime and immorality. I'm sorry to be blunt, but women make us men better people in most cases. I know I'm a better man for having Sonya in my life and it's the same for a lot of fellas.

"But repopulating Echo isn't the only issue we have to deal with. Morale is a big one. It's true that very few of us are monetarily rich, but we can be rich in other ways. We need to reach out to each other more and be willing to lend a hand to those in need. We're not doing a very good job of that right now, folks. We need to step forward and work together to find solutions to these problems.

"I'm not a conceited man and I'm not the most intelligent, so I know that I can't do all this on my own and I don't have all the answers. That's why I'm going to put together a town council made up of people who I know are smart and who are experts in different areas. My first order of business will be to put this council together so we can choose a new pastor for Echo. We need someone to lead us in our spiritual lives again, so please pray hard that we can find someone worthy of the post.

"In the meantime, I'll be leading some hymn sings on Sundays and a Bible study class on Wednesday nights at seven. Please join me for worship and fellowship. Regarding the economy, if you have any constructive ideas, don't hesitate in telling them to me—or any member of the council. Now, I'm going to do something a little strange, but that's not unusual for me. As I said, Sonya has been my right hand ever since I met her and also through this campaign, proving that women are just as valuable and intelligent as men. So that's why there may be a woman or two sitting on the council. I figure we can always use a woman's perspective on things."

Murmurs broke out and went through the crowd. There were both positive and negative comments.

"Like I said, it might not be the normal thing to do, but we're not living in normal times right now. We're in serious trouble, folks, and unless you want to see Echo die, we have to be creative here. So that's what I'm going to do; be creative. I'll work like a dog for the people of Echo, but everyone needs to do the same if we're gonna turn things around. Look around at our kids. If you won't do it for yourselves, do it for them. Well, that's all I have to say right now. Thanks again for voting for me and I look forward to working with all of you to secure Echo's future."

Applause broke out as Jerry finished. He held up a hand to acknowledge them and then began searching the crowd for the people he wanted to talk to. He located Edna Taft and made a beeline for her before Evan got her outside.

He put an arm around her and said, "There's the woman I'm looking for."

She smiled. "I do like being in demand. Congratulations Mayor Belker."

"Thanks, ma'am. Now, I have a huge favor to ask of you," he said.

"Anything for a handsome man such as yourself."

"Will you be my president of the town council?" he asked.

Edna's blue eyes widened. "Me? Why me? I'm a woman and I'm old."

Jerry laughed. "You're not old, Edna. You just have arthritis. I said I wanted a woman's perspective and I also want someone who's not a pushover and will speak her mind."

Evan said, "That's definitely you, Aunt Edna. You won't stand for any bull crap."

She narrowed her eyes as she warmed to the idea. "That's right. Our town doesn't have time for that. Ok, I'll do it."

Jerry kissed her cheek. "Great! Thank you. Ok, I hate to run, but there's some more people I want to catch before they're gone. Our first meeting is here tomorrow night at seven."

He ran off before she could respond.

Josie chuckled. "I'm very honored to be the niece of such an esteemed member of our community," she teased Edna.

Edna raised her chin proudly. "That's right. So mind your manners around me."

Josie grinned. "I think you need to tell yourself that."

"Get going before I give you a citation or something," Edna shot back as they moved towards the door.

The next person on his list wasn't one he really wanted to talk to, but he kept telling himself it was for the good of Echo that he did.

Marvin was surprised when Jerry approached him. "Well, Mayor Belker, to what do I owe the pleasure?"

Jerry scowled. "Look, you're a son of gun and God knows I don't want to do this, but I need to."

Marvin's expression darkened. "If you've just come to tell me what a terrible person I am, you can save your breath. I have better things to do than listen to you."

"No, I'm not here to do that. You're the best financially smart guy around here and everyone knows it. Will you be my treasurer?" Jerry asked.

Marvin wasn't taken by surprise very often, but Jerry's request caught him completely off guard. "Did I hear you correctly? You want me to be the town treasurer?"

"Yeah," Jerry said. "I know that you're turning things around out at your place and I think you can help do that for Echo. Will you do it?"

Marvin thought about Jerry's comment about working for the future of Echo's children and put aside his own possible motives for taking the position. He thought about Pauline, Bea's kids, Eva, and his new niece and nephew. If he did this, he could help ensure that they would have good childhoods.

"Yes, I'd be happy to. Where are the town ledgers?" he asked. "I need to know exactly how disastrous things are."

"Very disastrous," Jerry said. "They're here in the office. Our first meeting is tomorrow night at seven. Can you stay just a little bit and I'll get the ledgers for you? There are more people I need to talk to."

"Certainly," Marvin said.

Jerry nodded and went on his way. By the time he was done, not only had he gotten Edna and Marvin to agree to sit on council, he'd chosen Hank Winston as the town clerk, Spike as the town planner, and in another bold move, he asked young Adam Harris to sit on council so they could get a perspective from the young people in Echo. Since Adam would soon turn seventeen Jerry felt that he was old enough for the position.

As sheriff, Evan would automatically sit on the council as head of town security and whomever they chose as the new pastor would also sit on the council. By the time he and Sonya left that night, Jerry felt confident that with the diverse members of town council, they could help Echo come back from the brink of certain destruction.

Chapter Twenty-Two

"Where are we going?" Leah asked Lucky as they drove along the night after the election.

"Someplace special," Lucky said. "T'was another busy day, then?" He'd been busy himself and hadn't had much of a chance to talk to her when she'd arrived home.

"Yes and I'm glad. Keith is a Godsend. He's catching on quickly and he's willing to do anything I ask of him."

Lucky said, "He's a good boy and I know he likes workin' for ya. Of course, who wouldn't like workin' for a pretty lady like you?"

"You're such a flatterer," she said.

With a wink, he said, "I've been known to do that a time or two."

"More like all the time."

"I mean it, though," Lucky said.

"Thank you."

They turned off the main road and took a narrower one that started climbing, but she didn't say anything about it, knowing that Lucky wasn't going tell her anything. She'd come to see how stubborn he could be about things. It was funny to watch him and Win facing off about things.

Although she couldn't always see their lips clearly throughout a conversation they were having, she was normally able to get the gist, and it was usually funny. Lucky's temper ran hotter than Win's and he'd yell at Win and walk away. He'd soon return, though, and pick up the conversation again.

They continued to talk about their day as the horse took them further along the road that rose higher and higher. Then Lucky stopped the buggy and said, "We'll have to walk from here."

She was glad that he'd told her to wear sensible shoes because it wasn't an easy climb. However, with him helping her, it wasn't as difficult as it would have otherwise been.

"We're here," he announced as they reached the summit.

As she stepped up to stand beside him, she became a little dizzy when she saw how high they were. The panorama before them was breathtaking. It felt like she could reach up and touch one of the sparkling stars above them. Spread out below them was their farm. The moon shone down on the meadows and woods.

Small white dots that she knew were sheep shifted position as the animals grazed. She knew the darker shadows were the black sheep and saw a couple of fast moving objects that were the dogs as they did their job. The trees beyond the farm jutted up against the sky, the moon turning their tops a glowing silver.

She was able to make out Win and Erin's cabin, their house, the two tipis, and the barns. Light shone in the cabin and house windows and Leah felt as though she were gazing upon a live painting.

"It's beautiful," she said. "No wonder Billy likes to paint it so much."

Lucky sat down the lantern he'd used to light their way on a flat piece of ground. Then he put an arm around her and she leaned against him. "Aye, 'tis a pretty piece of land. When I first came up here with Billy and saw it, I knew that this was where I'd settle for the rest of my life. I started plannin' for it right away. I've always wanted a wife and family and a place to call home forever and I wanted that with Avasa.

"When she was taken from me, I thought it was a test that I had to get through. I don't give up and I didn't then, either. I worked and planned and dreamed and prayed for guidance. When Wild Wind got that letter to me, I thought the Lord had shown me what was to be. He did, just not the way I thought he had. There's nothin' I wouldn't have done to get Avasa and our child, and I went thinkin' that I was gonna finally have the future I wanted.

"But God still had a different plan in mind and that's why I only came back with Otto. I felt like my world had ended and in a way it did. Don't get me wrong; Otto is the biggest joy in my life, but at the time, I was crushed. I'm not ashamed to admit it. But with help, I got through every day, knowin' I had to go on, especially for Otto.

"And then I started lookin' for a wife and someone to be a mother to him. That's how it started out, anyhow. But then we started writin' and I began to see that the Great Spirit was guidin' me again. He was pointing me in a different direction than I'd started out in."

Lucky turned so that they were facing each other. He held her gaze unwaveringly. "Yer the direction He was pointin' me in, Leah. It's like yer the North Star and I believe I was meant to find you all along. And now yer here and ye've made me so happy again.

"I know ya still think yer defective, but yer not. Yer like me; ya have somethin' in yer life that's pushed ya to do more than a lot of people do with their lives. I'm Irish and yer deaf, but ya know what? There's not a damn thing wrong with either of us. We're determined to succeed no matter what and separately we've accomplished a lot, but together, there's nothin' we can't do.

"I want us to have the sort of future we've both always dreamed about and I want us to do it together. I know now I'll never find another woman like ya, Leah. Someone so smart and good and kind. Someone as beautiful and who makes me so happy. Or someone I love as much as I do you."

Leah's heart lurched at his admission and she swore she could feel it swell in her chest. She hadn't known he felt that way about her. Her vision blurred a little from the tears that suddenly welled in her eyes. He further shocked her by going down on one knee as he took her hand. She could barely breathe as he stared into her eyes and smiled at her.

Lucky tried to quiet the slight tremor in his hand, but he couldn't quite manage it. Taking a ring box from his coat pocket, he asked, "Leah Lucia Carter, will ya do this humble Irishman the incredible honor of agreeing to become my wife?"

Leah gasped, both at his beautiful proposal and at the beautiful ring nestled in the box. She realized that he was waiting for an answer and, reaching out to caress his cheek, she nodded and signed, "Yes, I'll marry you, Lucky."

His wide, happy grin made her heart swell even more. Slipping the ring on, he said, "This is a Celtic Trinity ring. Ye'll be able to see it a little better at home, but there are two Trinity Knots, one of either side of the diamond setting. They're the Irish love knot and represent my undying love for ya and unending loyalty. I'll give ya both of those, Leah. I promise ya that here and now."

As he stood up again, she signed, "It's such a beautiful ring and I'm such a lucky woman to have found someone like you to love me. You're honorable, so very kind, handsome, and a wonderful father. You've brought so much laughter into my life and you make me feel good about myself and you accept me just the way I am.

"You said you want us to work towards the future we both want, but we already have. The moment you answered my letter we began working on it. There's nothing more I want that to keep working on it. I can't wait to marry you and I can't wait to be a mother to Otto. I meant it when I said I'd never try to take Avasa's place, but I love Otto so much and I promise to take good care of him and help raise him to the very best of my ability." She stopped a moment and gathered her courage. Out loud, she said, "I love you, too, Lucky."

Lucky couldn't move or look away. It was the first time he'd heard her speak out loud and to have her first spoken words to him be so magical was such an intensely powerful experience that he was paralyzed for long moments. His eyes burned with tears at the beautiful moment and rolled unchecked down his cheeks.

When Leah had decided to speak, she hadn't known that it would have such a profound effect on him. He smiled through his tears and took her face in his hands. "Ya have such a beautiful voice, Leah, and for ya to say that to me out loud ..." He shook his head a little. "There just aren't words. Please talk to me more like that."

She said, "You think my voice is beautiful?"

When she spoke, it had a slightly nasal sound, but her voice itself was rich and throaty; a combination that was extremely pleasant to his ear. "Aye, 'tis. It's as beautiful as the rest of ya and I love everything about ya, lass."

She brushed hair away from his forehead and said, "I love you, too."

With a growl of need, he took her in his arms and covered her mouth with his in an urgent kiss that instantly kindled a fiery passion inside of her. She clung to him, pressing her body against his as she answered his unspoken expression of love with one of her own.

Leah felt like she was burning up as Lucky continued to kiss her and she couldn't get close enough to him. He must have felt the same way because he undid the buttons of his coat and then hers. Sliding his arms around her waist, he pulled her back to him, reveling in the feminine softness of her and warm sweetness of her lips.

Feeling emboldened by his actions, she allowed herself to explore his chest. She felt his muscles tense under her palms and wanted to feel his bare skin. To fight the urge, she fisted her hands against him.

Lucky felt the movement and knew it was time to end the embrace lest they get into dangerous territory. He hadn't meant for things to get so heated, but she brought out such an intense hunger in him that it was almost too much to control.

Slowly, he broke the kiss and smiled at her. "Yer torturin' me again."

She laughed. "You're torturing me, too."

"Good. I don't wanna be the only one with this problem," he said, buttoning up her coat. He then buttoned his, too, and took a deep breath. "I'd love to stay here with ya all night, but it's gettin' colder out and I don't want ya to get sick."

"Yes, I guess we should go home, but I'll never forget this night, Lucky," she signed.

He smiled. "Nor will I. Come, fiancée, and we'll go home. We'll start makin' weddin' plans right away." He put a hand to his forehead. "We don't have a pastor. Who's gonna marry us?"

Leah's eyes widened. "You're right!"

Lucky pursed his lips a moment. "Well, we could go to a church over in Dickensville," he said, helping her into the buggy and covering her lap with a blanket.

She nodded. "Yes, we could."

Lucky led the horse back the way they should go before getting in. The road was steep and narrow and turning around that way was safer. Climbing in the buggy, he said, "Don't worry, love, we'll get it figured out."

She snuggled up to him and signed, "That's right. We're very determined people and we won't let anything stop us."

"Right ye are," Lucky said, starting out their horse.

As they drove home, they talked about how they would get around that particular obstacle and were hopeful for a wonderful future together.

Chapter Twenty-Three

It had been week and a half since the election and Thanksgiving was only a couple of days away. Jerry sat in his and Sonya's parlor looking through response letters to their advertisement for a pastor. He sat the last one on the stand by his overstuffed chair and closed his eyes.

"What's the matter, honey?" Sonya said. She noticed his frustrated pose.

Jerry smiled a little. "I don't know where we're gonna get a pastor. All of these people that answered the ad are qualified, but they're all asking for more money than we can pay them."

Putting down the book she'd been reading, Sonya reached across to his chair and put her hand on his arm. "We'll find someone. We just have to be patient."

He took her hand and said, "You're right, but you know that's hard for me."

Sonya got up and went over to sit on his lap. Resting her arms on his shoulders, she said, "Well, I have something to tell you that'll make you feel better."

Jerry smiled at the enigmatic smile on her beautiful face. Looping his arms around her waist, he asked, "And what's that, my love?"

Sonya kissed him and then said, "In about five or six months, instead of two of us in this house, there will be three."

Jerry's eyes grew bigger as her meaning sank in. "You mean we're gonna have a little Belker?"

Her pretty smile said that he was right. He embraced her and they shared a celebratory kiss.

"I can't believe it's finally happening," Sonya said, with tears in her eyes. "We've been trying ever since we got married and I'm ashamed to say I started losing faith that it would happen. I was so afraid that I was imagining it when the signs started."

Jerry rubbed her midsection. "Well, our prayers have been answered and maybe it just wasn't time until now. Maybe it's a sign that things are gonna turn around for us and for Echo. I mean, just think about it. So many of our friends are having babies and now us. I really do think that the Good Lord is telling us that things will be ok."

Sonya hugged him again in joy. "I think you're right. I'm so happy."

"Mmm, me, too." He thought about the problem of finding a new pastor and said, "I'm married to such a smart woman. We're gonna just give this up to God because he'll find our new minister. Let's go to bed, sweetheart. We have another early day tomorrow."

She gave him a saucy smile as she got up. "I hope you're not too tired just yet."

He chuckled. "Just what did you have in mind?"

"I'll show you," she said, walking away.

Jerry eagerly followed his wife upstairs.

The next day, Jerry was busy replacing a wagon wheel when he heard a female voice say, "Mr. Belker?"

"Yep. That's me," he replied as he kept working.

"I've come about the pastor position you're seeking to fill."

He finished securing the wheel on the axle and turned to look at the speaker. He saw a tall, buxom woman with golden brown hair and brown eyes looking at him. Her brown, paisley skirt and white blouse were nice, but he could tell that she wasn't a rich person. Jerry wiped sweat from his face and said, "All right. You know my name. You are?"

"Andrea Thatcher," she said, holding out a hand.

Jerry wiped his right hand on his pants and shook it. "Well, Mrs. Thatcher, it's nice to meet you. Is your husband with you?"

Her brow furrowed. "My husband? I'm not married, Mr. Belker."

"Oh. Your father then?"

She smiled. "Mr. Belker, I'm the one applying for the position."

One of Jerry's eyebrows lifted. "You're a pastor?"

"Yes, sir. They've been ordaining women for a few years now," she said. "My father is a preacher and I've followed in his footsteps."

Jerry had never heard of a woman pastor before. "You don't say?"

She smiled again. "I have plenty of experience."

While he didn't want to doubt her, she didn't look very old. No more than twenty-five, maybe younger, he thought.

"I'm twenty-one," she said as though reading his thoughts. "I've worked with the Salvation Army as a nurse since I was sixteen and I went into the ministry and was ordained when I was seventeen, sir. I have several letters of recommendation."

That made sense to Jerry. He'd heard somewhere that the Salvation Army did allow women to be preachers. Something else occurred to him. "You said you're a nurse, too?"

"That's right."

Inside, Jerry jumped up and down. *Wait until Erin hears this. She was just saying last month that she could use a nurse. Dear Lord, You sure do work in mysterious ways, but I'm listening to You.*

"Well, Miss Thatcher, we'll have to call a town council meeting and talk to you about this more, but I'm keeping an open mind."

"That's all I ask. You can just call me Andi."

Jerry said, "Very well, Andi. Do you have a place to stay yet?"

"No, sir. I just arrived and had the sheriff point me in the right direction," she said.

"Oh. Well, allow me to show you the Hanover House. They take in boarders there and it's a nice place, too," Jerry said. He went outside to the horse trough, took out his handkerchief, and dipped it into the water. He wiped off his face and neck and felt more refreshed. "There. I'm a little more presentable now. Not much, but it's better than nothing."

Andi smiled. "Nothing wrong with some sweat from hard work. I get that way when I chop wood and so forth."

As he got closer to her, Jerry realized that she wasn't a whole lot shorter than his six-foot-three inch height. She was also broad in the shoulders and looked strong. He could believe she was capable of chopping wood.

"While I was serving, it was often up to us women to do those types of chores. As you can see, I'm much more capable of that particular job than most women," she said.

How does she do that? That's the second time she's read my mind. "Well, now that you mention it, I'd have to agree with you. I'm sure they appreciated having someone like you around."

She nodded. She liked Jerry. He had a nice vibe about him. Andi had a sixth sense about many things and people. They chitchatted about the town and Jerry filled her in on some of the townspeople and businesses. Upon reaching the Hanover House, Jerry introduced her to the owners, Gwen and Arthur Hanover.

Upon hearing that she was a pastor, Arthur said, "Well, we sure are getting some talented women around here."

"What do you mean?" Andi asked.

Gwen's blue eyes looked Andi over as she said, "Well, we have a lady doctor and a lady cobbler and now you've come about the pastor's position."

Andi replied, "Oh, I see." She saw Arthur looking at her. "I'm six feet tall and strong as an ox."

Arthur's surprised expression made Jerry smile. *I'm glad I'm not the only one she can do that to. It's a little spooky.*

"What room are you giving her?" Jerry asked.

"Uh, the, uh, green room," Arthur stammered in his deep bass voice.

Gwen said, "I'll show you."

"Thank you," Andi said, picking up her two suitcases.

"I'll take those for you," Jerry said.

Andi said, "Thanks, but I'm all right."

"Ok," Jerry said. "I'll see you tonight at the town hall then."

"I'm looking forward to it," she said.

Jerry nodded and left the Hanovers'.

It was rare for Andi to be nervous, but she did feel some trepidation as she sat in front of the long table the town council sat behind. This wasn't because she doubted her ability to perform the duties of a pastor. She'd been doing that for years, so that wasn't the issue. Andi was an extremely intelligent woman and she knew how most of society viewed women. She'd been surprised to find out that Echo had a female doctor, but it had given her hope that the council would be more open-minded.

Her gaze roamed over everyone and for the most part, she had good feelings about the one woman and six men, but her gaze kept returning to the very suave-looking blond man. There was something that disturbed her about him. Although she sensed a darkness about him, he didn't scare her. She felt sad for him. So sad, in fact, that it brought tears to her eyes. Taking out a hanky, she blotted her eyes.

Edna saw her and felt badly for her. It had to be scary sitting there in front of all of them like that. "Miss Thatcher, we're all very friendly people," she said and then cut a glance at Marvin who sat to her left. "Well, most of us, anyway."

Marvin smiled. "Edna, I'll try to behave myself."

Just the sound of his voice made Andi sad and she sniffed audibly.

Marvin grew concerned about the poor girl. "Are you all right, Miss Thatcher?"

"Yes," she nodded, trying to compose herself.

Spike asked, "Why are you cryin'?"

"It's just so sad," she said.

The council members all traded puzzled looks.

"What is?" Jerry asked.

Andi knew she had to get it out of her system if she was going to get through this. "May I approach, please? I need to pray with one of you."

Looking around at everyone, Jerry saw them all nod. "Sure, I guess."

Andi got up and walked straight to Marvin. "May I have your hand?"

For the first time in his life, Marvin shivered in fear of someone or some*thing* else as he looked into Andi's eyes. It passed through his body quickly, lasting no more than a few seconds, but it was a powerful feeling.

Andi grew insistent. "Your hand, please?"

Slowly Marvin gave it to her. Instantly Andi closed her eyes and although she couldn't see exactly why, she sensed rage, despair, and fear. *Dear Lord, what a twisted soul resides in him. Please shine Your light and chase away the darkness from him as only You can do. I haven't found anyone who needed Your help like this in a long time. I, Your humble servant ask that You show him Your great mercy and power so that he may be healed and restored. In Your great and precious name ...* "Amen," she finished aloud. Looking straight in Marvin's eyes, she said, "A blessing will come to you and when it does, you'll know that the Lord has forgiven you and that He loves you regardless of your past transgressions."

She gave him a beautiful smile and squeezed Marvin's hand before releasing it and sat back down again. Her sadness had dissipated and she was once again able to concentrate on the interview.

Everyone looked at Marvin, but he didn't notice. He was too preoccupied with trying to figure out what had just happened to pay them any attention. As he looked at Andi, he shivered again and wanted to run, which intrigued him.

Jerry cleared his throat and began the interview. By the time it was over, the council knew they'd found their new pastor. Her references were impeccable and Jerry and Hank had quizzed her on some theology. Not only did she get the answers right, she expounded on the information, completely surpassing Jerry and Hank's knowledge. It was evident that she was very well trained and had done extensive studying. They voted unanimously to hire her.

"Congratulations, Andi," Jerry said. "Can you prepare a sermon for this Sunday?"

"Certainly," Andi said. "Thank you all so much."

Hank asked, "Would you offer a prayer for us to end the meeting with?"

Andi smiled. "I'd be happy to." She came forward to take Jerry's hand and asked that the others join hands.

Marvin wasn't used to holding hands with people and he felt uncomfortable doing so. When he was slow to move, Edna grabbed his hand and held it tightly as though she thought he would let go. On his right, Evan eyed him with displeasure at the thought of holding Marvin's hand. The two men just looked at each other until Andi pointedly cleared her throat. Evan and Marvin barely joined their hands.

"Let us bow our heads," Andi said.

Everyone but Marvin lowered their heads and closed their eyes. Andi's prayer was eloquent, but Marvin only paid half-attention as he studied her. His belief fell in the agnostic category; he neither believed nor disbelieved in God. If there was a God, He'd certainly never helped him or Shadow. However, he was curious about what exactly had prompted Andi to pray for him and not someone else on the council.

When she finished the prayer, Andi opened her eyes to find Marvin looking at her curiously. She knew he was a nonbeliever, but she didn't take offense. She'd come across many of those and felt badly for them. With an inner sigh, she realized that Marvin was going to be a hard egg to crack. Andi liked a challenge, though, and was perfectly willing to take it on.

Marvin was so caught up in trying to figure Andi out that he forgot to let Edna's hand go.

"Marvin, I love holding hands with handsome men, but I'd like to go home now," she said.

"What? Oh, sorry," he said with a chuckle as he released her hand. "It's hard to let a beautiful woman like you go, Edna."

"Always a charmer," Edna said, rising.

Spike said, "Yeah. A snake charmer, maybe."

Marvin grinned. "I've never done that, but it does look interesting."

Spike grunted. "Try it once. If we're lucky, that cobra will bite you and get rid of the biggest snake of them all."

"Are you kidding, Spike?" Evan responded. "The snake would be the one to die, not the other way around."

It intrigued Andi that Marvin didn't mind these cruel remarks. In fact, he seemed to relish them. It was a part of the darkness in him, she knew. It troubled her as she left the town hall with everyone else.

Jerry stopped her and said, "I'd like to ask for your patience about moving into the parsonage. Bea and the kids haven't found a place to live yet that they can afford."

He'd explained why Echo didn't have a pastor. Andi asked, "I don't need a big house all to myself. If they have an extra room, I'd be glad to just use it. That way, they could just stay where they are and I wouldn't be lonely. It would be wonderful living with a family."

"I think they have a room. That would be a great solution," Jerry said. "Why don't you go over there tomorrow and talk to Bea about it? Oh, and since tomorrow is Thanksgiving, come over to the Tafts' house and have dinner with us. We'd love to have you."

Andi smiled. "I'll do that. That would be wonderful. Thank you again, Jerry. I'll do my very best for Echo."

"You're welcome and thank you," Jerry said and gave her the directions to Evan's house.

She gave him a parting smile and walked across the street to the Hanover House.

Chapter Twenty-Four

Thanksgiving dinner at the Tafts' house was boisterous and delicious. Andi was introduced to everyone and she felt nothing but positive energy around these people. Everyone joked and talked with her as though they already knew her. A few of the men flirted harmlessly with her a little, and everyone was curious to know all about her.

She noticed that many of the people signed to Leah and she was glad that Leah could read lips because she didn't know sign language. Andi decided she was going to have to learn so she could communicate with Leah. Lucky and Leah informed her that they had recently become engaged and asked if they could meet with her on Monday so they could make wedding arrangements.

Andi loved officiating at weddings and she was excited that she would be able to perform one so soon after securing her post. She happily agreed to the meeting. As she talked with everyone, she felt a warmth spread through her that told her that this was where she'd been meant to come. *Perhaps I've found my home.* That thought made her smile as she socialized and helped clean up from the meal.

Chapter Twenty-Five

After their meeting with Andi, Leah and Lucky rode home, holding hands along the way.

"I'll write our parents tonight and let them know about the wedding. They'll have plenty of time to make arrangements to come for it," she signed.

"Aye. I can't wait."

They approached the farm and noticed a couple of strange horses tethered outside of Lucky's tipi. He pulled the buggy up to the barn and they were just getting out of it when Otto came running towards them, shouting to Lucky in Cheyenne.

"Father! Come quickly! You have to see who is here!" The boy was grinning from ear to ear. "Come!"

He took off again and Lucky and Leah exchanged confused looks. Taking Leah's hand, they walked to his tipi and went inside. Lucky stopped dead upon seeing Avasa standing on the other side of the tipi. His voice failed him. Avasa smiled and stepped towards him.

"Yelling Bear, it is good to see you," she said in Cheyenne.

He frowned even as happiness rose inside him. "I do not understand.

How did you come to be here? Why are you here?" He looked around and although there was a man with her, it wasn't her new husband. "Where is Red Boar?"

Avasa's face fell. "He is dead. He became sick on the way to where they were taking us and died. I ran away." Her eyes turned to Leah and she noticed Lucky held her hand.

Lucky said in English to Leah, "This is my ex-wife, Avasa. Avasa, this is my fiancée, Leah."

Avasa smiled at her. "It is good to meet you."

Shock made Leah's smile wooden as she looked at the beautiful Cheyenne woman. "It's nice to meet you, too," she signed while Lucky translated. "Well, I'll let you catch up. I'm sure you have a lot to talk about." She left the tipi quickly, striding to the house just as Sofia came out onto the porch. "I don't want to talk about it," she signed to Sofia.

Going inside, she went to her room and shut the door.

Lucky sat by the fire looking over at the woman he used to love more than anything in the world and felt confusion and disbelief. Wild Wind and the man Avasa had introduced as William had taken Otto for a walk even though the boy hadn't wanted to go. Avasa was just as beautiful as ever.

"Your fiancée is very beautiful," Avasa said in Cheyenne.

Lucky nodded. "Yes, she is. Leah is a very good woman. I am a lucky man."

Avasa said, "I can see she makes you happy."

He smiled. "She does. Honestly, after what happened with you, I did not think I would be happy again, but she holds my heart now."

"The Great Spirit led both of us where we were meant to go," she said.

"Avasa, I hope you did not come here expecting anything to happen between us."

"No. That would be stupid of me," Avasa said. "I am still mourning my husband and I would not take advantage of you that way because I care about you too much."

"Good. Who is this man you are with?"

Avasa sighed. "He is taking me to a place in Canada where there are still a few Lakota living. He is friends with them. I will give him the engagement ring you gave me in return."

"You still have it?" Lucky asked. "I did not think you did."

Avasa sighed. "Yelling Bear, I do not want you to think that our time together did not mean anything to me. It did. I loved you very much and I still do. It is just different now."

"For me, too," Lucky agreed. He asked the question he dreaded to. "Will you take Otto with you when you go?"

She smiled sadly. "No. He belongs with you now. Even though I will go to these Lakota friends of William's, there is no guarantee of safety there. It is a chance I am taking for myself, but I will not take that chance with Otto's future. I just needed to see him one last time. Perhaps one day I will be free to see him again, but for now, I will take the memory of this visit with me. I know it is selfish of me, but I could not stay away."

Lucky understood that. He would most likely have done the same thing. After having Otto in his life now and loving him so much, he would give anything for just one more look at his son if the situation was in reverse.

"He looks well and happy," Avasa said. "Does he ask about me?"

"Sometimes, but it is becoming less frequent," Lucky said honestly.

"And will Leah be a good mother to him?"

Lucky said, "I would never marry any woman who would not be good to him. He is my son and comes first."

Avasa nodded. "We will leave in two days. I do not want to take the chance that the military has tracked us here. I do not want to bring trouble on you."

"I appreciate that."

They talked for a while longer until William and Wild Wind came back with Otto. He ran over to his mother and hugged her. She hugged him back and Lucky's heart was glad that they would have at least a little time together. Then his son's best interests rose in his mind; he'd been heartbroken over saying goodbye to Avasa the first time. What would it do to him this time?

Lucky said, "Avasa, can I speak to you outside a moment?"

"Of course. I will be right back," she said to Otto who frowned.

Joining Lucky outside, Avasa looked into his eyes. "What is it?"

His jaw flexed. "You should not have come. It took Otto a long time to get over you. Now here you are and he is going to have to say goodbye to you all over again. The longer you are here the worse it will be. You have to leave in the morning."

Avasa's bewilderment and hurt showed in her eyes. "What difference will one more day make? I do not know if William will agree to that. We are tired and need a few things from the store. Would you not have wanted to see him one last time?"

Lucky nodded. "I was just thinking about that very thing, but I now know that I would have stayed away because I love him enough to not cause him more pain by coming here only to leave him again."

Avasa's eyes filled with tears. "I understand, but you did not give life to him. It is different for mothers. Please try to understand, Lucky."

He sighed. "All right. Two days, but you must go after that so that he can get back to normal again."

She smiled. "Thank you. Wild Wind said that Otto and I can stay in his tipi and that he and William will stay with you."

He did, did he? "That will be fine." Lucky wasn't looking forward to playing host for the next couple of days, but he had no choice. His thoughts turned to Leah. "I will be back after a while."

Avasa nodded and he left her.

Lucky knocked on Leah's door hard enough that he knew she'd feel the vibration.

She opened it and smiled a little.

"Hello," he said. "Can we talk?"

"Yes. Come in," she said, admitting him into the room and leaving the door open a little.

Lucky continued the conversation in sign only to give them privacy. "I'm sorry about this. I didn't know she was coming."

"I know," Leah said. "It's all right. Why did she come?"

Lucky explained Avasa's situation. "She wanted to see Otto one last time before she goes to Canada."

"I can understand that. He's her son," Leah said. "But she doesn't want you back, does she?"

"No, lass. She said she can see how happy ya make me. Even if she had, I don't love her anymore. Yer the only woman in my heart, Leah," he assured her.

He hugged her then and she was reassured by his embrace. Leah wanted to be a good sport about things for Lucky and Otto's sake, so she said, "Let's go make dinner your way since we have guests. Besides, I want to hear some more stories about you from when you were with the Cheyenne." She gave him an impish grin and scooted out into the hallway.

He laughed and shook his head. "I have the feeling I'm gonna regret this," he said, following her.

They didn't go to bed until late because they'd stayed up talking and telling stories. After a couple of hours of this, Leah realized that she'd made a mistake in insisting on spending the evening with Avasa. As she listened to the stories Avasa, Lucky, and Wild Wind told, she could see how close Lucky and his ex-wife had been and that they still cared for one another. It made her extremely jealous, but she worked hard not to show it. Otto was glued to Avasa's side and, while Leah knew that it was only natural for Otto to want to be with his mother, it made her jealous, too.

Finally she pleaded fatigue and rose from where she sat in Lucky's tipi. "Goodnight, everyone. Sleep well."

Lucky got up and walked her to the house. "Yer a great woman, Leah."

"What makes you say that?" she asked.

"Because even though I know ya didn't want to sit there all night with the woman who used to be my wife, ya did it. I didn't want to, either, really, but I was tryin' to be a good host," Lucky said. "I'll be glad when she goes so that Otto doesn't get too attached to her again. It'll still be hard for him, but not as bad as if she was goin' to be around longer."

"I agree," Leah said. "And what about you?"

"What about me?"

"Do you think you would get attached to her again if she were around longer?" Leah asked.

"No. I told ya; I'm in love with *you*, not her." Lucky took her left hand and ran his thumb over her engagement ring. "Unending love and loyalty, remember?"

She smiled and hugged him, nodding against his chest. They kissed goodnight and Lucky watched her go inside, just like he always did. With a sigh, he went back to his tipi to settle in for the night.

The morning that William and Avasa were supposed to leave, William was missing. He'd gone in town the night before, but he hadn't come home apparently. Lucky was on his way to town when he met up with Shadow.

"Mr. Quinn. Just the person I was looking for," he said.

"I'm not gonna like this, am I?" Lucky asked.

"I'm afraid not. Your friend met an unfortunate end last night when he got into an altercation with another gentleman during a card game."

Lucky swore a blue streak. "Thanks, Shadow. How are yer little ones?"

Shadow grinned. "Beautiful. They're growing already. I can't believe it."

"It doesn't take long," Lucky said. "Well, I guess we'd better be havin' a funeral."

"I'll let the preacher lady know," Shadow said.

"Thanks," Lucky said and turned his horse around.

Two days later, Otto came down with a cold and couldn't shake it. It turned into the flu. Lucky felt like his world was turning upside down.

Avasa was still there since there was no one to take her to Canada and now Otto was seriously ill. He sat on one side of Otto and Avasa sat on the other. Otto burned with fever and it was hard getting anything in him because he was so weak. Erin was doing everything she could for him and worried over him constantly along with everyone else.

Leah helped whenever she came home from work, but there was only so much she could do except be there for Lucky. His concern over his son's welfare grew every day and Leah understood how he felt. She'd come to love the little boy and would be devastated if he didn't make it and that possibility was a very real one.

One evening, she came out of the house to go to Lucky's tipi to see what she could do to help. She was halfway to the tipi when Lucky and Avasa came outside. They said something to each other, but she was too far away to be able to read their lips. Lucky put his arms around Avasa and hugged her. Leah stopped walking as anger and jealously ignited inside her.

Lucky pulled away from Avasa and they went back in the tipi again. Leah couldn't move for several long moments. Then she went back to the house. She didn't go to the tipi at all that night.

The next morning, Lucky went up to the house and found Leah drinking some tea before she went to the shop.

He kissed her cheek. "Good mornin', love. I missed ya last night."

"Good morning. I knew you were busy. How's Otto?" she asked.

Sitting down, he said, "About the same. He's a fighter, though. He'll make it through." He reached for her hand, but she drew it back.

"He *is* a fighter," Leah agreed. She finished her tea. "Please give him a kiss for me and I'll see him when I get home from work."

"Aye. Are ya all right?" he asked.

She smiled tightly. "Just worried about him. See you later on."

He watched her leave, bewildered by her behavior.

Chapter Twenty-Six

Over the next week, Leah watched Lucky and Avasa together with Otto and she could see that they were becoming closer. Their son's illness was creating a strong bond between them again. She kept trying to tell herself that it was only because of Otto and that of course they would draw comfort from one another, but finally she couldn't deny what she was seeing any longer.

Then one morning, Lucky came running into the house, a huge grin on his face.

"Leah! His fever broke a little bit ago!" He picked her up and planted a kiss on her lips. "He's gonna get better now."

Leah hugged him back, genuinely thrilled over the news. Then she remembered what she'd been witnessing and pushed away from Lucky. At his questioning look, she signed, "I want to go see him."

Lucky's smile returned as she put on her coat. As they walked to the tipi, Lucky sent up a prayer and reached for Leah's hand, but she wouldn't take her hand out of her pocket. Ducking inside the tipi, she went directly to Otto, barely looking at the woman who was taking her fiancé from her.

Otto's dark eyes were still dull, but he seemed a little more alert as

Avasa gave him some broth to drink. He smiled when he saw Leah and reached his little hand towards her. She took it and kissed it.

"Hi," she signed. "You seem better."

He nodded and smiled. He drank a little more broth and then started getting sleepy again. Avasa laid him down again and covered him up.

"I'm so happy his fever broke," Leah said. "He'll get better now."

Avasa grinned, tears in her eyes. "Yes. The Great Spirit has answered our prayers."

Leah smiled and left the tipi. Lucky followed her.

"What's the matter?" he asked her.

"Nothing. Why?"

He stared into her eyes. "Ye've not been actin' right lately. What's wrong?"

"I've just been worried about Otto like everyone else."

"That's not all that's wrong," Lucky said. "Tell me the truth."

"It is the truth," Leah insisted.

"No, it's not," Lucky said becoming very irritated. "Why are ya lyin' to me?"

Leah said, "I can't do this right now. I have to get to work."

Lucky's jaw set. "Fine, but we're talkin' about this tonight."

Leah nodded and hurried away.

After supper, Lucky asked Leah to come outside so they could talk in private. They went to the barn so they were out of the bitter winds.

Lucky lit a lamp and said, "All right. Out with it. What's wrong?"

Leah said, "Lucky, you don't belong with me. I've been watching you and Avasa and she's the one you should be with. It's obvious that you still love he, and you have Otto to consider. She's his mother and you're his father. You should be a family now. Maybe this is God's way of showing you that that was what was meant to be all along."

"Yer wrong, Leah. I don't love Avasa like that anymore. Sure, I love her, but as a friend now. *Yer* the woman I love, not *her*," Lucky said.

"I think you want to believe that, but if you look deep inside, Lucky, you'll see that I'm right," Leah said. "Avasa and you were meant to be together. I can see that."

Lucky came close, looking down into her eyes. "Leah, I'm in love with *you*. Can't ya see the truth in my eyes? Can't ya see how much I love ya?"

"What I see is a man who's deluding himself into thinking he's in love with me, but who should be with the mother of his child," Leah said. "I'm moving into town in the morning."

Lucky's eyes widened. "What? Ya can't do that. Are ya that jealous that ya can't see what's right in front of ya?"

Leah couldn't deny her jealously. "I'm jealous, but I *am* seeing what's right in front of me. I've been seeing it ever since Avasa arrived here. You two share a son and a strong bond and you should be together. I'm leaving in the morning, Lucky. You'll see that I'm doing the right thing. I love you so much, Lucky. So much in fact that I have to do the right thing and let you go."

"No, ya don't. It's *not* the right thing," Lucky said, his brows drawing down in anger. "I love you, not Avasa, and you and I belong together, Leah. Yer my future, not her." He took Leah in his arms, kissing her ardently, trying to convey to her all the love he felt inside for her.

Leah relaxed in his arms, letting herself have a few more moments with him before saying goodbye to him. His kiss was insistent and she couldn't resist him at the moment. She allowed him to deepen the kiss, wrapping her arms around his neck. She felt him growl against her lips and was thrilled by it even though she knew it would be the last time she would ever feel it. She only let the kiss go on for a few more moments before breaking it abruptly and pushing her way out of Lucky's arms.

Lucky's breathing came in shallow pants. "Don't you see how much I love ya? Can't ya feel it?"

Leah shook her head as tears filled her eyes. "It doesn't matter, Lucky. I don't love you like that anymore after seeing you with Avasa over the past couple of weeks. It's just not the same," she lied. "I can't complete with what the two of you have together."

Lucky watched in numbing disbelief as Leah took off her engagement ring and held it out to him. He couldn't take it. Looking back at her, his gray eyes pleaded with her to change her mind and put it back on. When he made no move towards it, Leah took his hand and put the ring in his palm. Then she ran from the barn and Lucky's heart split in two.

Billy watched Lucky stare sightlessly into the fire and frowned over the pain in his friend's eyes. He'd hoped to never see Lucky look like that again. And yet, here he was again, mere weeks away from when he and Leah were supposed to get married. Lucky wouldn't tell anyone why he and Leah had called things off and Leah wouldn't enlighten anyone either.

Most of their friends surmised that it had something to do with Avasa, but no one knew for sure. Avasa felt terrible about it and also watched Lucky. Had this been the way he'd looked after losing her not once, but twice? She thought it must have been and her heart broke anew for him. It had taken her a long time to get over him, so she understood. Her heart was still broken over the death of her second husband, too.

Her eyes met Billy's and she shook her head a little. Billy nodded his agreement. He hated to leave, but he wanted to get home to Nina who was due to have their baby any day now.

"I'm heading home, but come see me tomorrow," Billy said. "Nina misses you."

Lucky gave him a wan smile. "Aye. I will."

"Ok. Goodnight, everyone," Billy said, going out into the night.

Lucky's gaze returned to the fire again, his mind returning to Leah once more. He ached to see her, hold her, and kiss her. He missed laughing with her, talking to her about their hopes and dreams, and teasing her. Otto kept asking for her so Lucky had had Wild Wind take the boy to see her. He couldn't bring himself to do it because he knew he'd beg Leah to come back and he wouldn't embarrass himself that way.

Avasa couldn't stand seeing Lucky like this. She knew that Leah had left because of her even if Lucky wouldn't say so. Looking over at her sleeping son, she knew that there was only one thing left to do. She kissed Otto, told Lucky goodnight, and went over to Wild Wind's tipi.

Leah's head was bent over a pair of ladies' dress shoes so she didn't notice anyone come in her shop. When she felt a touch on her shoulder, she started a little and was surprised to find herself looking up into Avasa's eyes. It also surprised her that Avasa looked angry.

"May I sit down?" Avasa asked.

Leah nodded. "Yes. Of course."

Avasa sat and looked around the shop then back at Leah. "You are being stupid and stubborn and you do not strike me as a woman who is usually stupid."

Leah was taken aback by her statement. "Who are you to call me stupid?"

"I am someone who cares a great deal for Lucky and I am Otto's mother," Avasa said. "I know you think that Lucky and I are still in love, but we are not. I am still in love with my husband. Lucky has told you that he loves you and not me, but you will not believe him. I do not understand why."

Leah said, "I watched the two of you together with Otto and you should be a family, Avasa. We both know it."

Avasa shook her head. "No, we should not. My time with Lucky is over. He is miserable without you. He is an honorable man, so when he tells you something, it is the truth. He has never lied to me or to himself. He knows his heart. Do you still love him?"

Leah couldn't lie either. "Yes, but you—"

"Yes, yes! I am his former wife and the mother of our son! I will be leaving tomorrow, Leah. It is time for me to go."

"Why are you leaving? What about Otto?"

Sadness entered Avasa's eyes. "My place is not in white society. I know that. Now that Otto is well again, it is time for me to go. I never meant to stay here. I cannot live as you do and I know that in my heart. I would wither and die. Otto no longer belongs to me. I have seen how much he loves it here and loves his father and everyone else. That includes you. He talks about you all the time and does not understand why you are not there. He calls you his second mother and wants you back.

"And Lucky wants you back. He will not talk about it, but I know him so well that I can see it. Lucky is good at hiding his heartbreak, but there are moments when his guard is down when I can see it. You need to go back to the man who is your future and to our son, yours and mine, Leah. For he is now yours and will need you for the rest of his life. I have already talked to Otto about this; one day I will see him again, but you and I hold different places in his heart and while he is sad I am going, he understands.

"Because I love the both of them so much, I will plead on their behalf for you to once again become the wise woman I have come to know and like and do the smart thing for all of you. There is no need for all of you to be miserable, but if you do not do something soon, that is what will happen. Please think very hard about everything I have said," Avasa said.

She held out a hand to Leah and Leah hesitantly gave it to her. Avasa took it in both of hers. "Yelling Bear would only love a woman worthy of him and our son. I will say this to you now in the hopes that I have reached your heart. I am entrusting my wonderful friend Yelling Bear to you and also my son, Otoahnacto, to your care. I ask that you love them with your whole heart and I wish you happiness with them for all the days of your life. Goodbye, Leah. Be well."

Leah watched the lovely Indian woman leave her shop, her mind racing as she went over everything Avasa had just said to her. She tried to go back to work, but she mostly just sat staring at shoes while her brain and heart were busy.

Thad arrived at the farm the next morning at the appointed time he'd agreed to meet Avasa so they could start out for Canada. William had told them where the Lakota camp was the first night he and Avasa had arrived and Thad was certain that they could locate it. It actually didn't sound too far from the Canadian border, so Thad didn't figure it would take too long.

Lucky and Thad finished packing their horses and Avasa came to stand before Lucky.

"Yelling Bear, thank you for allowing me this time with Otto. It has been good seeing you and I wish you every happiness," she said.

Lucky tried to smile, but couldn't. "I don't think I'll have much happiness outside of Otto and my friends. I don't think I'm meant to have anything more than that."

Avasa took his face in her hands. "This is not the Yelling Bear I know who goes after what he wants. Find that man again and do not let your happiness get away. You are a good man and deserve to be happy. I love you and want that for you. Do not give up! You never have before. Do not do so now!"

"It's too late," Lucky said.

Avasa gripped his face a little tighter and her expression intensified. "No, it is not!"

"I was too late comin' to get you."

"That was meant to be. You said that she is your future and that is still true as long as you are too stupid and stubborn! Do not let your future go," Avasa said. "It is time for me to go. Please listen to me."

She embraced Lucky for a few moments and he hugged her back. Then they released each other and she knelt in front of Otto, whose expression was one of resigned sadness. She stroked his curly, silky hair.

"My son, I love you so much. It is because of my great love for you that I came and also that I must go. Do not be sad. I will see you again, but for now, our paths must part. I will be with you always in your heart," she said tapping his little chest. Then she leaned forward to whisper in his ear. "I will always be your mother, but Leah is your mother, too. Remember that and help your father to remember how much he loves Leah. Will you do that for me?"

Otto smiled and nodded. "Yes, Mother."

"You are such a smart, handsome boy, and I am so proud of you." Avasa hugged him tightly, fighting the tears that welled up in her eyes. "Never forget how much I love you."

Otto said, "I will not forget. I do not want you to go. Do you promise that I will see you again?"

"I promise. Be a good boy," she said, kissing him. "I love you."

"I love you," Otto said.

Avasa kissed him one last time and stood again. She smiled at them both and then mounted her horse.

Lucky said, "Thanks for takin' her, Thad."

Thad smiled. "Sure. What are friends for?"

"Be careful," Lucky said. "I'll be prayin' for yer safety."

"Appreciate it," Thad said as he picked up Otto. "You keep your da in line, ok?"

Otto smiled. "Ok."

Thad hugged him. "Ok. I'll see you soon." He put Otto down and mounted up.

Lucky and Otto watched them ride off. Avasa turned to wave at them once and then kept looking straight ahead. She cried silently as she followed Thad's horse out to the main road. Leaving Otto again was so difficult, but she knew it was best. She was determined to keep her promise to him that she would see him again. As she rode along with Thad, she prayed to the Great Spirit for Him to help Lucky and Leah find their way back to each other.

Chapter Twenty-Seven

"Tell me why we're climbing up here again?" Lucky asked Billy as they trekked up the mountainside past the abandoned mine early the next afternoon.

"I told you. I want to make a sacrifice to the Great Spirit to help with the birth of our baby. It's gonna be anytime now and I want to make sure it goes well."

"But why up here?"

"It's closer to the sky and maybe it'll make it easier for Him to hear me or something. You told me that up high was a good place to pray," Billy said.

Lucky said, "I did. Yer right. I'm sorry I'm so cranky. I can't hardly stand myself sometimes."

Billy smiled. "It's ok. I understand. Everything will be fine." *I hope.*

"Maybe someday," Lucky said as they rounded the last bend before reaching the summit. He saw a large tipi lodge and a bunch of their friends gathered around it. "What's goin' on here?"

Billy said, "You'll have to go inside and find out."

Lucky gave Billy a perplexed look as he dismounted.

Otto ran over to them and gave Lucky a very stern look. He put his hands on his hips and said, "Don't be stubborn, Da."

Lucky's confusion grew. "All right."

Otto took his hand and pulled him to the tipi. "Get in there and behave."

Lucky's gaze traveled around, touching on each person gathered there, but no one offered any explanation. Annoyed and puzzled, Lucky stepped through the lodge opening to see Leah standing inside.

Joy at the sight of her hit him so hard that it was painful. He didn't understand what was happening at all.

"Hello, Lucky," she signed to him. How she'd missed him. She drank in the sight of him; his broad shoulders, blond hair, and those fantastic gray eyes of his. Since their parting, she'd ached to be held in his strong arms and kiss him. Avasa had gotten through to her and she'd decided to try her best to make it up to Lucky for hurting him and not believing in him.

"What is all this?"

Leah swallowed. "I have been a complete idiot, Lucky. I didn't listen to what you were telling me. I thought I knew what was best for you and Otto, but I was so wrong. Breaking things off with you was the worst thing I could have ever done and I'm so, so sorry. Avasa made me see how foolish I was to do that and how much I hurt you and I am so ashamed of myself. I love you so much, which is why I did what I did. Your happiness matters so much to me and I thought you'd be happier with Avasa and Otto, together as a family.

"When she visited me, she made me see that you, me, and Otto was what was meant to be. You proposed to me up here and said that we were each other's future and you were so right, Lucky. I know that you believe you're lucky and you are. My luck changed the moment I read your first letter and I found the love of my life. I'm done being stupid, Lucky, and I want to have the future together that we talked about."

Hope rose in Lucky's heart, but he tread lightly, not quite ready to believe it was possible to reconcile. "Leah, I want to believe that we can, but I don't know. Ye've hurt me, cut me to the quick, and I can't do it again. Ya ran away from me while I professed my love for ya over and over. That's not an easy thing to forget."

Tears of remorse ran down her face as she moved closer. "I know you'll never forget it and neither will I. I'm asking for your forgiveness. Will you forgive me for being a stupid, foolish woman and give me the chance to show you how much I love you and that I'll love you with my whole heart for the rest of my life? Can you find it in your heart to forgive me for being so blind and not listening to you? Will you let me make it all up to you? I promise that if you forgive me and take me back, you'll never regret it."

Leah went down on her knees. "Please forgive me, Lucky. I love you and I need you and I promise I'll never leave you and Otto again. I love you so much."

Lucky watched her shoulders shake and he couldn't hold back his feelings any longer. He knelt in front of her, taking her face in his hands. "I still love you, Leah, so much. I've missed you every minute of every day," he said, looking into her lovely dark eyes. The eyes he'd missed staring into every day. "If ya can honestly promise me that ye'll never leave me and Otto again, I'll forgive ya, but if ya do, ya have to honor that promise."

She put her hands over his. "I vow to you right this minute to never, ever, ever leave the both of you again. I promise it with my whole heart and soul, Lucky," she said aloud.

Her words had been said slowly and carefully so that she got them right. He smiled at hearing her voice. He loved it when she spoke out aloud and she knew it. That she had, told him that she meant what she said. "Then I forgive ya and I promise the same thing. I'll never leave ya and I'll never let ya go again."

She broke down completely and Lucky gathered her to him, holding her tightly, crying with joy and relief over having his love back again.

After a time, Leah drew away so she could look at him. "I don't want to be apart from you one minute more. Will you still marry me, Lucky?"

Lucky wasn't going to miss the opportunity. He shoved his hand in his pants pocket and pulled out her engagement ring. "I've never stopped carryin' it," he said, putting her ring back on. Then he kissed it. "There. It's back where it belongs."

Leah hugged her hand to her chest. "I've missed this ring so much because it's a symbol of unending love and loyalty." Meeting his gaze, she asked, "Lucky, will you marry me right here and now?"

Lucky's brow furrowed and he looked towards the lodge opening. He could here everyone outside talking quietly. Looking back at Leah, he asked, "You really mean right this minute? As in right now?"

"Yes. Right this very minute," she confirmed.

"That's why everyone's here, isn't it?"

She nodded. "Yes. I was hoping and praying so hard that you'd take me back. I wasn't going to take any chances that something else would happen before we could get married. Please marry me right now."

"But how? We need Andi."

"She's here and ready. We already signed the marriage license and all of our friends are here."

"But what about your dress and all?" Lucky asked.

Leah said, "Does any of that really matter? Isn't the most important thing that you and I love each other and want to spend the rest of our lives together?"

"So you don't care that I'm not dressed either?"

"Lucky, you are the most handsome, delicious man I've ever seen, no matter what you're wearing," Leah said. "I'd marry you if you wore a burlap sack or a blanket. I don't care."

"What about our weddin' bands? And a honeymoon? We didn't finish plannin' that," Lucky said.

Leah signed. "Billy has our rings. How do you feel about a Cheyenne honeymoon to honor that side of you and a part of why I love you? Besides, Christmas is almost here and I don't want to go anywhere."

"But what about yer parents? Don't ya want them here?"

Leah's smile grew. "They are. They arrived yesterday. Evan had Shadow go to Dickensville at the beginning of the week and send them an urgent telegram. They're hiding out there. I didn't want you to see them until it was the right time."

Amazement struck Lucky dumb for a couple of minutes. Then he asked, "Ye've thought of everything then."

"I had a lot of help," Leah said. "Will you marry me right now?"

With tears in his eyes, Lucky nodded. "Aye. I'll marry ya right now, love."

She threw her arms around his neck and kissed him. He responded to her, holding her tightly until the kiss ended.

His smile was beautiful to Leah. "I think we're s'posed to wait for the 'I do's' to kiss," he said.

She shook her head a little and mouthed, "I don't care."

He chuckled and got up, pulling her with him. "Well, I guess we oughta let them in here so we can get married."

She grinned and went to the lodge flap. Opening, she waved at them and said aloud, "We're getting married!"

Everyone cheered and clapped. Soon the lodge filled with people. Lucky had been paying so much attention to Leah that he hadn't noticed that a small altar area had been set up at the back of the lodge. Andi came inside, dressed in a smart black and white suit befitting her position.

She said, "I'm so happy for you and glad that I can share in your joy."

"Me, too," said Billy as he took his place by Lucky's side.

Lucky watched all of their friends, who were now his family, file into the tipi. He was surprised to see Marvin and Ronni there. Marvin saw his expression and came over to him.

"We helped get her here," he said, smiling smugly. "You didn't think we were going to miss your wedding did you?"

Lucky laughed. "That's right. I'll always be grateful to ya for all of yer help. So, ya can stand right here by Billy. I think it's only right. If ya hadn't gone with me, I might not have Leah."

Marvin was surprised. "I didn't mean—"

Billy cut him off by grabbing his arm and yanking him over by him. "Just stand here and shut up before he changes his mind," he said, smiling.

It was strange for Marvin to have Billy smiling at him, but he smiled back and chuckled. "Yes, Mr. Two Moons."

"That's right," Billy said.

Broderick and Constance approached Lucky.

"It's good to see you, Lucky," Broderick said.

"The same to you, sir," Lucky responded.

Constance said, "This is the oddest wedding I've ever been to, but also very sweet. Thank you for forgiving our daughter for being so foolish."

Lucky smiled bashfully. "Well, I was foolish, too. I shouldn't have let her end things. I forgot about my tattoos for a while, but I won't ever again."

Broderick's brow puckered. "Tattoos?"

Lucky explained about his tattoos. "So ya see they're supposed to remind me that I can't ever stop when I want something. I lost sight of that for a while and it took Leah doin' all of this to remind me. I won't repeat that mistake."

Broderick's dark eyes twinkled a little. "Something tells me you would've remembered before too long."

"I'd like to think so," Lucky said.

Andi said, "Is everyone ready to begin?"

Leah took her place beside her father. Broderick's eyes grew moist when he saw the happy light in her eyes as she looked at Lucky. He'd always dreamed of giving her away to a good man when the time was right. It was something all fathers wanted for their little girls, but in that dream, he'd never seen her getting married in a Cheyenne lodge high on a mountain. In a strange way, he found it fitting for his daughter who'd overcome so many odds and had reached pinnacles of success that many people had never thought she would.

Sofia stood up at the altar, so happy for her sister and Lucky. She'd come to love him since she'd come to Echo. Originally, she'd planned on going back to Glendale at some point, but she'd decided to stay permanently in Echo. Lucky and all of his friends had become another family to her and she didn't want to leave them now. As she watched her father hand Leah off to Lucky, she wondered if romance might be in the cards for her someday and found that her heart had healed enough for her to actually hope so.

Erin stood by Sofia, a hand on her rounded belly. Her and Win exchanged a smile, their happiness over their baby almost overwhelming sometimes. Billy and Nina did much the same thing. Nina had been carefully carried to the summit and she was excited about the wedding.

Leah had another surprise for Lucky. He'd expected her to sign her vows, but she'd decided to say them out loud so that she could hold his hands and also because she knew how much he liked hearing her voice. He and everyone else had reassured her that she didn't sound stupid so she had grown more comfortable in doing it.

As she spoke carefully and clearly, Leah tried to show all of her love for Lucky in her eyes and in her voice. The message got through to Lucky and he listened with rapt attention every time she spoke. He tried to convey his strong feelings by squeezing her hands and staring unwaveringly into her eyes.

Andi had to keep a tight rein on her emotions because of all she was picking up from those around her. There was so much joy flowing through the tipi that it made her feel giddy and it was only by exerting the utmost control was she able to keep from laughing in delight. She guided Lucky and Leah through the ceremony with a smile on her face the whole time.

Leah had insisted on bands that matched her engagement ring. They were silver with Irish Love Knots on either side of small diamond insets. When Lucky slid Leah's on, pride that she was now his forever filled him. Leah put Lucky's on and vowed in her heart to never allow anything to come between them again. Barely did Andi have the words, "You may now kiss your bride" out than Lucky took Leah in his arms.

When they parted, the tipi was filled with applause and people rushed forward to congratulate them. The wedding might not have been what he'd planned, but Lucky was glad that his bride had come up with this idea. He thought that maybe the Great Spirit had moved her to do it.

Josie and Billy had brought their guitars and played so that Lucky and Leah could dance. She didn't hesitate to step into his arms because she knew that he would guide her and never let her fall. Lucky was that sort of man. People knew they could lean on him and that he'd never let them down, so she had no fear of that. But she also wanted to be there for him to rely on and she wanted to take care of him. She would do that to the best of her ability every day.

Lucky held his new wife as they swayed to the music and knew that he'd finally found his own happiness. She was so courageous, as her putting the wedding together proved, and he was fortunate to have found a strong woman like her on whom he could depend. Yes, she'd hurt him, but everything she'd done to make their wedding happen and her honest contrition had quickly erased that pain, leaving behind only gladness.

As the guests began leaving, Lucky and Leah gave them heartfelt thanks for all of their help in making their wedding so wonderful and for coming even though it was so cold. No one had minded, the joy of the occasion overpowering a little discomfort. The happy couple stood outside the lodge in their coats waving everyone goodbye.

When they were alone, Lucky saw that the sun was setting and led Leah around the lodge so that they could watch the sunset together. The vibrant colors matched their mood and it seemed as though the Great Spirit was smiling upon them. When the sun was almost down, they went into the lodge and out of the cold.

Lucky said, "Never a prettier lass than you did I see."

"Never a handsomer lad than you did I see," she returned.

He smiled as he shrugged out of his coat and looked around at the lodge. "I still can't believe ya did all this."

"I didn't do it alone," she said as she shed her coat, too. It was plenty warm in the lodge. "I never thought I'd get married in a Cheyenne lodge, but I'm glad I did."

"Me, too." His gaze turned hungry. He closed the distance between them and slid his arms around her waist. "Yer the loveliest bride. I don't care what *you* wear, either. Ya look fetchin' in anything ya wear and I'll bet ya look even lovelier without one stitch on."

His bold statement made her blush, but also excited her. "You do?"

A wicked gleam entered his eyes. "Aye."

Pulling her close against him, Lucky stared into her eyes a moment before giving her a slow, lingering kiss. Although he wanted her fiercely, he wasn't going to rush things. It was a meaningful experience for both of them and he wanted to savor it. He released her hair from the combs she had it pulled back with and watched the inky tresses fall over her shoulders and down her back.

Delving his fingers into her thick mane, he captured her lips again, desire flowing through his body when she sighed. Slowly they were bared to one another. Lucky reassured her with words and in sign that there was no need to be nervous. Leah gave herself up to his kisses and caresses, delighting in the way he felt and tasted. Something occurred to her and she stepped away from him.

"What's wrong, love?" he asked.

"I want to see your tattoos. I've never seen them," she said. "Of course, I've never seen you like this, either," she signed and then began walking around him, trailing her hands over his hard muscles. She smiled when they flexed under her touch.

His patience and playfulness made her feel as though walking around naked in an Indian lodge was the most natural thing in the world. The bull and griffin were beautiful and she thought that their meanings fit him perfectly as she traced their shapes over his powerful back. She was fascinated by him and couldn't stop touching him as she came back around in front of him.

Lucky didn't mind a bit. He wanted her to be completely comfortable with him. "What do ya think of them?"

She smiled and said, "They're beautiful, my stubborn, determined, loyal, loving Irishman." Putting her arms around him, she stood on tiptoe to give him a passionate kiss that told him how much she desired him.

He growled and the vibration of it under her hands, which rested on his chest, thrilled her. She'd missed that sensation; it made her smoldering passion turn into a full-blown flame. Lucky suddenly found himself holding the temptress he'd gotten glimpses of here and there. Even as she kissed him, he picked her up and carried her to where sleeping robes had been made up for them and sank down onto them with her.

In her low, husky voice, she said, "Make love with me, Lucky."

"Aye. I will," he said, his eyes turning a smoky hue. "I intend to do just that and make ya mine from now 'til eternity. Ye'll never get away from me again. Do ya understand me?"

She grinned and said aloud, "Aye. I do."

He laughed and said, "I know ya don't like to talk out loud, but ya have a beautiful voice and I especially like hearin' ya laugh. And ya know what else?"

"What?" she asked. His praise of her speaking voice gave her more courage to do it.

He said, "It's pretty, um, stimulatin'."

She giggled and asked, "Really?"

"Aye. It's sort of smoky."

"Smoky?"

He searched for the right word. "Sultry. I'm no writer, but that's the word that comes to mind."

She wiggled against him a little. "Sultry. I like that. So my voice is sultry?"

"Yes. Very sultry." She was driving him crazy and he could see that she knew it.

That he'd actually said "yes" let her know how emphatic he was about it. "If you make love to me right now, I'll keep talking, Irish."

"It's a deal, lass," he said, rolling her over.

They talked, laughed, and loved all evening as he introduced her to lovemaking and Leah was filled with wonder over the tender way he showed his love for her. She was glad for the firelight so that she could see what he was saying to her as well as hear what his body told her. She answered him back and before too long, there was no more need for words.

Epilogue

The lodge situated on the mountain that overlooked their farm became their oasis of love for the next several days. Wild Wind brought them food every day, but only scratched on the tipi flap and melted away into the trees again. They never saw him, as was the Cheyenne tradition when a couple was on a honeymoon.

However, on the fourth night they were there, Wild Wind did stay there after scratching. He also called out to them even though it was late.

When Lucky opened the flap, Wild Wind said, "I'm sorry to interrupt your honeymoon, but Nina is in labor."

Lucky's face lit up. "Praise be! We'll be right along."

Wild Wind grinned and left again.

Lucky told Leah what was going on and she let out an excited little cry. They got themselves put together and left right away.

Billy sat on the sofa in his parents' parlor, Josie sitting right beside him holding his hand. His mother was in with Nina and Erin. His leg bounced continuously and he winced every time Nina made a sound. He wanted to be with her so badly, but he most likely would have passed out or gotten sick at the sight of any blood. That would be distressing to Nina, and she was under enough stress.

Nina let out a particularly loud moan and Josie thought Billy was going to break her hand.

"Billy, can you ease up a little?" she asked.

"Sorry," he said sheepishly. "I know I don't have any of the pain involved, but I'm a wreck here. How's she doing? I mean, can someone get me a progress report or something?"

Evan grinned at Billy. "You should just do what I did. Go on in there. I've never regretted it and when this next baby comes along, I'll do the same thing."

Josie and he had recently announced that there would be another little Taft arriving around the end of April. She smiled at him. "You'd better be. I need you to fight with me so I can push harder."

"I'll do that," he said proudly.

Billy said, "I can't go in there. I'll be on the floor in a matter of seconds."

Lucky said, "Well, I'll go." He got up from his chair and said, "I'll let ya know how things are since yer too chicken to do it."

Billy stood up and put a hand on his chest to stop his progress. "Oh no, you don't. That's my wife and you are *not* going in there right now."

Lucky said, "Then get in there and help bring yer wee bairn into the world."

"Are you gonna do that whenever more little Quinns come along?" Billy challenged.

"We haven't discussed it," Lucky said.

"Well, when you do discuss it, are you gonna do it?" Billy asked.

"I don't know. We haven't discussed it. How can I tell ya if I'm gonna do somethin' if I haven't discussed it yet?"

"Do you want to be there?" Billy asked.

"Of course. I think," Lucky said uncertainly.

"Well, I do, and I am. We'll just see who's chicken!" Billy asserted. He knocked on the door to their room off the parlor and said, "I'm coming in there."

Nina looked up at him as he entered the room and grinned. "Good. You can make me laugh by falling on the floor when you pass out."

"I'm not going to fall on the floor," he said. "I have another way to amuse you."

She laughed and then moaned. "That's how I ended up like this."

Billy blushed while Erin laughed. "That's not what I meant." He picked up one of the numerous sketchpads and a couple of the pencils that lay around their room. He still sometimes painted there so there were art supplies handy. Carefully averting his eyes from what Erin was doing, he dragged a chair over to the bed and placed it up near her head.

He kissed her and sat down. Nina loved watching him draw and in between contractions, he entertained her by drawing all kinds of things for her. When the time drew nearer for the baby's arrival, he put the drawing things down and held her hand while she pushed. He focused on helping Nina and his squeamishness vanished as she held onto him, gritted her teeth, and pushed.

When the baby was born and Erin announced the sex, Nina laughed smugly. "I was right! We have a boy!"

Billy laughed with her and said, "Mother's intuition. No fair." Then he kissed her, looking lovingly into her eyes.

Erin was getting used to fathers being in the birthing room here and there and she smiled over how cute the young couple was. "Billy, would you and Nina like to meet your son?"

Billy took the baby and was struck by a rush of love so strong it left him feeling weak. He put the baby in Nina's arms and sat on the bed with them.

She smiled at the baby. "He has your hair color and your nose."

Billy said, "Yep. I hope he has your eyes." He wiped away tears as he looked at their baby and he saw Nina do the same thing. "He's so beautiful."

Nina nodded a little and leaned her head against his chest. "Thank you for letting me name him after my father. His name is one of the few things I remember about my first family."

Billy smiled and said, "No thanks needed, honey. It's a good name and I like that it has such a positive meaning to it."

She kissed the baby's forehead and then handed him to Billy. "Let Grandma have him a moment before you have to leave. You can take him to meet everyone then."

Arlene came over to them. Tears welled in her eyes at the sight of her grandson, whom Billy put in her arms. "Oh, he's such a handsome boy! I can't tell you how happy I am for you two and for the rest of us!" she said quietly. She gave him back to Billy. "Ok. Out you go."

"Thanks, Ma," Billy said. He kissed Nina. "I love you. I'll be back."

When he went into the parlor, he beamed and said, "I'd like you all to meet Thomas Remus Two Moons. Here, Grandpa. Would you like to hold, Tommy?"

Remus took Tommy. "Of course," the big man said.

The others crowded around so they could see Tommy, and they all congratulated Billy and Remus. Josie saw Billy start to cry and wrapped her arms around him. She sat him down on the sofa and hugged him as relief, joy, and gratitude swamped him.

"I can't believe he's here. He's so beautiful and Nina's so beautiful. You're beautiful, too," he said through his tears. "I was scared and happy and Nina was so strong and she liked my drawing and I held her hand and I didn't pass out or anything."

His rambling was touching and funny and Josie chuckled along with everyone else.

Evan patted his shoulder. "I completely understand how you feel, buddy. You did good, Billy."

"Thanks. It'll be your turn next, Win."

Win nodded. "That's right, and I'll be right there since I'm delivering our baby."

Lucky asked, "Yer deliverin' it?"

Win said, "Sure. Who else is going to do it? You?"

"Don't be daft. Of course not," Lucky said. "There's women around who can do that."

"True," Win said. "Charlene is going to be there, too, but so will I, just in case. I am a doctor, after all."

Edna said, "Yes, you are. If you can deliver calves and foals, I'm sure you can deliver a human baby."

"Thanks, Edna," Win said, smiling.

"Of course, if it comes out looking like a horse, you're gonna have some explaining to do."

Everyone laughed and little Tommy was passed around to meet the rest of his family.

Christmas was a wonderful holiday for many people, the Earnests included. Shadow was a great father and loved their twins intensely. He was with them as much as possible and always had one or the other in his arms. He knew it was a little silly, but he divided his time equally between them, never wanting either to feel less loved than the other.

Bree loved watching her husband with them. He read stories to them, told them about his day at work, and even played piano quietly for them, which helped to put them to sleep. Marvin also did similar things with them and Eva. The little girl was on the move now and Marvin often chased her around the house, keeping her from harm. Eva loved the twins and they were teaching her to be careful around them.

They spent the day playing with the children and eating a very nice meal. In the evening, Travis came over with Pauline to spend a little time with them and open gifts. It was difficult, but the father and daughter were getting through each day with help from their family and friends.

Marvin would never reveal that he'd paid Jenny to leave town—he knew that it would hurt Pauline even worse if she knew how easily Jenny had left. He would help Travis and Pauline any way he could to come back from the ordeal.

The New Year came and with it many changes in the lives of some of Echo's residents.

On a night near the end of January, Ronni left the washroom and came into Marvin's room ready for bed. Marvin was just beginning to undress.

"I think I just heard Eva cry," he said.

Ronni's brow puckered. "You did?"

"Yes. Why don't you check on her and I'll turn down the covers?" he said with a suggestive smile.

"All right, but I didn't hear her," Ronni said, slightly irritated.

Marvin grinned when she walked out of the room.

Ronni went into the nursery and saw that Eva slept peacefully, but there was a little box sitting inside the crib up in the corner. She smiled, figuring that Marvin was playing some sort of game with her. Picking it up, she took off the lid and found a little piece of paper inside. Unfolding it, she read, *Marvin loves you and me whole big bunches and wants to know if you'll marry him so he can be my daddy and argue with you for the rest of your lives? Please say yes. If you do, he'll put that shiny thing in the box on your finger.*

Looking back in the box she saw an exquisite diamond ring lying on a velvet bed. She put her hand to her gaping mouth to muffle her gasp of surprise. Quietly, she left the room, closed the door, and then ran flat-out to Marvin's room. It was a good thing he was just getting into bed when she launched herself at him because she barreled him over backwards onto the mattress.

"Oof!" he said as he landed on his back with her on top.

Ronni kissed him hard and then laid the box on his chest. "Yes! My answer is yes! Put it on!"

Marvin laughed with immense joy over her answer and reaction. "Ok. Quit bouncing! I can't get a hold of the ring!" He laughed when Ronni bounced harder. "If you keep doing that, I'm going to get distracted and I'll have to wait to put the ring on."

Ronni stilled and held out her hand for him.

Marvin cleared his throat and said, "Let me do this properly. Veronica Hendricks, will you—"

"Yes! I'll marry you!" she said, bouncing again.

Marvin groaned. "What did I tell you about that? Now, shut up! Will you please marry me and make me so very incredibly, unbelievably, unendingly happy?"

"That was a lot of adjectives," Ronni said, laughing. "Yes! I'll marry you!"

Marvin managed to get the ring on before she kissed him again and they laughed together as they rolled and ended up side by side.

"You challenge me, piss me off, and aggravate me so much, but you also amaze me with your kindness, sense of humor, and beauty," Marvin said. "I know being married to me won't always be easy, but it won't be boring, either."

She smiled at him. "I can say the same about you. I'll always love you, even when I'm mad at you."

"And I'll always love you, even when you make me mad enough to want to throw something."

He kissed her and then she took a hard hold on his face.

"Marvin, you need to listen to me. I have something to tell you."

He grinned and tried to move her hand, but she wouldn't let go. A strange, very intense expression settled on her face. "Very well. I'm listening."

"You know that I love you, right?"

He nodded. "Yes."

"And that I would never, ever cheat on you, correct?" It was almost a plea.

Rubbing her back, he said, "Yes, of course. I know you're not that sort of woman. What's this about? Why are you so upset?"

She bit her lip and then said, "Marvin, I'm pregnant."

His hands stilled and he paled. "What?"

"I'm going to have a baby. *We're* going to have a baby."

Disbelief showed in his gorgeous eyes. "How? I can't m—are you sure? That's impossible. My hernia—I can't—"

She covered his mouth with her hand. "Yes, I'm sure. I've already been to see Erin and she confirmed it."

Marvin still couldn't fathom what she was telling him. He couldn't process the fact that he'd sired a child when he'd been told that he never would and when no one he'd ever been with had gotten pregnant.

"She's sure? You're sure? Certain? Positive? Really and truly, you're pregnant? With child?" he asked.

Ronni smiled at his rambling. "Yes. Absolutely positive. I recognized the signs from when I was pregnant with Eva and I thought I was mistaken given, well, you know. But it's true. We're having a baby, honey."

Marvin didn't want to allow himself to hope that he wasn't dreaming, because it felt surreal to hear the woman he loved tell him that they were having a baby. It had been his dream to have a wife and family for so long and he'd desired children so much that to have it all coming true was scary. Good things didn't happen to him very often, and something like this was beyond his comprehension.

Ronni understood his reaction because she'd been amazed, too. She let his face go and put her arms around him. "It's true, Marvin. It's real. I couldn't believe it at first, either."

For the second time in a matter of months, Marvin embraced Ronni and cried his heart out. But this time he cried with joy and wonder instead of sorrow and anger. Finally, he pulled back and looked at her with tear-stained cheeks. "What's the matter with you?" he said and sniffed.

"What do you mean?" she asked.

"You're pregnant with my baby and yet you're running around like that! You will not ride a horse or run or go outside when it's icy without someone walking with you. I'll write you a list so you won't do them. I mean, you should not do the things on this list, the list I'll write. No doing them."

Ronni laughed and he grew very angry. Suddenly, he got out of bed, ran his hands through his hair and walked out of the room.

"Marvin! Get back here! You're naked!"

"Gets pregnant with my baby and then runs and jumps and there's going to be a list," he mumbled as he went downstairs as bare as he was on the day he'd been born.

Ronni muffled her laughter as she grabbed the pair of pants he'd draped over a chair and went downstairs. He stood in the parlor, pouring scotch into a tumbler. He downed it and poured more. When he saw her, he said, "You are not allowed to drink this or any other spirits."

"Yes, honey. I know that. Are you forgetting that I've done this before?"

"Oh. Yes. You have. I didn't forget, exactly, it's, well, you understand."

Marvin couldn't stay still. He wanted to share their joy. Walking past her, he ignored the pants she tried to give him and went to the bottom of the stairs.

"Shadow! Bree! Shadow! Come here!" he shouted.

"Marvin! Don't do that! You'll wake the twins and Eva!" she reprimanded him.

Shadow came to the top of the stairs and started down. "Marvy, are you all right?"

"I am splendid," Marvin said.

"Well, I know you're proud of yourself. Is that why you're running around naked while you're drinking?" Shadow asked, joining Marvin at the bottom of the stairs.

"I'm naked?" Marvin looked down. "Oh, dear God, I am!" He looked at Ronni. "Why did you let me come down here naked?"

Ronni said, "I tried to stop you. Here, put these on!"

Marvin handed Shadow his drink and put his pants on just as Bree came into the room.

"Am I mistaken or did I just see your bare backside, Marvin?" she asked.

Marvin grinned. "No, you're not mistaken. You did see it, but there's a good reason for it."

Bree looked at Shadow, but he just shrugged. "I have no idea what's going on."

Marvin hugged Ronni and kissed her forehead. "A miracle has happened, that's what's going on. A miracle. I never used to believe in them, but I'm starting to. A miracle. Ronni and I are having a baby and I don't mean adoption. A baby that I made. We made. I sired it. Everything worked. My baby."

Ronni held onto Marvin as she shook from the force of her laughter.

Shadow asked, "He's serious? You're really pregnant?"

Ronni nodded. "Yes. Erin confirmed it. I'm pregnant."

Bree and Shadow let out noises of delight and came to hug them.

"No wonder you're running around acting stark raving mad," Shadow said. "I would certainly call that miraculous."

Bree hugged Marvin. "You're right. It *is* a miracle. I'm so happy for you two."

Marvin said, "We have even more good news. Ronni has agreed to be my wife."

This brought on more celebration and it was a long time until they were all sufficiently calmed down to go to bed.

As Marvin took Ronni in his arms that night, he said, "As happy as I am about this baby, the first miracle was finding someone who loved me the way you do. So you're miracle number one. Then there's Eva. She's another miracle and I'll be just as good a father to her as will to this baby."

Ronni loved the gentle way he put a hand over her stomach and the loving way he looked at her. "Marvin, I know you will. I know how much you love Eva and I know you won't play favorites."

His expression turned fierce. "No, I won't. I'll never make any of our children think they're not loved as much as one of their siblings. Never."

Ronni caressed his cheek. "I know. Don't think about all of that, honey. It's all in the past. Don't go there. Look ahead to all of our miracles."

He grinned. "You're right. I want to get married right away so that I can give Eva my last name and so that this little one doesn't arrive out of wedlock."

"I think that's a good idea."

"What sort of wedding do you want?"

"We could have an Indian wedding," she teased.

"I think not," he said.

They pretended to argue about the wedding for a little while before getting lost in each other and celebrating all of their miraculous events.

Not everyone was so fortunate that January, as Thad found out when he came home from his latest job. He'd been in a hurry the whole time because for some reason he felt a burning need to get back to Echo.

He got home about four in the afternoon to find a note from Evan on the front door, telling him to come to the Tafts' as soon as he got there. He got back on his stallion, Killer, and raced over to their house.

When Josie let him in, there was such sadness in her blue eyes that his heart lurched in his chest.

"Josie, what the heck is going on? I just got home," he said.

She took him out into the kitchen. "Evan is still at work. We have the Daughtry kids here for now. The last time they saw Darlene was the day after you left."

Thad became furious. "Damn her hide! I'm gonna give her hell like never before once I find her!"

Josie put a stilling hand on his arm and shook her head a little. "You can't. She's dead," Josie almost whispered.

Thad felt faint for a few moments and took a steadying breath. "How?"

"Someone stabbed her and hid her behind some brush at the Burgundy House. Evan's investigating."

"Where are the kids?" he asked. He knew the investigation was in good hands with Evan, so in that moment, Thad's main focus became those three children.

"Upstairs playing with Julia. I was just going to start cooking dinner," Josie said.

Thad ran through the parlor, acknowledging Edna with a nod, and then took the stairs two at a time. He entered the nursery and as soon as the kids saw him, they ran to him. He knelt, taking the girls into his embrace as they cried. He hugged them tight and tried to comfort them. Porter stood off to the side a little bit. Thad could see the boy was trying to be brave, but tears trickled down his face.

Thad said, "C'mere, Porter. C'mon. It's ok, son."

Porter ran over then and Thad held the three brokenhearted children as they cried out their fear and sorrow. It reminded him of when Evan was ten and had watched while the rest of his family had been killed. He'd been through so much trauma and Thad had been glad that he'd had Rebel and Edna to take him in. These poor kids had no one. There were no family members waiting in the wings to love and raise them.

As the vision of an orphanage rose in Thad's mind, he muttered, "Like hell they'll go there."

Porter said, "I don't know what we're gonna do. I can't support us. I'm not old enough."

Thad kissed each of their heads and then stood up. "You won't have to, buddy. It's gonna be ok."

"You don't know that!" Porter said. "We got no money and nowhere to go!"

Thad put a hand on his shoulder. "Porter, it's gonna be ok." Thad sighed.

"No, it's not! They'll put us in one of those orphanages and we'll get split up. I'll run away; I swear I will!"

Thad shook him a little. "Porter! Listen to me. I'm not lettin' you kids go to one of those places. You'll stay with me and that's that. Now, I don't want to hear any backtalk about it. We'll get it figured out and it'll be all right."

J.J. looked up at Thad. "Do you promise?"

Thad put his hand under her chin. "I promise, sweetheart."

Porter wiped away his tears and gave Thad a half-smile. "Well, ok, on one condition."

"What's that?"

"You go get a bath. You stink like hell," Porter said.

"Hey, no swearin'," Thad said even though he laughed. "I just got back in town not a half hour ago and already you're bitchin' at me about a bath."

The kids laughed.

"I can see that this is gonna be real fun. Ok, I'll go get a bath and be back. You help Josie with supper while I'm gone. You hear me?" he asked going downstairs.

"Ok," Porter said.

"Just stay up there a minute, ok?"

"Why?"

"Because I said so!" Thad shot back, smiling when he heard them laugh. In the parlor, he sat on the sofa and looked at Edna, who smiled at him. He sighed, ran a hand over his face and then stared back at her. "Are you busy right now?" he asked her.

"Nope. Not at all."

Thad groaned and got up again. He went out to the kitchen, rummaged around in a drawer while Josie peeled potatoes and then went back into the parlor. He handed Edna a tablet and pencil. "I guess you better write me up one of those ads of yours. Looks like I need to get married real quick since I have kids now."

Edna tried valiantly not to snicker as she said, "So what would you like it to say?"

"This isn't funny, Edna," Thad said.

She shook her head. "No, I know. It's not funny about what happened to their mother. That's horrible of course, but the thought of you raising children?" She couldn't write for a few moments. Then she cleared her throat and asked, "What kind of woman are you looking for?"

"It doesn't matter to me as long as she can get here quick and understands that this is out of necessity and not romance," Thad said, sitting back down.

Edna eyed him, still smiling. "Thad, this is going to be for the rest of your life, so think about this seriously."

"Yeah, says the woman laughing at me. Hey, kids! Get down here!" Thad called, making Edna jump.

The kids joined them.

Thad said, "Now, look, I know that this is a rough time for you, but we have to think about something. You know what I do for a living and I'm not always able to be in town, right?"

They nodded. Edna had never seen the way Thad dealt with the Daughtry kids before, so she didn't understand their relationship. Evan had told her and Josie about it, but seeing it was a different thing entirely.

"Ok," Thad continued. "If you're gonna stay with me, we have to find someone for me to marry so that you have a mother figure in your life and someone to take care of you when I have to go out on a job. Agreed?"

Again, three heads nodded.

"Well, Edna wants to know what kind of woman I'm lookin' for, but I figure it ain't up to just me. So sit down here with us and tell us what you want, too, and then Edna will write us up a nice ad for the paper, ok?"

Three heads bobbed.

"Ok, go ahead and tell her," Thad said.

J.J. said, "She should be pretty."

Porter said, "She should be able to shoot a gun."

Liz said, "She should cook and like dogs because I want one."

Edna wrote down everything that the kids and Thad told her and then Thad went to the Hanover House to use the big tub in their bathhouse. He hadn't done that since Phoebe had died, but he knew that it was time to move on. There were three kids counting on him now. As he bathed, it felt as though he was washing away the past along with the dirt that clung to him.

When he was done, he dressed and said, "Ok, Lord. You gave 'em to me, now give me the right woman to raise 'em with."

Putting his coat on, he looked around at the bathhouse, making sure it was neat again. As he blew out the lamp and stepped through its doorway, Thad knew that in leaving the bathhouse that night, he was leaving his old life behind, too. He closed the door on the bathhouse and that chapter of his life. Then he walked to where he'd left Killer, mounted, and rode away towards his future.

The End

Thank you for reading and supporting my book and I hope you enjoyed it.

Please will you do me a favor and review "Montana Luck" so I'll know whether you liked it or not, it would be very much appreciated, thank you.

Linda's Other Books

Echo Canyon Brides Series

Montana Rescue
(Echo Canyon brides Book 1)
Montana Bargain
(Echo Canyon brides Book 2)
Montana Adventure
(Echo Canyon brides Book 3)
Montana Luck
(Echo Canyon brides Book 4)

Montana Mail Order Brides Series

Westward Winds
(Montana Mail Order brides Book 1)
Westward Dance
(Montana Mail Order brides Book 2)
Westward Bound
(Montana Mail Order brides Book 3)
Westward Destiny
(Montana Mail Order brides Book 4)
Westward Fortune
(Montana Mail Order brides Book 5)
Westward Justice
(Montana Mail Order brides Book 6)
Westward Dreams
(Montana Mail Order brides Book 7)
Westward Holiday
(Montana Mail Order brides Book 8)
Westward Sunrise
(Montana Mail Order brides Book 9)

Westward Moon
(Montana Mail Order brides
Book 10)
Westward Christmas
(Montana Mail Order brides
Book 11)
Westward Visions
(Montana Mail Order brides
Book 12)
Westward Secrets
(Montana Mail Order brides
Book 13)
Westward Changes
(Montana Mail Order brides
Book 14)
Westward Heartbeat
(Montana Mail Order brides
Book 15)
Westward Joy
(Montana Mail Order brides
Book 16)
Westward Courage
(Montana Mail Order brides
Book 17)
Westward Spirit
(Montana Mail Order brides
Book 18)
Westward Fate
(Montana Mail Order brides
Book 19)
Westward Hope
(Montana Mail Order brides
Book 20)
Westward Wild
(Montana Mail Order brides
Book 21)
Westward Sight
(Montana Mail Order brides
Book 22)
Westward Horizons
(Montana Mail Order brides
Book 23)

Connect With Linda

Visit my website at **www.lindabridey.com** to view my other books and to sign up to my mailing list so that you are notified about my new releases.

About Linda Bridey

Linda Bridey lives in New Mexico with her three dogs; a German shepherd, chocolate Labrador retriever, and a black Pug. She became fascinated with Montana and decided to combine that fascination with her fictional romance writing. Linda chose to write about mail-order-brides because of the bravery of these women who left everything and everyone to take a trek into the unknown. The Westward series books are her first publications.

Made in the USA
Monee, IL
22 August 2020

38943744R00142